EVERY EXQUISITE THING

content warnings: *disordered eating, parental addiction, emotional abuse, animal death, body horror, disfigurement, violence, suicide threats, death*

AUTHOR'S NOTE

When I first pitched this reimagining of *The Picture of Dorian Gray*, I hadn't planned on writing something that dealt with body image and disordered eating so directly. I originally intended to use Penny's fear over her hair loss to tackle our collective obsession with beauty – and the way it's hailed as a young woman's most vital currency.

Yet the further I got into the story, the more I realised that for girls entering into a portrait bargain like this, a huge part of the appeal would be no longer having to restrict themselves to achieve a certain physique. To skirt around that fact felt cowardly, so I decided to tackle the issue head-on.

This is something I find terrifying, for a variety of reasons, but this story feels important enough for me to tuck that fear away – or at least to write alongside it.

That said, I oppose the culture of authors feeling obligated to disclose private information in order to defend themselves against scrutiny, especially when exploring thorny and inherently problematic issues. So I ask you to please trust that I write this story from a deeply personal place. It's the book I so badly needed when I was eighteen.

Finally, your mileage with body image may vary. I don't seek to represent every story, struggle or perspective – just Penny's.

Laura x

EVERY EXQUISITE THING

Laura Steven

First published in Great Britain in 2023
by Electric Monkey, part of Farshore
An imprint of HarperCollins*Publishers*
1 London Bridge Street, London SE1 9GF

farshore.co.uk

HarperCollins*Publishers*
Macken House, 39/40 Mayor Street Upper,
Dublin 1, D01 C9W8

A CIP catalogue record of this title is available from the British Library

ISBN 978 0 00 862735 5
Special Edition ISBN 978 0 00 866287 5
Printed and bound in the UK using 100% renewable electricity at
CPI Group (UK) Ltd

1

Typeset by Avon DataSet Ltd, Alcester, Warwickshire

MIX
Paper from
responsible sources
FSC™ C007454

For the girls who were
born hungry.

"Behind every exquisite thing that existed, there was something tragic"

— Oscar Wilde, *The Picture of Dorian Gray*

PROLOGUE

A full moon hung low over the mirrored surface of the lake, round and silver as a ten pence piece.

A darkened figure knelt on the shore, screaming like a wounded animal.

Blinking sleep from my eyes, I squinted through the arched window in my dorm room. With a sickening lurch, I recognised the spidery limbs and the short black hair.

Davina.

I don't know what made me run to her. We hated each other with a venom I'd never experienced before – our every exchange left puncture wounds – and yet there was something so existentially terrible in her cries. Something that called to me like a siren.

Stuffing my feet into sheepskin boots, I tossed a trench coat over my pyjamas and hurtled out of the flat. The night air was so cold it felt solid, and the Great Lawn was slicked with dew as I sprinted down towards the lake. A low mist gathered in the Crosswoods beyond, swirling with moonlight to cast a spectral glow over the grounds. Everything smelled of frost and silt.

As I grew closer, Davina's howls ebbed to a low sob, and somehow that was worse.

Breathless, I skidded to a halt beside her. Her head was in her hands, narrow shoulders shaking violently inside her leather jacket. Her knees pressed into the wet lakeshore, and damp was spreading up her black jeans – she must have been freezing.

'Davina,' I said, torn between softness and ferocity, the words coming out somewhere in between.

She stilled at the sound of my voice. 'Leave me alone, Penny.'

'No.' I pulled my coat tighter around me, teeth chattering. 'You're upset.'

Her hands clasped her face with a kind of fierce desperation, as though trying to hold her features in place. 'Just fuck off.'

'*No.*'

Usually she would fight back, spar for spar, dodging and parrying with vicious words, but her ferocious spirit seemed to abandon her. Instead she began hyperventilating, rollicking gasps wracking her whole body as she tried to take in air.

Then she said something else, but it was so obscured by her laboured wheezes that I didn't catch it.

'What?' I asked. I'd been crouching beside her, but had to give in to my trembling muscles and lower my knees to the ground. The cold wet earth turned my silk pyjamas into ice in an instant.

Slowly, silently, Davina lowered her hands from her face, turning to look at me.

My stomach heaved, and I fought the urge to cry out.

Her left eye was *gone*.

But there was no blood. The socket was simply welded shut, bisected by a ragged gash from the arch of her brow to the ridge of her cheekbone. Even in the silvery moonlight, it was clear the scar was a faded purple, as though the wound was weeks or even months old.

Impossible. I'd seen her only hours before.

Planting a palm on the ground, I stared at the earth and fought to keep from fainting. My vision blurred, shimmering like mist and silk and shadows.

'Oh my god,' I whispered, bile stinging the back of my tongue.

I looked up at her again, dizzy and disoriented, the feeling of landing into a parallel world where everything was *wrong*.

Davina was shaking uncontrollably now. 'It's real, then. Not a nightmare.'

Pull it together, I told myself. *This isn't about you.*

Except it was.

'I'm so sorry,' I all but moaned. Blood thundered in my ears. 'I'm so sorry.'

She covered her face once more, and my heart broke for her. She started murmuring lowly, urgently, like a litany. 'Not my eye. Please, not my eye, I – it can't be gone. No, no, *no*. I'll do anything.'

My skin prickled with vicarious dread. 'Does it hurt?'

A frantic sob. 'I felt the blade, I – it doesn't make sense. There was no real knife to my face. How can – *arghhhhhhh*.' She drove her fingers through her cropped black hair, grabbing desperate fistfuls of it.

'Were you awake?'

She shook her head fiercely. 'The pain woke me up pretty quickly.'

'And you came here?' My stomach was gripped in a vice, threatening to empty at any moment.

'I don't know why I was compelled to.' She dropped her bone-white hands into her lap and stared out to the eerily still water. The swans barely caused a ripple as they circled hypnotically. 'It was like my feet dragged me of their own accord. I didn't even scream, at first. I thought it was a dream.' Her whispering voice rose an octave. 'It *has* to be a dream, Penny. It has to.' I'd never heard her sound so young.

A strange kind of protectiveness came over me. I grabbed her by the shoulders, looking at her straight on, not flinching at the sight of the wound even though I so badly wanted to. 'We're going to find who did this.'

But her trembling only intensified. She once again began praying to a faceless deity. 'No, no, no, *please*, please don't be real, please –'

'Davina . . .'

Then she let go, let the pain and anguish and fear roll out of her in visceral screams. She dug her fingers into the earth, dragging deep claw marks along the shore. 'No, no, no, no . . .'

The ghostly swans on the lake watched with funereal ambivalence.

Fear gripped me by the ribs as I ran a finger over my own warning scar – carved as I slept by an invisible blade, a disembodied hand.

There were already three dead bodies in the Masked Painter's wake.

The message was clear: if we didn't find the killer soon, we would both be next.

CHAPTER ONE

Several weeks earlier

The spotlights shone white-gold from the back of the theatre, making the row of casting directors in front of them look headless.

I clutched a blank sheet of paper in my hands. A fake letter from Macbeth.

"'What thou art promised. / Yet do I fear thy nature; / It is too full o'th' milk of human kindness / To catch the nearest way. Thou wouldst be great, / Art not without ambition, but without / The illness should attend it. What thou wouldst highly, / That wouldst thou holily; wouldst not play false / And yet wouldst wrongly win.'"

My voice was a staccato rattle, fraught but also restrained, heated but controlled, like stoking a coal furnace. I imbued the Lady's scornful lines with an undercurrent of jealousy, hunger, letting her need for power burn through the words. Ambition was not too difficult an emotion to access, given how much I wanted this lead.

And I knew in my bones I was going to get it.

I'd spent my whole life playing the part of Penny Paxton, daughter of an icon. Acting felt as natural to me as breathing. So if the old adage was true – that it took ten thousand hours to master a craft – then nobody could come close to me.

But god, I was nervous. I was so nervous that my vision blackened and starred, and I had to blink furiously to bring myself back into the room. Fear coiled around my stomach like a python crushing its prey, and I couldn't fight the feeling that I wanted to be somewhere else. *Anywhere* else.

It was the first week of a three-year undergraduate programme at Dorian Drama Academy. The auditions for the winter production of *Macbeth* were open, and my fellow first years sat along the front few rows, watching, enraptured, something like envy written on their faces. Everyone here was excellent – you had to be, to get into Dorian – but they could feel the palpable tension in the room. A crackle in the air, mingled with the scent of hairspray and dusty velvet chairs.

I just had to hope it was for my talent, not my name.

When I finished the audition piece, murmurs rippled through the small crowd. The stern-faced casting director puffed air through her lips. Fraser Li, the favourite for Macbeth, climbed to his feet and clapped rapturously. I fizzed with pride. None of the other auditions had garnered such a response – it was very much the modus operandi to pretend not to be impressed by your rivals.

I left stage right, and a blonde girl with bright red glasses was wringing her hands in the wings. She was up next, and looked exactly how I felt inside: small, terrified. Detached from her peers. Alone in some fundamental way.

'You were amazing,' she whispered, clicking her knuckles. Heavy red curtains fell around us in stiff waves. 'How do I follow that? Shit. I should have chosen a different soliloquy.'

Her self-consciousness yanked me back to my first-ever audition. I was ten years old, vying for the role of Mary in the primary school nativity play. By then I had started to understand my mother's fame in a more real sense – the stares, the gasps, the way people literally fainted in her presence. I also understood the fact that she did not shower me with love the way the other parents in the playground did. My young brain had drawn a wobbly line between the two realities, concluding that if I could follow in her footsteps, maybe I would finally earn her love.

Unfortunately, I could barely get the words out during the audition, and pure terror caused quite a serious accident in my daisy-print underwear. Rebecca Murray was cast instead. Mum didn't even blink at the news. I'd thrown the pants in the tampon bin at school, so she wouldn't have to see what I'd done.

I never wanted anyone to feel how I'd felt back then – even if they were my competition.

'You're here for a reason, okay? You've got this.' I reached out and squeezed the nervous girl's shoulder, even though physical affection didn't come naturally to me.

She was white as a sheet. 'The words have totally left my

brain. I'm going to forget my lines, and everyone's going to think I'm a moron. What if Dorian's my flop era? Oh god. Youth theatre was one thing, but this . . . maybe I'm not cut out for . . .'

Sympathy twisted through me as she trailed off. Dorian was no am-dram. The stakes were so much higher, the audiences so much more discerning, the pressure of being perceived so much more debilitating.

'Do you want me to wait in the wings?' I suggested quietly. 'I'll mouth the words along with you. If you get stuck, just cast a dramatic look over at me, okay? Pretend it's a character choice to have her stare off into the middle distance every now and then.'

She blinked several times. 'You'd do that?'

'Of course.' Perhaps it was foolish, but I couldn't fight the feeling that we were both just insecure little kids. And I had spent so long wishing that someone would do the same for me. A reassuring hand on the shoulder. Kindness and affection without ulterior motive.

'Thank you, Penny.'

She smiled gratefully, but I felt that familiar burst of heat, the intense prickling sensation that came from strangers knowing your name when you did not know theirs. A fundamental power imbalance. A scale tipped too far in one direction. The generational curse most would consider a gift.

Play the part. Pretend to be your mother. Nobody needs to know the real you.

'You're welcome,' I said, painting the sanguine mask onto my face the same way I'd been doing for eighteen years. Smearing the persona over myself like red lipstick. 'What's your name?'

Something shone in her eyes, as though she was dazzled by my mere presence. 'Nairne.'

I nodded. 'I'll be right here.'

As it happened, Nairne only needed one cue, and while her performance was good, it was too timid, too apologetic. We both exited the stage and took our seats in the front row. Even in the unforgiving leather of my Louboutins, I felt like I was walking on air.

The part was mine. It had to be. Because there was only one actor left to audition for Lady Macbeth, and she was horribly late.

Hadiya Lazar, the casting director, rose to her feet. A high-necked purple poncho draped over her arms in folds of expensive cashmere. 'Well, if Ms Burns does not deign to join us, perhaps we should wrap things up here.'

Professor Drever, the show's director, gritted his teeth. 'Let's give her five more minutes.'

Lazar scoffed. 'If she does not respect our time, we do not respect –'

'Five. Minutes.' Drever's jaw was clenched, and he stared rigidly down at his notes.

Shooting him a filthy look, Lazar cast her gaze around the rest of the students. 'By all means, you're free to go.'

But nobody moved. We all wanted to see how this would play out. Would the final actor show up – and receive the tongue-lashing of the century? Or had she disappeared off the face of the earth, the pressure of Dorian already too much to handle?

I looked reverently around. This theatre was what most people thought of when they heard the words Dorian Drama Academy. Fronted by a facade of towering stone columns, the neoclassical auditorium inside was all grand proscenium arches, gold-leaf boxes and tiers, and an ornate ceiling fresco depicting the wedding night from *A Midsummer Night's Dream*. It was one of the few student theatres in the world that regularly attracted flocks of patrons, all eager to watch the budding talent of the future – and earn the bragging rights of *I saw them before they were famous.*

While we were waiting in tense silence for the final actor, my phone vibrated with a call in my pocket. *Mum* flashed on the screen, and with it came a pulse of conflicting emotion. I slipped up the aisle into the atrium of the theatre to answer.

'Hi, Mum.'

'Darling, listen, can you send me the names of your new flatmates? I'm going to have Ballantyne look into them. We must make sure they're not moles.'

I took a deep, steadying breath. Ballantyne was the private investigator my paranoid mother kept on retainer. She wouldn't let anyone new into my life without a thorough background check, though it was not completely clear what she was afraid of leaking. Hers was more of a vague, directionless paranoia – a fine mist rather than a sharp point.

'Okay.' A taut beat. I waited for her to ask, but of course she didn't. 'I just had my audition.'

'Oh, of course, darling!' The words were fond, but the tone was not. A common affectation of the upper class – the ability to sound emotive while remaining utterly detached. 'How did it go?'

'Really well. Really, really well.' I couldn't stop the beam spreading across my face. 'I think I nailed it, Mum.'

'How wonderful! I'm so proud of you, darling.'

I stilled, those words I'd chased for so long casually tossed in my direction, but there was no warmth behind them. A simple stock phrase, proffered in the correct social situation.

'You are? Proud of me, I mean.' Maybe I could jostle loose some genuine emotion by forcing her to elaborate.

'Of course,' Mum said. 'You know, I was cast as Lady Macbeth in first year myself.'

'Really?' The revelation was at once moving and anxiety-inducing – yet another benchmark for direct comparison.

A curious pause. 'It's a wonderful achievement, Penny.'

I swallowed hard. 'Thanks. You know, I wasn't sure whether you remem–'

'Listen, darling, I've got to dash. But congratulations! I can't wait to come and watch.' The thought of my ultra-famous mother stalking back into these hallowed halls filled me with a dread I didn't quite understand. 'Send me those names, won't you? Soon as you can.'

As we hung up, I tried to convince myself that the words I'd chased for so long were worth the effort. Worth crapping my pants in primary school, worth the debilitating stage fright, worth mimicking her every move since I was a child. And yet I felt more hollow than ever, as though the figure on the horizon I'd been chasing for a decade was nothing but a shadow.

Maybe it would've felt better to receive them over text, I reasoned. Then I wouldn't have to examine the porous words for tone and tenor. I could read them in my own voice. Stare at the screen until they sank in. *I'm so proud of you, darling*.

Just as I was preparing to go back into the auditorium, the rotating gold doors leading from the quad into the lobby swivelled and squeaked, spitting out one of the most beautiful girls I'd ever seen.

She was ghost-pale, with black pixie hair that stuck up in tufts. Her make-up was Parisian-bare, with just a slick of rose-pink lipstick and soft black mascara. Thinner than me, I noted – a score the demon in my mind always kept – and dressed entirely in black, but it was more biker chic than gothic. Leather jacket, tight jeans, cropped tank top exposing a strip of toned white stomach.

Attraction fluttered low in my belly, like the wings of a moth around a candle.

Seconds later, understanding clicked into place. She was the last student to audition for Lady Macbeth.

My rival.

And yet she was not rushing at all.

She drew closer, carrying with her the scent of fresh cigarette smoke and musky perfume. I couldn't tear my eyes away; it was as though she had her own magnetic field.

I was no stranger to raw charisma – my mother bled the stuff – but it was rare in people my age. I'd always believed it was something you grew into, something that became more powerful with time, like the dark matter of the universe expanding.

I waited for the girl to notice me, but she never did. The experience was entirely foreign. I was used to stares, to whispers, to feeling like a rare species in a city zoo, but the girl in the leather jacket didn't even look at me as she strolled calmly past, her footsteps unhurried, as though she wasn't dangerously late to an audition that would define the next three years of her performing career.

I followed her back into the theatre, hypnotised, and slid into the second row back from the stage. The late girl was having a terse, low-toned conversation with the casting panel, and *everyone* had turned to watch.

'That's Davina Burns,' muttered Nairne beside me. 'I heard her entry audition brought grown men to tears.'

After a few moments of chastising from the director – which seemed to roll off Davina like rain off an umbrella – she walked down the aisle towards the stage with the elegance of a ballerina, her feet barely grazing the red carpet. Climbing up the narrow stage steps, she shrugged her leather jacket off and tossed it into the wings.

And then she began.

The transformation into Lady Macbeth was immediate – and silent.

Her whole body snapped with tension. Her face was at once blank and haunted.

She cupped her empty hands together, as though clasping the bottom of a candle. I felt immediately silly for bringing a blank sheet of paper to use as a prop. A ridiculous amateur. A pantomime of a person.

Then she started to walk fearfully around the stage.

The sleepwalking scene right before Lady Macbeth's death.

Ghosts we could not see slipped over her face like swathes of silk. Her footsteps grew increasingly frantic.

The theatre was crypt-quiet, the air taut with tension.

Nobody moved. Nobody breathed.

I waited for Davina to speak, but she never did. My mind filled in the lines – *Out, damned spot! Out, I say!* – but it was almost like she didn't *need* to utter them. The emotions of the scene writhed through her entire body. Fear and shame and frantic remorse.

She pulled one hand off the invisible candle, staring blankly into her palm. Her breath hitched in her chest, horror dawning over her pixie features.

Here's the scent of blood still: all the / perfumes of Arabia will not sweeten this little / hand.

Goosebumps covered me from head to toe. The scene played out not in words, but in *her*. I had never seen anything like it.

The silence in the auditorium swelled; metastasised. All the hairs on the back of my neck stood to attention.

Davina's ears palpably pricked up, as though suddenly hearing a knocking at the gate.

What's done cannot be undone.

And then the scene was over. She broke character immediately, jarringly, and it was disorienting, the way she slipped from one person back into herself, as though the character had been her true persona all along.

Nobody clapped. She did not bow.

Instead she aimed a sarcastic little thumbs up towards the casting panel, scooped up her leather jacket and stalked out of the auditorium as soundlessly as she'd arrived.

A few moments after the door to the lobby closed, the spell was shattered. Murmurs rose like a tide, and the air dropped several degrees. The casting panel stared at the spot on the stage where Davina had stood, as though seeing her ghost, her after-image.

And I knew in my heart that I had just lost the lead.

CHAPTER TWO

A lock of copper hair circled the shower drain.

I froze, as though perfect stillness would undo it somehow.

It was thick as a rope, long as a tree branch, and it swirled and eddied in the water like seaweed on a tide.

I ran my fingers over my shampoo-lathered head in disbelief. Sure enough, there was a bare patch of scalp at the base of my skull where it had been coaxed free. A shudder rolled through me like a clap of thunder.

Over the summer I had lost a few strands – a thin ribbon from above my ear was the worst of it – but nothing like this. Nothing that made my cheeks burn with dread. Nothing that left me so quietly devastated.

My great-aunt had suffered from trypophobia. It was illogical, on the face of it, the way she recoiled from honeycombs and pomegranates as though in mortal danger. As a child I found it entertaining, this utter irrationality. What harm could clusters of small holes do to her? But as I grew older, the more I understood the fear was something ancient and evolutionary. It was in the sinister images those holes conjured up: tarantula eyes and black mould, poisonous snake scales and deathly diseases.

That was how looking at the cord of hair felt: as though my subconscious mind knew something dark and threatening lurked beneath the surface. Something viscerally frightening.

Shutting off the shower, I tried to quell the panic surging in my chest, but it was no use. The water drained, but the hair remained coiled around the plughole, lank and defeated. Grabbing it in a fistful of paper towels, I dumped it in the bin beneath the sink and covered it with a purple tampon wrapper, ashamed of the fact I was shedding in brutal clumps.

Would it be contained to a single sorry patch? Or would I slowly shed it all until not even an eyelash remained?

Ten minutes of research into alopecia over the summer had told me there was no cure.

My single dorm was crypt-cold away from the steamy heat of the en-suite shower, and I crossed to the white-arched window to pull it shut. The campus grounds rolled away from Abernathy Hall like a bolt of emerald silk. At the foot of the lawn was a kidney-shaped lake patrolled by vicious swans, next to which was a small, rotting boathouse painted flaky white and sky blue. Beyond the glassy water lay a dense woodland of birch, holly and hawthorn, and above the canopy was the distant Edinburgh skyline, smudged by a low haze.

As I blotted my hair dry with a towel – flinching at the slightest follicle tug – a sense of fraudulence settled over me like the mist over the city. What if I didn't deserve to be here after all? What if I'd only got into Dorian because of my name and my beauty?

What would happen if I lost one of those things?

Davina had been officially cast as Lady Macbeth. The announcement went up a few days after the audition.

I was one of the three witches.

Throwing on a white Givenchy shirt dress in broderie anglaise and a cream cashmere sweater, I padded through to the communal kitchen I shared with three other drama students. It was a high-ceilinged room with tall, bright windows, bare white walls and Victorian tiles of black, cream and terracotta.

My flatmates Catalina and Maisie sat on stools at the dark wood breakfast bar, but Fraser was nowhere to be seen. The space was already homely, thanks to Catalina. Her menagerie of green plants spilled from the windowsills on to the countertops, and Kilner jars of coffee and sugar were lined up next to a vintage tea kettle. An assortment of Gentileschi prints hung opposite the windows, cast in slatted daylight, and the row of bookcases were already overflowing – Murakami next to Agatha Christie, a *Lord of the Rings* special edition next to the complete Sherlock Holmes collection.

Catalina was brewing a cardamon-scented tea in a silver infuser, chatting about a textual analysis she'd needlessly performed on the fourth act of *Macbeth*. Maisie, by comparison, preferred to discuss other people.

'Apparently Davina Burns has been getting a little *too* friendly with Professor Drever,' Maisie said, slicking red polish on to her fingernails. Her blonde hair was French-plaited, and she wore a matching white sweatshirt and jogger set with fluffy pink slippers.

Catalina blinked behind enormous tortoiseshell glasses, visibly bemused. She'd been discussing alternative interpretations of the love potion, and Maisie's tendency to derail conversations with childish rumours was jarring.

'Oh. I hadn't heard that.' Her accent was underpinned with a subtle Spanish warmth.

She immediately went back to the textbook she was reading, but Maisie didn't take the hint. 'She's been staying behind after class a *lot*, and Portia Bianchi said she saw her leaving the other night looking "flushed".' She threw exaggerated air quotes around the latter word, her tone a conspiratorial hush.

'No wonder she got Lady Macbeth,' I grumbled. I didn't believe for a second this was the reason, but it made me feel a little better to imagine a world in which I was unjustly robbed of the role by a girl who couldn't even show up on time.

Too late, I realised I'd forgotten to slip into the polished Paxton persona. I forced a twinkle into my eye, a pep into my tone, a gentle arch into my back, and added, 'I'm kidding. Her audition was flawless.'

Maisie practically glowed with self-satisfaction – someone had given her the reaction she wanted. 'I also heard that she got caught shoplifting when she was younger. But you didn't hear that from me.'

I opened the cupboard and pulled out a rose-painted teacup. My flatmates all had sentimental mugs – tacky photo-memories and cheesy slogans from mums and uncles and old school friends – while I had a set of floral Emma Bridgewaters with zero personal meaning.

At the sight of Catalina's open packet of cookies, my stomach growled like a feral thing. But I never ate breakfast: a small test of willpower I made sure to win every morning. Over time these rules I set for myself had become more restrictive, more severe, like the ribbons of a corset constantly pulled ever tighter.

You have to wait until midday to eat. If you can just make it to eleven, you can have another coffee. An apple at three. Diet Coke at four.

You can last a few more minutes. A few more hours.

My mum maintained her supermodel body without even trying, but for me it took significantly more effort. I reached instead for the ornate silver cafetière I'd bought in Paris during last year's fashion week.

'What did your mum say about you not being cast as Lady Macbeth?' Maisie asked. 'I bet she was livid.' She put on a pretentious accent, the exaggerated vowels scraping at me like the shrill metallic screech of sharpening knives. '"The *dean* will be receiving a letter any *day* now."'

I laughed light-heartedly, but my heart sank. 'Bold of you to assume my mother knows how to write.'

In truth, I hadn't spoken to my mum since I'd sent her my flatmates' names. I was afraid to tell her that I didn't get the lead, and more than a little humiliated. Not because she'd be disappointed – ambivalence was far more her style – but because my pride couldn't take the admission of failure, especially after I'd told her the lead was all but mine. Especially after she'd told me she was proud of me. That it was a wonderful achievement. I couldn't bear to have those long-chased sentiments withdrawn.

'What's it like, having such a famous parent?' Maisie asked, screwing the lid back on to her polish and blowing at her clawed nails.

'It's all I know.' A careful, practised answer. I adjusted the low messy bun at the nape of my neck. The bare skin beneath felt tender and exposed, as though a scab had just been torn from the top.

'She came to Dorian too, right? Back in the day?'

I nodded, spooning dark-roast coffee into the French press and topping it with water from the recently boiled kettle. 'She dropped out after first year, though.' I ran some quick mental calculations, trying to remember how much of my mother's messy history was public domain.

Pausing her forefinger over the paragraph she was reading, Catalina looked up, blinking twice in rapid succession and pushing her glasses up the bridge of her nose. 'Why? That's so sad. Passing up an opportunity like this.' Her auburn curls fell to her shoulders, swept back from her olive face with a sage-green claw clip.

'She was scouted for modelling.' There were also the twin pillars of depression and addiction for her to contend with, but I couldn't say as much.

Maisie leaned forward on the breakfast bar, fixing her hazel eyes on me so intensely that I had to look away. 'Do *you* know who your dad is?'

Ah, the gossip-rag subject *du jour*. My mother's publicist had 'accidentally' dropped a pseudo-hint to drum up excitement for Peggy Paxton's upcoming memoir, *Life Between the Lines*. Ghostwritten, of course, but sure to be a bestseller. Everything my mum touched turned to gold. Every *Vogue* cover she graced, every record she sang on, every feature film she cameoed in.

Everything except me.

Keen to shut the topic down, I simply said, 'Nope. And I don't care.'

A well-trodden lie. Deep down, the question of my father had always gnawed at me. I'd spent most of my childhood fantasising about a warm, jocular man who'd throw me over his broad shoulders and call me *kiddo*. A dad who'd teach me to tie my shoes and make mud pies and fix broken bike chains and roast the perfect chicken.

But my mother had always insisted it would do me more harm than good to know who he was – and why he didn't want anything to do with us.

'Are we boring you, Catalina?' Maisie asked with a chuckle, but the laughter was brittle.

Catalina had started reading again, and sighed at the interruption. She looked up reluctantly. There was a rectangular bulge at the waistband of her vintage jeans – an insulin pump. She pulled her chunky taupe cardigan tighter around herself.

'Sorry. I'm just not into gossip, unless it's a critical part of a Dungeons & Dragons campaign. Convincing the blacksmith to tell you who bought the magical sword, et cetera.'

I chuckled. I'd only lived with her for a week, but I'd never seen Catalina without either an open book in her hand or a rolled-up fantasy map under her arm. Some might find it rude, the way she was only ever half listening to you, the way her mind wandered mid-conversation as though she was chasing orcs that very second, but I found it endearing.

'Oh, come on,' Maisie said, leaning forward on the counter. 'Not one part of you wants to know who Penny's dad is? What if it's someone really famous?'

'Not really.'

The whole exchange was making my skin crawl – the heat of Maisie's gaze, the unbearable sensation of being perceived, of being talked about like a newspaper headline instead of a person – so I dropped my teaspoon into the white Belfast sink with a clatter. 'See you both in the voice seminar?'

As I walked away with my coffee, I heard Maisie stage-whisper, 'Do you think it's true that she was dragged along on massive benders with her mum when she was, like, four years old?'

Memories flitted through me unbidden. Crystal-studded lighters held beneath silver teaspoons, spider-thin limbs tangled on chesterfield sofas, rows of white powder lined up like playground chalk tallies. I blinked the images furiously away.

Even though my flatmates were all attending the same

seminar, I finished my coffee and walked across campus by myself. My own company was the only company I could honestly say I enjoyed. It was the great paradox of my existence – I wanted to be loved, but I also wanted to be left alone. A dichotomy I could never quite reconcile.

It was late September, and the heat of the summer had faded to an orange ember. The wych elms clustered in the quad had been kissed yellow at the tips, and the air was tinged with woodsmoke and clove. The fountain at the centre of the courtyard babbled merrily, streams of water arcing from the mouths of rough-hewn stone swans, and a group of students lounged around it, talking in absurd Austen accents.

Flicking one end of my tartan scarf over my shoulder, I cut through the tall, red-bricked Drummond Building to get to Kern.

The entrance hall of Drummond was lined with portraits of the school's founders: four exaggerated busts painted in rich, jewel-toned oils. Unlike the old cliché, their eyes didn't follow you around the room, but rather my eyes had no choice but to follow *them*, so magnetic was their lure.

As I was exiting the rotating doors, something snagged my attention in the back alley behind Kern: a dark green estate car, with two people in the front seats bowing their heads together.

Professor Drever was one of them; salt-and-pepper hair, a coarse beard, a tweed jacket and navy-blue tie. His middle-aged eyes were crinkled, with permanent commas etched around the mouth.

Davina was the other.

Black pixie-cropped hair, paper-white skin, leather jacket, ballerina limbs.

I remembered what Maisie had said back in the kitchen: *She's been staying behind after class a lot.*

Some strange instinct told me to back into the building and watch from a distance. Suspicion burned at me, along with something altogether shameful and self-serving.

Indignance bucked like a steed in my chest.

What if the role really *had* been mine to lose?

I remembered how Lazar wanted to end the auditions without Davina, only for Drever to insist they wait five more minutes.

As they sat in the car, Davina was hard-faced, fixing Drever with her idiosyncratic glare. He shook his head, one hand clasped over the top of the steering wheel, staring unseeingly ahead.

For a few moments, nothing happened. Neither spoke. Neither moved an inch. Still, I had the curious sensation of intruding on a private moment – something at once charged and vulnerable.

I don't know what made me pull out my phone and open the camera. I don't know what made me press record. I don't know what I was expecting to see, or what I was intending to do with it.

Yet when Davina leaned in and kissed Drever on the stoic cheek, I caught it all.

The kiss was almost nothing; a feathery brush. But it *looked* like something.

Just as I took a step forward to get a clearer shot, Davina drew away from Drever, opened the car door and stepped her long legs out. She slammed it shut without a backward glance at the professor, and when her gaze lifted from the pavement her eyes fixed on me.

My stomach lurched as violently as it had watching my hair circle the drain.

From the look on Davina's face – equal parts fearful and furious – she knew *exactly* why my phone was cradled in my outstretched hand.

She stormed over to where I stood rooted to the cobbled pavement, her features morphing from malignance into faux amity. Behind her, Drever reversed out of the alley and back on to the narrow road that looped around campus.

Davina stopped a few feet away from me, curling her red-slicked lips into a crooked smile.

'Penny, isn't it?'

CHAPTER THREE

'And you're Davina.'

My pulse skittered and flared like a snare drum. I was mortally afraid of conflict – mostly because it involved eye contact and saying the right things, neither of which came naturally to me. *Put on the mask, Paxton.*

'Nice to meet you,' I added, but it seemed absurd given the circumstances.

She arched a thin black brow. 'Listen, I'm not sure what you think you just saw, but it was nothing.'

'Okay.'

'Or at least it wasn't what you think it is.'

I nodded, tucking my phone into my back pocket. 'Alright.'

Her eyes flitted to my hip, narrowing almost imperceptibly. She shifted from one ballet flat to the other. 'Did you take a picture?'

'It shouldn't matter if I did, considering it was nothing.' I kept my tone cool and measured, careful not to inflame the situation, but it came out more bluntly than intended. Story of my life.

'Could you just delete it, please?' She ran slender white

fingers through her cropped hair, making it stand on end, and visceral envy licked through me. *She* wasn't balding by the day.

'Why?' A gaggle of students left one of the terraced houses from the row opposite Kern, and their pops of laughter chafed against the tense situation.

'I – look.' Davina sighed, her narrow jaw clenching. Then she dug a hand into her jacket pocket and pulled out a hand-rolled cigarette, perching it between her lips without lighting it. 'You and I both know we're the most talented bitches on this programme.' I frowned. When had she seen me act? 'Realistically we're going to spend the next three years competing against each other for the lead. But I don't want there to be any bad blood between us.'

I frowned, not fully comprehending. 'There isn't.'

Was she threatening me? I tried to scour the words for hidden meaning, but as usual my brain couldn't parse the subtext.

Tilt your jaw up, I reminded myself. *Smile without your teeth.*

This time the noise Davina made was more of a scoff. 'Why are you being like this?'

'Like what?' I was genuinely bemused. I hadn't said anything that could be considered incendiary or hostile.

Davina took a step forward, and some primal instinct forced my own feet back.

And she *laughed*; a short, sharp bark.

'Are you . . . *afraid* of me?' Her eyes darted from side to side, scanning my face like an ancient text. There were traces of a smirk curled around her mouth, the skinny cigarette still dangling unlit. 'There's no reason for someone like you to be –'

'Sorry, someone like me?' Finally I allowed some heat into my tone, and Davina rocked back on her heels, pleased by the rise.

'You know,' she said, sneeringly. 'Wealthy. Privileged. Powerful.'

I met her spiteful energy with my own. 'You have no idea what you're talking about.' All the times I'd been powerless as a child crested in my heart.

Davina only rolled her eyes. 'Come back to me when you've spent a summer sleeping in your car.'

'Oh, so you *do* have a car?' I snapped. 'Strange that you had to get a lift with Drever.'

The mask was slipping, despite my best efforts. How had Davina pried it off me so effortlessly?

'Okay, I'm done playing nice,' she hissed, stepping forward again until she was so close to my face I could smell the tobacco and her musky perfume. 'I got Lady Macbeth because I'm better than you. And you know that, and it's why you're resorting to petty pictures instead of *proving* yourself like every other student who earned their place here instead of buying it.'

The words were like whips across my back, raw and true, and I loathed her for how easily she honed in on my deepest insecurities. But I couldn't let her see that. Pride ran through the Paxton women as undeniably as our copper hair and green eyes; a perpetual undercurrent of stubbornness.

So instead I said sweetly, 'So much for "we're the most talented bitches on this programme".'

She laughed again, high and cruel. 'Oh, *I'm* talented. I'm so fucking talented that I had to choose between Dorian and the Royal Ballet School.' Her expression was almost feral. 'You're just rich.' She made the final word sound like a hideous disease.

Tears stung at my eyes, and I hated myself for it, I *hated* how easy it was to make me cry. In an instant I was four years old, my knees grazed and raw, my nose snotty and pink, sobbing and sobbing for a mother who was too comatose to comfort me. I'd never been taught how to regulate my emotions, and so they often ran away from me, gathering speed as they hurtled downhill.

Before I could respond to Davina's jibes, the rotating doors of Drummond swivelled behind me.

'What's going on?' Maisie's voice was filled with a kind of vicarious thrill.

I turned to face my flatmate. Catalina stood next to her – at least a foot shorter, with soft curves and elfish brogues – hugging an annotated script to her chest with one hand and an open library textbook with her other. At the sight of my pink-rimmed eyes, she took an instinctual step forward, her head tilting with concern.

Yet that Paxton pride prevailed. I didn't want Maisie to feed on the drama like a leech. I didn't want Catalina to comfort me like some pathetic kid.

'It's nothing,' I muttered, staring down at my ankle boots.

They weren't yet worn in, and I could feel my skin beginning to blister and bleed. 'Don't worry.'

Davina shot me a final glare, tundra-cold, and stormed away. Her footsteps were almost silent on the pavement; she glided with an impossible elegance.

'What was all that about?' Maisie asked, not even bothering to hide her excitement. 'Was she having a go at you?'

'It's fine.' I picked at a flake of loose skin on my lip; a compulsive habit my aunt Polly always lectured me about. 'Just a misunderstanding.'

Catalina's brow furrowed with concern. 'I heard what she said. It's not true, you know. You totally deserve to be here. You slayed your audition. Slayed it like Smaug. Absolute Bard the Bowman energy. Which you should be pleased with, since he is at least my second-favourite Bard.'

My phone buzzed in my back pocket, and I pulled it out to see Mum was calling me. The thought of talking to her right now made my stomach curdle. I slipped it back in until it rang out.

We started walking to Kern.

'Thing is, though,' Maisie said earnestly, 'even if you weren't quite as good as the rest of us, so what? Use the tools at your disposal, I say. And if those tools are your mum's name and your fat bank account, so be it.' She held up her palms. 'It's a cut-throat world. No judgement here.'

For some reason, Maisie's facetious support felt even worse than Davina's venomous onslaught. I cringed away from her words, fighting the urge to curl up in a ball like a hedgehog.

Would I ever know if they were right?

Frustration ebbed at my temples. My brain naturally gravitated towards indisputable facts. They were a comfort blanket to me, bringing order and structure to an unwieldy world. It was why I loved chess so much as a child, the pieces moving along ranks and files according to predetermined rules, the mathematical certainty that if you made the best calculations, you would win. There was no luck or opinion involved. No unfavourable rolls of the dice, no begging your opponent to sell you Mayfair.

No messy human emotions. Just logic. Beautiful, simple logic.

Yet I would never be able to quantify Davina or Maisie's comments, never be able to prove them true or false in any real sense. Why had I gravitated towards a profession that was built on art, in all its glorious subjectivity? Why hadn't I pursued maths, or physics, something with right answers and definitive formulae?

If I had been cast as Lady Macbeth . . .

But I hadn't. Davina had – because of the special allowances Drever had granted her.

As we entered the oval atrium of Kern, an ugly idea surfaced. I now had photographic evidence of Davina and Drever at my fingertips. Could I use it to force Drever to recast my rival? He might name me Lady Macbeth in her stead. If he did, then I'd know I had the acting chops to be here. And I wouldn't have to admit to my mother that I had failed.

I thought of my ten-year-old self auditioning for Mary, hiding her soiled underwear in the girls' loos, mortified that her very best efforts still hadn't been enough. I thought of the turmoil I'd put myself through to get here. I thought of how good it would feel to receive a standing ovation, after almost two decades of wishing I was *enough*.

For all my flaws, indecision was not one of them.

As soon as the idea had come to me, I knew I was going to do it.

Davina would survive. Like she said, she was extremely fucking talented.

Call it blackmail, call it extortion, but I'd always been told that Dorian was a cut-throat world. Besides, Davina was hardly morally unimpeachable. Even though revenge was not my primary reason for the ploy, I couldn't deny the forked tongue of satisfaction at the thought of wiping the smugness from her face.

'You go ahead,' I said to Catalina and Maisie, stopping abruptly just outside the lecture hall. 'I'll meet you in the seminar.'

Catalina stopped too, resting a hand decked in gold rings on the back of my elbow. 'Are you sure you're alright?'

'Yeah.' I forced a smile, despite the shame baying at me. 'Just need to grab something from the library.'

The Narciso Trevisan Library – named after one of Dorian's most esteemed alumni – was almost deserted, since it was so early in the semester that even the final year students hadn't started panicking about their dissertations yet.

It was housed in another old red-brick building, with gleaming chequerboard floors, mahogany bookshelves with gilded sliding ladders, and the aphrodisiac scent of old paper and ink. There were countless display cases filled with trinkets and miscellany: old programmes and strange props, golden compasses and curious hourglasses in which the sand was suspended mid-trickle. The wood-panelled walls were hung with more oil paintings, plus a row of ornate masks from the school's first-ever production of *The Merchant of Venice* back in 1894.

After finding a quiet nook in the cloister near the printers, I played back the video on my phone, pausing it at the point of the cheek kiss. Davina's fingers were resting languidly on Drever's shoulder, and his eyes were closed in a way that could've been either sensual pleasure or existential despair. Her other arm was ambiguously placed – it might have been resting on the gearstick, but it was also suggestive of something far more career-jeopardising.

I took a screenshot of the still, then added a text overlay. A single block-capped word, both an instruction and a threat:

RECAST.

CHAPTER FOUR

The day after leaving the printout on Drever's desk, I spent his entire acting seminar feeling sick to the stomach.

Because Davina was nowhere to be seen.

Had he already dropped her from the production?

Worse . . . had she been booted off the programme entirely?

It was a possibility that came to me late at night, tossing and turning as an old oak tree outside Abernathy scraped at the rattling windowpane. As cruel-tongued as Davina was, she didn't deserve to have her entire career ruined before it had even begun. And if someone other than Drever had found the photo first, who knows how far they might have escalated it?

Horrified with my knee-jerk actions, I arrived at Drever's classroom twenty minutes early that morning, hoping the blackmail would still be on his desk and that I could scoop it up before any severe action was taken. But the classroom was locked, and when Drever finally arrived to let us in – five minutes late and distinctly harried-looking – I saw that the printout had already gone.

The printout was gone, and so was Davina.

I reassured myself that if it had been escalated to the dean,

Drever would not still be standing here gesticulating about the Stanislavski method. I scanned his face for any clues about what had transpired; purplish bags under his dark brown eyes, a slouched weariness to his usually upright posture. I even sniffed the air when he strode past my rickety pine desk, hoping to catch a scent of Davina's musky perfume or earthy tobacco on his tweed blazer.

Nothing.

The classroom was both shadowy and bright, with dusty sunlight filtering through dramatic bay windows. A green chalkboard hung at the front of the room behind a squat desk laden with leather-bound volumes and a mounted *Phantom of the Opera* mask – Drever had got his start in musicals, much to the admonishment of Dorian's sniffier professors.

The oak floorboards creaked and groaned whenever Drever shifted his weight from one foot to the other, and his cavernous voice echoed and boomed in the rafters.

I stretched in the loose-legged chair. My body ached from a week of movement sessions. I'd always been naturally fit – running was my preferred method of maintaining my physique – but the way Madame Lavigne combined Lecoq with yoga and pilates was stretching my muscles in ways they'd never been stretched before. Combined with the five miles I'd forced myself to jog that morning, I was hurting.

As I moved, I felt half a dozen sets of eyes fixing on me. Not because I was doing anything especially noteworthy, but because in the presence of extraordinary beauty, people stared.

My appearance afforded me a certain privilege in the way I moved through the world, but it also cast a constant spotlight on me at times when I would prefer the luxury of anonymity. For someone so mortally afraid of being perceived, it made perception an inevitability. Yet I played into it, always. I starved and jogged and preened. I chose the show-stopping outfits, the perfect light make-up, the long, flowing hairstyles. I spent undue energy on keeping my waist small and my nails painted in pretty pastels. It was exhausting, and yet I was so terrified to stop – because who would I be without it?

And now my hair was falling out.

I'd been too afraid to wash my hair that morning, and it felt heavy on my scalp. Once again I'd tucked it into a low pony, attempting to make it chic with a leather scrunchie.

'Of course, Stanislavski's method has downsides,' said Drever, his hands animated as he talked, 'and the murky concept of emotional memory is probably the most controversial. With this technique, an actor activates the memory of a lived experience to connect to their character – but in the pursuit of heightening emotional memory, some actors merge their personal lives with their characters' lives in psychologically unhealthy ways. On occasion, they may unearth deep-rooted trauma in their own pasts – and, disturbingly, they cannot remember whether it is real or an implant from their character. The bounds of their identities become blurred, and that is a dangerous thing.'

My phone buzzed in my Hermès backpack, and my stomach

clenched itself into a fist. Mum again. I still hadn't returned her call, and it was rare for her to persist in trying to reach me.

I thought back to the Dorian open day, which she was supposed to attend with me. I'd spent the morning agonising over the perfect outfit to wear, eventually settling for a floral Valentino dress and an oversized Balmain tote.

Your looks are your greatest currency, as she had always taught me.

A few minutes before we were due to set off, though, she decided she couldn't face it after all.

'Oh, sweetie, it would just be so *strange* to set foot there again.' She wrung her hands, skin so pale it was almost blue. 'All those memories, and . . . I'm sorry, darling. You'll be fine without me, won't you? Anyway, it's probably not cool to have your old mum floating around behind you, is it?'

Old was a stretch – she looked the same as she had twenty years ago.

Part of me was relieved that she had bailed. I'd be far less likely to be stared at without my iconic mother striding around the campus. But I was stung, nonetheless. She'd always been flaky, missing out on the youth theatre production of *Cabaret* to have drinks with a former manager, skipping my cross-country championships to attend Milan fashion week.

I tried to convince myself that her flaking on the Dorian open day had nothing to do with the fact I'd come out to her as gay two days prior. Intellectually I knew she wasn't pretending when she said she didn't care – she'd participated in enough orgies in her day to be lax about that kind of thing – but the insecure little girl at the heart of me needed the reassurance.

She insisted that she loved me the same as she always had. But maybe that was the problem.

'You look like a goddess, though,' she'd purred as I was clambering into a hastily summoned Uber. 'Your beauty will open doors for you that are locked to most other people. Always remember that. Love you, darling.' The last three words were uttered out of some vague sense of good manners.

Around me in the classroom were the sounds of pencil cases zipping and notebooks snapping shut, and I realised Drever had dismissed us.

'Lunch at the Costumery?' asked Maisie, who'd been sitting to my left and texting under the table the whole time. Catalina sat to my other side, still scribbling furious notes.

The three of us – plus Fraser, our fourth flatmate – had got into the habit of eating in the students' union after our morning seminars. The schedule at Dorian was punishing, with four hours of academic classes lasting until midday, a quick sustenance break and then four hours of rehearsals in the afternoon. On one or two evenings a week, we also had private sessions with our individual mentors. Mine was a stand-offish male professor, Dr Keddie, who had an honest-to-god 'countdown to retirement' calendar hung behind his desk.

My head rushed dizzily as I stood up.

'Sounds good,' I said to Maisie, still irritated about her comments about whether or not I deserved to be at Dorian.

'*Unff*,' moaned Fraser, who had been clubbing in the city last night and was still suffering immensely. He'd been cast as Macbeth in the first-year production and was still in the throes of celebration.

I couldn't get a strong read on Fraser. He was handsome and he knew it, with chiselled Asian features, a tall, carved physique and thick black hair swept to one side. His energy was somewhere between golden retriever, guffawing rugby lad – he was the only other student at Dorian that reminded me of the kids at my private school – and unfairly talented classical actor. Fraser was also absurdly good at improv. I'd never seen anyone switch so effortlessly into different personas.

Maisie gazed at him while she thought he wasn't looking. She was, without question, completely infatuated.

As we were traipsing out of the airy classroom – Catalina lagging behind as she finished an urgent paragraph – I'd almost forgotten about the Davina situation. About her conspicuous absence, and what it might mean. About what I had done, and why I had done it.

Until Drever fixed me with an impenetrable gaze and said, 'Penny, can I have a word?'

CHAPTER FIVE

'Of course,' I said, my throat arid, my gaze drawn determinedly to the swathes of sunlight sweeping across scuffed floorboards. Shame rose in me, a furious heat spreading from my toes to my brow, a searing paranoia that he *knew* it was me.

Had I been careless? Was my student ID stamped across the footer of the printout? Had he caught a damning glimpse of my altercation with Davina before pulling away in his car?

Maisie cast me a look that said, *Ooooh, drama!* while Catalina furrowed her dark brow in my direction. Fraser looked simply like he might vomit Jägermeister into the wicker basket by Drever's desk. They filed out with the other dozen students in our cohort, leaving just me and Drever standing by his desk. I watched from the corner of my eye as he crossed around to the back, shrugged off his faded blazer and sat slowly into his chair.

'Unfortunately, Davina Burns has had to withdraw from the role of Lady Macbeth,' he said. A muscle feathered in his jaw.

A pit opened up in my stomach. 'Oh. Why?'

'Scheduling conflict.'

The booming tenor of his teaching voice had quieted to a melancholy murmur, with an unmistakable underpinning of emotion. Had Davina actually meant something to him? Or was he thinking only of her unique talent, and the way it had been squandered so soon?

What exactly *was* the nature of their relationship? Romantic enough that he had succumbed to blackmail with such ease, at least. But just how many lines had they crossed?

'Oh,' I said, my pulse high and thin in my temples. I forced my gaze up, but he was staring out of the bay window onto the quad. Students milled around in merry clusters, mostly in the direction of the Costumery or the little campus grocery shop. It was a sea of Fjällräven backpacks and high-top Converse, with the occasional roll-neck jumper and plaid peacoat.

Finally, as though the very words pained him, Drever said, 'We were wondering whether you might like to take her place.'

My heart skipped.

There it was.

Undeniable proof that I deserved to be here.

So why did it taste so sour?

A rhetorical question. I knew exactly why.

Thoughts pinballed around in my mind. I wasn't the only one at fault, I reasoned. Davina should have considered the potential consequences before she laid her lips to Drever in plain sight. And yet I had exploited her mistake for personal gain without a second thought, and now the victory felt hollow.

The dizziness in my head intensified – whether from low blood sugar or from stress, I did not know. I leaned back against a desk to steady myself.

When I said nothing for a few moments, Drever misinterpreted my silence for reluctance.

'I know the lead carries a certain pressure.' He steepled his fingers in front of him. 'I understand if you'd rather stick with the weird sister. A fine role, in the right hands.'

'No,' I said, with more ferocity than intended. *Raise your chin, drop your shoulders, smile graciously. Don't forget the Paxton polish.* 'I want to do it.' I beamed, flashing pearly white teeth with the slightest vampiric points. 'Thank you. You won't regret it.'

He smiled. 'I'm so glad. Your audition was very strong.'

It didn't bring anyone to tears, though, did it? I thought bitterly.

'You have a lot of potential, and I look forward to seeing what you bring to the role.' He opened his top desk drawer and pulled out a fresh script, white and crisp and full of promise. He handed it to me. It was still printer-warm. 'And I'm here to offer guidance whenever you need it, alright?'

It was strange not to have his gaze roam over me, not to hear a flirtatious crackle in his voice. Strange, but nice. Knowing about his relationship with Davina should have set my teeth on edge, but there was nothing that felt predatory about him. His presence was almost a paternal one – but having grown up fatherless, I supposed I had little to compare it with. All I knew was that the offer of guidance nearly brought a tear to my eye.

Before I could stop myself, I thought of how I might have grown up – swimming lessons and hot chips on a weekend, flying kites with big, strong hands clasping mine – then of how I *actually* grew up. Ice cubes clinking in vodka sodas, the clack of stiletto heels dancing on coffee tables. The pounding bass and intoxicated shrieks blaring through the house as I tried to sleep. Strangers stumbling into my room, passing out on the futon where I read my *Goosebumps* books. The next day, my mother's eyes never quite meeting mine. The connection between us never quite knotting, never quite deepening.

I swallowed the lump in my throat. Now was not the time for childish imaginings. My life was what it was. Once I was a decorated actor in my own right, I would be adored in a way my mother had never been able to muster.

Wasn't that what everyone wanted, at the heart of themselves? To be adored?

'There's one more matter left to discuss,' Drever went on, as I stared fixedly at the script, praying he wasn't about to rightly accuse me of blackmail. 'It is tradition for the first-year female lead to be mentored by Professor Orlagh Camran.'

I stifled a gasp. Orlagh Camran was RSC *royalty*.

Her career had come to a famously devastating end a little over two decades ago, when merciless throat cancer left her voice hoarse and painful. After a final encore as Lady Macbeth on the West End, she'd taken up a tenured position at the drama school she herself had attended. She only taught one class – tutoring the third years on mastery of Shakespeare – and spent the rest of the time swanning around campus in exquisite ball gowns, eating fresh figs and reading battered old paperbacks.

She was a goddess.

Again, Drever filled my silence before I could find the proper words.

'I understand that you have already commenced your sessions with Dr Keddie, and given the unusual circumstances you're welcome to remain under his wing. But Professor Camran has a . . . unique ability to pull diamonds from the rough. She is a common thread between the girls who leave Dorian and catapult to stardom.'

A dark thrill flickered in my chest. Perhaps this would be the thing that *made* me extraordinary. That hauled me up to Davina's level. To my mother's level.

'I would love to be mentored by her,' I answered, cradling the script to my chest. 'Thank you.'

'The pleasure is all mine.' Another paternal smile. 'I'll see you in rehearsals this afternoon. You're going to be great, Penny.'

Still light-headed, I left the classroom feeling equal parts exhilarated and sickened. I was about to be mentored by one of the best living actors of all time. She could polish me. She could take my supernatural beauty and my rough talent and gild it in gold.

The hallways of Drummond were already deserted, and my heels squeaked on the parquet flooring. Lining the corridor were more of the eerie portraits from the entrance hall: famous alumni and hallowed directors, as well as deans and professors alike. Drever's portrait looked freshly painted, the gentle jowls hanging from his once stoic jaw a cruel reminder of the passage of time. His expression was deep and forlorn, and I couldn't tear my eyes away.

Hung over the stone staircase that swept down into the atrium, there was an ornate gold mirror the size of a terraced house, refracting light into every darkened corner. For a reason I couldn't name, I was afraid to look in it.

In fact, I was struggling to look at anything. My vision swam and swooped, like two swallows chasing each other. I really needed to eat something.

As I was about to make my way down the steps, a shadowy figure stepped out from a narrow alcove and grabbed me by the ponytail, hauling me into the darkness.

Adrenaline spiked into my veins from the shock of it, but I couldn't get my vision to focus on the perpetrator.

Fear coursed through me as the hand tightened around my hair.

My *hair*.

Stomach lurching, I was swivelled around and slammed against a cold stone wall. The impact somehow dissipated the spots across my vision.

Davina's lupine eyes bore into mine, one forearm pressed against my clavicle, and the other hand curled around my ponytail.

'I know what you did,' she whispered, and it was more terrifying than a fully fledged scream, every hushed decibel low and venomous.

We were mere inches apart. Her breath was tobacco-laced and cool as it brushed my lips.

There was no sense in lying. 'You would have done the same.'

'No.' She shook her head slowly, threateningly. 'I would never have needed to in the first place.'

'Why did you get involved with Drever?' I asked, hating the pressure of her forearm against my chest but feeling too weak and dizzy to push her back. 'Why would you jeopardise yourself like that? Your talent won you the part. You didn't need to seduce the director.'

Something impenetrable flickered across her face. Then she put even more pressure over my clavicle, to the point where it started to hurt. 'I don't owe you an explanation.'

'Maybe not,' I said, as evenly as possible, 'but you owe yourself one.'

Her lips curled, and I noticed her lipstick was hastily applied and smudged at the corners. 'You won't need to worry about my peace of mind for much longer.'

Even my overly literal brain sensed the threat.

I swallowed, and the rise and fall pushed my collarbones into her arm. 'Why? What are you going to do?'

The question was not intended to goad. I was genuinely curious – and afraid. She was several inches taller than me, and I fixed my glassy eyes on a point over her shoulder. The corridor behind us was deserted. Drever had not left his classroom. I didn't know whether it would be good or bad if he found us like this. It would make me safer, yes, but it would also become extremely obvious who had placed the printout on his desk – if he didn't already know, that is.

Shit, what if he already knew? What if that was the real reason I got the part – to buy my silence?

No. He wouldn't have been nearly so kind if he knew the truth. There would have been a tension between us. A bitterness from him, instead of paternal smiles and words of affirmation.

Without warning, Davina tugged my ponytail sharply downward, as though forcing me to look up at her. There was a hot flash of pain on my scalp, a sharp gasp loosed from my lips, followed by a look of confusion on her part.

She pulled her hand away, and with it came a lock of hair as thick as a chopstick. Horror played out across her face as she held it up to the dim light in the alcove.

There were a few terrible beats in which neither of us spoke. My vision blurred again, and my skull *stung*. Taking in ragged breaths, I fought the urge to bend at the waist and vomit my morning coffee onto her ballet flats.

Davina shot me a meaningful glare as she curled her hand around my lock of hair. 'You're going to regret fucking with me.' A wide, cruel smile. 'Maybe not today. Maybe not this week. But sooner or later, I will come for you. When you least expect it.'

She stepped out of the alcove and strode down the stone steps into the atrium, her slippered feet making almost no sound.

She took my hair with her.

CHAPTER SIX

The Costumery hummed with thespian energy: elevated voices, vivacious hand gestures, exaggerated laughter, a bourdon drone interspersed with bright cackles, all of it clashing in a way that made me want to curl into the fetal position.

The student union was an acid trip of a place, filled with blank-faced mannequins in absurd costumes – fur coats and feather boas, regal gowns and a musketman's breeches, sequinned boleros and a Tudor king's robe. The fairy-lit bar was backed by a long, dusty mirror, which didn't seem to truly correspond to the real-life reflection. Kaleidoscopic fragments danced where there should have been none. Disco lights twirled balls of colour around the room at all hours of the day. It was camp and brilliant and overwhelming.

Students were notched into leather-upholstered booths, sipping at pints of cider and frothy cappuccinos, scripts and textbooks sprawled out on the ring-marked mahogany tables. The whole place smelled of vodka and cranberry, and it made my stomach churn.

There was only half an hour left until I had to be at my first rehearsal as Lady Macbeth. Nerves rattled in my ribcage, my bones jittering and jarring as I spotted my flatmates. The new patch of exposed scalp on the back of my head seared like a brand.

Wear the Paxton costume, I told myself, and I felt myself slip into the skin like it was second nature. High chin, squared shoulders, a subtle arch to the back. An aloofness to my gaze, as though I were above everything and everyone around me.

Almost as soon as I slipped into character, the stares and whispers began. An electric crackle filled the air. *That's Penny Paxton. Yeah, Peggy Paxton's daughter. I can't believe she's here.*

Feeling detached from the world in some fundamental way, I sauntered over to the booth my flatmates were piled into. Maisie was sitting next to Fraser, nudging his shoulder and laughing highly at something I hadn't heard.

'Hey,' Catalina said, moving her brown leather satchel to make more room next to her. A hand-painted sepia map fluttered out of the front pocket, the name *Atalandia* scrawled over the mountains in cursive script.

As well as poring over a non-fiction book about the psychology of Shakespeare, Catalina was also folding up a receipt into something crane-shaped – she turned every scrap of paper she could find into origami. 'Forgive the stack of books. They are, in all seriousness, my best friends.'

I couldn't help but crack a smile as I slid in beside her. 'You do love the written word.'

Catalina nodded earnestly. 'If there are three wolves inside of us, all of mine are encyclopaedias.'

'What was all that about?' asked Maisie, turning to look at me. She used the final crust of a cheese toastie to mop up her almost-empty bowl of tomato soup. I envied the casualness with which she ate, as though the very act didn't fill her with self-loathing. 'With Drever, I mean.'

The thought of telling them about the recast made my guts clench even harder, but they were about to find out at rehearsals anyway.

'Davina had to drop out of the play.' I stared down at the laminated menu, then forced my gaze back up. *Paxton mask. Come on.* 'Drever asked me to be Lady Macbeth.'

'Oh my god!' squealed Catalina, dropping the paper crane in surprise. 'That's amazing! Congratulations, Penny!'

Fraser gave me a dopey grin from across the booth. 'Nice. Looks like we're fictionally married, hey.'

Even though he was slouched in the corner, nursing a black coffee, his eyes twinkled with something I recognised all too well: infatuation. Most of the boys at my private school had looked at me the same way, but barely any of them actually pursued it. Almost as if they knew it was pointless – maybe because I was way out of their league, or maybe because I was a raging lesbian.

Maisie looked between me and Fraser and then back at Fraser, frowning. 'Wait, why did Davina drop out?'

'I don't really know,' I lied, picking at a loose flake of skin on my lip. It came away red from my lipstick. 'Drever just said it was because of scheduling conflicts.'

The frown on Maisie's face deepened, as though she was performing some taxing mental arithmetic. 'Right after you and Davina had that blow-up argument yesterday?' She raised a brow. 'You still haven't told us what that was about.'

Fraser scoffed and tipped more sugar into his coffee. 'You're literally the nosiest person I've ever met, bro.'

Maisie looked stung, and I hated that she was turning into collateral.

'No, Maisie's right,' I said, smiling at her in a way I hoped was warm and non-threatening. 'The timing is weird.' I shrugged, but my chest was pounding. 'I honestly don't know what's going on with Davina. She arrived late, did that amazing audition, then dropped out anyway.'

'What were you arguing about?' Maisie asked again.

'Okay, Inspector Cluedo. Why does it matter?' Fraser shrugged, tucking his chin into his navy half-zip sweater. 'Penny's just as talented as Davina. Maybe more so.' He smiled broadly at me, and the lie made me feel queasy.

'If you say so,' Maisie muttered, taking a pointed drink of Diet Coke.

Now it was my turn to feel stung.

Catalina raised her hands like a UN mediator, and her gold rings twinkled in the light. 'Okay, let's all take it down several notches. It's a student production of *Macbeth* that literally not one person on earth cares about except us. Probably not worth murdering each other over.' Her amber-flecked brown eyes crinkled at the corners. 'I mean, no offence, Penny. It's big news and I'm so excited for you. It's just, you know, a bunch of teens prancing around on stage. It's not that deep. *Anyway.* Can I buy you a drink to celebrate?'

'Thanks,' I replied gratefully, still aware of Maisie's scorn searing into me. 'But I don't drink, remember?'

'Of course.' Catalina tucked a curly lock behind her gold-cuffed ear. 'Some cheesy chips, at least?'

Nothing sounded better in that moment than cheesy chips. But if I was losing my hair, I had to make sure my body was *perfect*. And the demon lodged in my brain told me I didn't deserve food anyway.

'No. Thank you, though.' My stomach growled defiantly.

Catalina's face folded into concern. 'Are you sure?' She searched my face, as though she knew I was lying – about my hunger, if not about Davina. 'You didn't have breakfast, and you ran this morning. You look a little pale.'

Her concern felt strange. Neither good nor bad, but unnatural in some way. My mother had always turned a blind eye to my eating habits – or lack thereof. And the few times my aunt Polly had brought it up, I'd been able to deflect easily, since she didn't live with me.

I should have been touched by Catalina's worry, but the twisted part of my brain told me it was going to be a problem. I didn't want to have to lie constantly, to lay out bowls with a trickle of milk at the bottom so she'd think I'd eaten cereal, to order food in restaurants just to push it around my plate. It would be so much easier if she'd just let it go.

'I'm fine.' Dizziness fuzzed at my eyes, just to spite me. 'Just not hungry, I guess. I'm not a big food person.'

A lie. Such an outrageous lie. I'd loved food since I was a child, when my aunt Polly taught me how to bake. I used to pore over her old-school recipe books, dog-earing the pages I wanted to try next. I think I was just born hungry.

Maisie grabbed her backpack and slid out of the booth. 'Whatever. I'm going to find Davina. See if she's okay.'

Another lurch in my stomach. The last thing I needed was the gossip bloodhound sniffing around my new-found nemesis. I just had to hope that Davina wouldn't tell Maisie the truth – it would implicate her too, after all.

'I'm heading off as well,' said Fraser, shrugging his shoulders into a puffy gilet. 'Congrats again, Penny.'

Catalina clapped her hands together once they'd left. 'Okay, I'm getting you a coffee at least.' She grabbed a woven coin purse from her bag and slid towards the bar. 'And there will be sugar in it.' She raised a stern finger, but with a smile. 'And you will drink it, because you cannot say no to a type one diabetic on sugar-based matters.'

Smiling back as sincerely as I could, I said, 'Thanks.'

As I watched her walk up to the bar, I pulled my phone out of my back pocket. Another missed call from my mum.

I tapped her name before I could talk myself out of it.

She answered on the second ring, which was unusual for her. There was a time when it took at least seventeen attempts to ever get hold of her.

'Penny?' Her voice sounded a little off-kilter, and it gave me a prickle of apprehension. She'd been sober for two years now. I could not bear to see her unmoored yet again.

'Hi, Mum,' I answered, making sure my own pitch was steady.

'Darling! I thought you might be dead in a ditch.'

The tension in my shoulders relaxed somewhat. Maybe I had imagined the strange tenor in her tone.

'Sorry.' I chuckled. 'I've been busy practising the art of standing still.' It was true – Professor Lawrie had us spend hours on end *rooting ourselves to the ground like trees*. 'A very sane and normal thing to do. Not at all pointless.'

Mum laughed, and it made me glow. 'Oh, I remember those seminars. I still never learned to stop wearing high heels. The *blisters*, darling.' Although we'd lived in Edinburgh for almost a decade, her accent was still upper-class Kensington. 'But if you think that's uncomfortable, just wait for the master and slave class.'

'I think they call it master and subject now.'

'Mmmm. Just make sure you're wearing your good knickers.'

I couldn't hold it in any longer. I cupped a hand around my mouth to disguise my excited shriek from the students clustered in nearby booths.

'Mum, guess what?' A minuscule beat. 'I got the lead! I'm Lady Macbeth!'

Perhaps now that it was confirmed, official, I'd get more of a reaction.

'Listen, sweetheart,' Mum said, her words slightly

overlapping with mine as though she hadn't heard me. 'The reason I'm calling is that I suddenly had the *horrible* realisation that someone might leak your whereabouts to the tabloids. And once those rotten journalists know where you are, they might come after you.'

Now I realised what the odd pitch of her 'hello' had betrayed. It wasn't intoxication. It was paranoia. My mum's constant bedfellow. Even though Ballantyne's reports into my flatmates had come back clean as a whistle, she always found *something* to latch onto. Always saw ghosts where there were none.

Her lack of acknowledgement about Lady Macbeth wounded me, but I knew that once she was in one of her spirals, nothing I said permeated the surface of her brain.

'I know not to say anything personal to anyone,' I said flatly. 'So it won't matter.'

'But they can be so tricky, these journalists.' She was talking rapid-fire now, the mania mounting, and I could've sworn I heard the sound of pacing footsteps. 'You have no idea, Penny. They can poise as your friends or peers, and get you drunk enough that you'll spill anything they ask.'

'I don't drink. And it seems unlikely that any journalists would also be gifted enough actors to waltz into Dorian on a whim. You know how rigorous the selection process is.'

'Well, you know what I mean,' Mum muttered darkly. I wondered if she was alone. 'Don't trust anyone, alright?'

I watched as Catalina beamed at the bartender and ordered

my coffee. She must've said something funny, because his face melted into easy laughter.

'I won't. I promise.'

When Mum didn't say anything else, I rerouted. 'Did you hear what I said? About Lady Macbeth.'

'Oh yes, darling. Didn't you already tell me that?' She was still jittery. 'But congratulations again.'

An aching hollowness opened a well in my ribs. The praise felt entirely empty. It was missing the earnest fervour – the heartfelt zeal – I so sorely craved.

'Thanks.'

Another strange beat, laden with something I couldn't identify. Then she said, so quietly I almost didn't catch it, 'Did they mention anything to you about private mentoring? Or is that a thing of the past?'

I frowned. A peculiar question. 'Erm, yeah. With Orlagh Camran. She mentors all the first-year female leads.'

Mum didn't reply for a long stretch. Catalina set off towards the booth once more, the coffee cup rattling in its blue saucer.

'Mum?' I prodded, unease spreading over me like a winter frost. 'Are you there?'

'Just be careful, alright?' She sounded almost strangled, the words pulled taut by an invisible noose.

I sighed. 'I told you I'm not going to talk to any journalists.'

'With Orlagh, I mean. Just . . . be careful.'

And then the phone went dead.

CHAPTER SEVEN

Professor Drever cleared his throat. "'To be an interesting actor – hell, to be an interesting human being – you must be authentic, and for you to be authentic you must embrace who you really are, warts and all. Do you have any idea how liberating it is to not care what people think about you? Well, that's what we're here to do.'" He closed the textbook he was reading from. 'Sanford Meisner. A master from whom we can learn a great deal about our craft – and about ourselves.'

The classroom was hot and woozy, and I was struggling to concentrate. My hunger-addled brain felt like a withered hand trying to grasp at something out of reach. And while I knew – I *knew*, okay? – that a simple sandwich would probably fix the situation, I couldn't bear to admit defeat. Defeat, or failure, or something else that made no sense at all.

Drever folded his arms over his chest and leaned back against his desk. He rolled a small gold drawing pin between his thumb and forefinger. 'We'll be spending the next few weeks immersed in the teachings of Meisner, working our way through a series of interdependent exercises that gradually build in complexity and intensity. First, we will hone our ability to improvise, and then we will work on accessing our richest emotional selves. Finally, we will practise bringing the spontaneous and the personal together in a powerful response to the dramatic texts upon which we work. How can we bring our innermost identities to Banquo? How can we bring originality to Macduff? Impulsivity to Lady Macbeth?'

Maisie and Davina both turned to stare pointedly at me. They had arrived together, firing disdainful glances in my direction. It had been three days since I was recast, and I hadn't spoken to either of them since. I had no idea how much Maisie knew.

Drever pushed off the desk, then gestured for us to stand up and start shoving our tables and chairs to one side. Everyone but me obliged. When I climbed to my feet, my vision swooped and blackened away from me, and I had to collapse back into my seat, hoping desperately that nobody had noticed. All I heard was the distant scraping of chair legs against floorboards, and Drever's continued drone.

I was dimly aware of the dark drain I circled, but felt powerless to pull myself out of it.

'For today's exercise, we're going to pair off and sit on the floor opposite our partners. One actor will speak first, making a benign observation about the other, such as "you're wearing a blue shirt". The recipient will then repeat this observation back, before moving on to another. Initially, you'll repeat the exact same sentence, such as "you're looking at me", then you'll advance to repeating the observation from your own points of view, as in "I'm looking at you". As the exercise progresses, it should become more about what's going on between you in the moment. "You look unhappy with me." The hope is that you'll stop thinking about what to say and do, and respond more freely and spontaneously, both physically and vocally.

'You'll be surprised how quickly an emotional connection forges between you and your partner – if you fully immerse yourself, that is. Now pair off. And let's begin.'

There was a tap on my shoulder. I turned to see Catalina smiling hopefully at me.

'Want to work with me?'

I breathed an inward sigh of relief. If Drever had paired me up with Davina, it could have got ugly fast. Catalina was the easy presence I needed right now.

We arranged ourselves on the floor, sitting cross-legged facing each other. The bare wooden floorboards pressed into all my sharpest angles, and I was painfully aware of every knobbly bone on my legs and bum. No matter how much I shifted my weight, I couldn't get comfortable. I wanted so badly to use my scarf as a rug, but I didn't want to draw any more attention to myself.

So I donned my Paxton mask – easy smile, high jaw, disaffected gaze – and we began.

'You're wearing a cream cardigan,' I said evenly.

She nodded. 'I'm wearing a cream cardigan.'

I couldn't remember exactly what to do next. Was I supposed to repeat the same sentence again? Or say something else? I'd been so busy trying not to faint that I hadn't been fully listening. I inwardly chastised myself. Dorian was a life-changing opportunity. I'd worked myself into the ground to get here, and now I was squandering it.

Thankfully, Catalina took the reins.

'You keep looking at the clock.'

I frowned. I'd barely been aware of my doing it, but she was right. I'd just checked – 11.44 a.m. 'I keep looking at the clock.'

Now she searched my face, and I forced myself to hold her gaze. The apples of her olive-toned cheeks were smattered with tiny freckles. Her irises were burnished copper pennies, dark pupils darting back and forth across them.

'You're dreading something,' she said finally, plainly.

A yank of recognition in my gut. 'I am dreading something.'

The mentoring session with Orlagh was tonight, and my mother's strange warning burned bright in my mind.

'You think you should feel excited, but you don't.'

Drever hovered behind Catalina, arms folded, staring down at us as we performed the exercise. His presence loomed like a shadow, making me hyper aware of what we were saying. At Catalina's statement, his eyes narrowed almost imperceptibly.

I didn't want him to know she was right – he'd trusted me with the lead, after all – and yet it wasn't in the spirit of the game to lie, to refute your partner's statements. I had to agree with her, no matter how vulnerable it made me feel.

I swallowed hard. 'I think I should feel excited, but I don't.'

How was she doing this? Honing in on my precise

feelings – some I hadn't even quite processed myself? I was so used to seeing her with her head in a book that I had no idea how astute her emotional intelligence was. It was a curious blend of comforting and unsettling to have someone stare so effortlessly into the heart of you. It didn't feel like it did to be perceived by strangers, or audience members, or journalists, or my mother's fans . . . it was far more intimate. Not quite so unbearable. The sensation of being understood carried a subtle underpinning of warmth.

Yet it worried me that my Paxton mask didn't seem to be fooling the people around me at Dorian. First there was Davina, and the way she'd so effortlessly provoked me into dropping it. And now there was Catalina, who didn't need me to drop it at all – because she could see right through it.

The thought made me feel distinctly panicked, but I couldn't say for certain why. Maybe it was my mother's paranoid mutterings, the way she'd spent eighteen years warning me against letting anyone get too close. Maybe they'd left more of a mark than I thought.

You have no idea, Penny. They can pose as your friends or peers, and get you drunk enough that you'll spill anything they ask.

Don't trust anyone, all right?

'You feel uncomfortable.' Catalina's statement was plain – she hadn't begun to imbue her own emotional reactions yet.

I nodded, jaw tense. 'I feel uncomfortable.'

Mercifully, Drever moved on to another pair, and Catalina glanced over her shoulder to make sure he wasn't listening.

Then: 'You wish you weren't here.'

Another simple observation, and yet it was so profoundly true that I almost didn't know what to do with it. She wasn't saying it to be cruel, or to draw undue attention to me. She was just calling it as she saw it.

'I wish I wasn't here.' My voice cracked like a frozen lake over the final word.

The silence that followed was like a rolling snowscape – a blank, brilliant, confronting white. Fresh and new, waiting for someone to make another footprint.

Yet I didn't know how to fill it. I felt so horribly exposed, like a scab as old as myself had been suddenly ripped off, revealing the bright, fresh skin beneath.

Should I turn it back on Catalina? Find something about *her* for us to focus on instead?

I studied her the way she had studied me, searching every plane of her face for a flicker of emotion, a betrayal of how she was really feeling. Something upon which I could impose thought or meaning. But it was impossible. I'd never been able to read people in that way.

Or I was just so hungry and exhausted that I couldn't concentrate on anything outside my own immediate suffering. Starvation made you feel like you were trapped inside yourself. A brain beating against the bars of the body. An excruciating interiority.

I wish I wasn't here.

Sensing how much I was struggling with the exercise,

Catalina reached out a hand and squeezed mine. The sudden touch was like a lightning bolt, and while I usually flinched away from physical contact, it felt oddly pleasant.

Pulling her hand away, she smiled conspiratorially and said, 'You find an enchanted amulet and receive bonus health points.'

'I . . . what?' I could still feel the imprint of her warm skin on mine.

She nodded sagely. 'You are on a quest to obtain a new bow.'

Suddenly I understood. She was leading me into an impromptu game of Dungeons & Dragons. Still improvisation, but less personally confronting.

Gratitude coursing through me, I repeated, 'I am on a quest to obtain a new bow.'

'You want to hit an Owlbear with an arrow.'

I fought the urge to laugh. 'For reasons unknown to me, I want to hit an Owlbear with an arrow.'

'You want to breach the castle walls.'

'I want to breach the castle walls.'

We were talking in low voices, so that Drever wouldn't pick up on what we were doing, and it felt like being two pre-teens at a sleepover, whispering our biggest secrets under the blankets at night, hoping our parents wouldn't hear. At least, that's what sleepovers looked like on television. I'd never actually had one.

Catalina's eyes were twinkling now. 'You want to win the treasure inside.'

'I want to win the treasure inside.'

'Which is . . .' she prompted, breaking the rules of the game to forge her own.

Emboldened, I grinned broadly, chivalrously, playing a character. 'I want to win the hand of the princess.'

'You want to win the hand of the princess.' Another meaningful flicker of those dazzling eyes. 'You want love.'

God. How did she do that so easily? Was Dungeons & Dragons a technique used by therapists the world over? Or was I just an extremely easy nut to crack?

'I want love.'

It could have been a weakening moment, but instead Catalina mimed rolling a dice.

'Ooooof,' she said, blowing air through her lips. 'You roll a one on the D20. No love for you. Only barbarian gnomes. And they're armed! With fire swords! Arghhhhh!'

We couldn't help ourselves, then. We collapsed into laughter, earning furious glares from Davina and Maisie, and a disparaging sigh from Drever.

Little did he know that the exercise had *worked*.

'Thank you,' I whispered to Catalina, once we'd finally calmed down.

And I meant it. She had achieved the impossible, and distracted me from the impending session with Camran – if only for a moment.

But nothing could stop the clock marching forward, and before I knew it, it was time to meet my fabled mentor.

CHAPTER EIGHT

Orlagh Camran's office was hung with more art than I had ever seen in my life. And I'd been to the Louvre.

At some point the walls had been oak-panelled, but there was barely a square inch visible. The effect was a disorienting mosaic of faces staring down at me as I walked into the echoing room. Every painting was a portrait, in every major artistic style from the last thousand years. Rembrandt warred for space against Van Gogh, Picasso battled against Kahlo, Raphael and Géricault and Da Vinci hung in clashing gold and silver frames. Most of them looked like prints, but several could fairly convincingly be originals, given Orlagh's enormous wealth.

Orlagh was seated behind an enormous desk topped with vases of dark red roses. Glossy auburn hair fell to her breastbone, and a delicate golden tiara perched on her crown. She wore an empire-waist Aesthetic dress in deep navy and emerald green, folds of rich silk and sheer overlays skimming her ample curves. She must have been at least sixty or seventy years old, but the rounds of her cheeks shone pink and smooth, her complexion waxen and glowing from within. A stranger might think her thirty, at most. Her surgeon must be incredibly gifted. Not even her hands were wrinkled with age.

At the sight of her my stomach flipped, but not in the anxious roil of the past week – it was a fluttery starstruck feeling I had thought myself immune to, given my mother's countless famous friends. This woman was a living legend. She was everything I aspired to be – wildly successful and talented beyond measure, yes, but also beloved as a kind of national treasure, wrapped in a blanket of adoration that would always keep her warm.

'Penny,' she said, her voice remarkably smooth and lustrous considering her purported throat cancer.

In front of the desk were two chesterfield sofas bracketing a low coffee table, which was strewn with newspapers in several languages – including Russian and Arabic. She gestured for me to take a seat, and swanned over to perch on the sofa opposite, her gown gliding along the rich Persian rug. As she moved, all the hundreds of portrait eyes seemed to follow her at once. There was an almost religious reverence to their gaze – though it was perfectly possible I was just imagining things.

They were, after all, only paintings.

She studied me intently. 'It is true what they say about you. A rare beauty, indeed.'

My mouth went to say thank you, but for some reason the words stayed lodged in my throat.

Orlagh tilted her head to one side. Her eyes shone green as clover, shot through with hazel and sage.

'You think of it a curse,' she said silkily. 'The ugly have an easier ride of it, no?' She laughed, gentle yet bitten with something darker. 'They can sit at their ease and gape at the play. But we, Penny – we are the players. It is what we were fated to be. And while we shall suffer for what the gods have given us, we will also prosper. If we so choose, of course.'

There was an old-fashioned cadence to her speech, as though she had been born a century too late. Perhaps it was a side effect of living and breathing Shakespeare for so long.

I shifted on the sofa, uncomfortable under her searing stare. 'My mum always says that beauty opens doors for us that remain closed to most people.'

Orlagh showed no glimmer of recognition at the mention of my mother, despite Mum's ominous warnings. 'It is true, yes, but it can also lock certain others.' Her gaze roved over my body, and her eyes narrowed. 'Tell me, child. If you so resent your beauty, why do you inflict such agonies on yourself in order to maintain it?'

I felt a flicker of apprehension. How had she honed in on that so quickly? 'I don't know what you mean.'

She leaned back in the sofa, smoothing her skirts with an elegant hand. 'I have a rare ability to sense starvation. There is a rabidness to the gaze, a lack of substance to the posture, a weakness to the thoughts. And in you these qualities are sorely manifest.'

Ouch.

'A weakness to the thoughts?' I all but stuttered.

'I do not mean to offend, my dear,' she said, but her tone

was plain and unapologetic. 'Tell me, is acting your true passion? Is acclaim in this arena the thing you desire most in the world?'

I nodded, but mostly because I thought it was the correct answer. The real one was far more complicated.

'Unless you can conquer this destructive behaviour, I fear your desire may be left unsated. For if you must insist upon shrinking yourself, how do you propose to command a stage? If you cannot hone and sharpen your thoughts, how will you ever master Shakespeare? If you know not who *you* are, how can you truly embody another character?'

Her words wounded me, because I knew she was right.

I looked out of the enormous windows, past crimson tussore-silk curtains to the rolling Great Lawn. A cluster of students lounged by the lake, sipping cider from bottles, laughing and rolling over each other. Their careless joy was alien to me. I was too earnest, too serious, too painfully self-aware. Would I ever feel like that? So . . . free?

Orlagh folded one leg over the other. 'You know, I often think about how much more prevalent such sicknesses have become in the last half a century. My conclusion is usually that mass photography is to blame.'

'What do you mean?'

'Well, historically we had significantly more control over the ways in which we were immortalised. One might sit for a portrait once a decade, if one was particularly affluent, and the working classes never had to worry about such trivialities because they were simply inaccessible to them. And so as long as one was comfortable moving about one's daily life, and one could afford clothing of decent quality and soap with which to wash oneself, comparatively little thought was given to one's appearance or shape. There have always been beauty ideals, of course, but not so rigorously documented or upheld – especially among the lower echelons.

'Yet nowadays there's so much photography that there exist hundreds if not *thousands* of photos of every single one of us. For me, it is likely millions. Statistically speaking, not all can be flattering, so we must sit with the discomfiting knowledge that this "ugly" image of us will exist, in some sense, forever.' She shook her head. 'It is neither normal nor natural to be so aware of our every unfortunate angle, our every perceived flaw. And it is neither normal nor natural for us to be so frequently immortalised. It carries with it a certain anxiety.'

Every single word chimed true as a tuning fork. I was utterly enraptured by Orlagh, by her eloquence and intellect, her clarity of wisdom. I had a new appreciation for the insult she'd levelled at me: *weakness of thought*. It was horribly, helplessly true.

I didn't want to be like this. I wanted to be like *her*. I wanted to be able to polish my thoughts into rare jewels, to captivate with my mind, not just my body. Being in her presence made me want to swell, not shrink.

'So how do we stop fixating on it?' I asked. 'Cameras aren't going anywhere.'

She patted a vintage black analogue phone on her desk. The handset was a faded gold. 'Well, I don't have one of those ghastly smartphones for one thing. This was all we ever needed as a species.' She shrugged, the luxurious folds of her dress shimmering and flowing as she shifted. 'Plus, you would do well to remember that everyone looking at said images will be dead in a hundred years.'

And then she started to laugh. Big, bold, lavish laughter, so roomy and palatial that I felt I could roam around inside it like a bell tower. I couldn't help but smile, although it lacked the same zeal.

'Sorry to take up our mentoring session with this,' I said finally, once the raucous laughter had bubbled away. 'I know we should be talking about acting.'

'Nonsense.' Her eyes were dewy with mirth. 'It is all part and parcel. This ailment is, as it stands, the greatest barrier your acting faces. If I can help you overcome it, I will have performed my role as mentor quite nicely.'

A pair of postbox-red dragonflies danced past the window, fluttering and chasing.

'I guess . . . I don't know who I am without my beauty,' I said finally.

Orlagh was right. My thoughts were weak, shallow. The most dominant image in my mind was the bare scalp at the back of my head. I'd examined it earlier – it was as small and round as a ten pence piece, but it felt so much larger. And as I'd coaxed the hair into a simple ponytail, another lock had shaken itself loose. I felt frozen by the fear of it – by how quickly it was happening. How soon would I be bald?

Orlagh raised a perfectly hooked brow. 'Tell me, are you afraid to be fat?'

I thought of Catalina and her rolling curves, of the Raphaelite figure before me, and felt immediately guilty. I hadn't meant to equate thinness and beauty. 'No. I'm not fatphobic. At least, I don't think I am.'

It was both true and untrue, in a way I couldn't quite unpack.

She shrugged. 'Who could blame you if you were? Thinness is very much the ingrained Western beauty standard – for a plethora of reasons I won't bore you with – and humans are biologically hardwired to want to be attractive. So that we might find a mate, of course, and perpetuate the species. No matter how intellectually and socially sophisticated we become, we are still animals. And so we must compete for sex.'

'I don't think finding a mate would help me perpetuate the species,' I laughed. 'I'm extremely gay. And honestly, I don't think bigger bodies are unattractive. They're beautiful.'

She nodded, as though this is what she suspected all along. 'And so your self-starvation is about control. You cannot control much, but you can control your body. And so you do. Ruthlessly.'

A strange sense of vulnerability washed over me. Orlagh had torched through the tangled undergrowth, straight to the root of my pain. It left me feeling raw and exposed.

This legend in front of me – an icon who had enraptured

millions – seemed genuinely invested in my petty problems. Coupled with Catalina's concern, I felt cared for in a way I never had been before. And yet I couldn't understand it. Why would they want to help me when they had nothing to gain from it? Why did they care about the self-inflicted starvation of a relative stranger?

'I do want to overcome it,' I whispered. 'I don't want to live like this.'

For several moments, Orlagh stared up at the crystal chandelier hanging from an ornate ceiling rose. She looked deep in contemplation, as though making a difficult decision.

Eventually she murmured, 'What if there was a way to free you of these particular shackles? To let go of the need to obsess over your appearance?'

'I've tried therapy,' I said. It was a lie – my mother was far too paranoid to allow a stranger to unpack our most sinister secrets – but I could not face a lecture from Orlagh about getting help.

Another tense beat.

'What do you know about the portraits of Dorian?' she asked.

I frowned, searching my mind for a clear answer but landing on none in particular. 'There are a lot of rumours.'

'Many of them balderdash, in truth. The portraits cannot predict fortunes, or change the past, or bewitch their beholders into suicide. But certain others . . .'

Orlagh smiled a peculiar smile, and I stilled, frozen by

the inexplicable sense that something fundamental was about to shift. She had the air of a forest witch luring me to her lair.

'There is one tale in particular that has its roots in truth,' she murmured. 'You may have heard it, but I shall share it with you as if it is brand new.'

'Okay.'

She took a deep breath, then began talking on the exhale. 'Beneath the campus lies an underground gallery containing a few dozen portraits, painted by an enigmatic hand. Those portraits – of Dorian alumni, mostly, many of whom you might recognise as some of the most famous faces in the world – are said to age on behalf of their subject. To grow old and wrinkled and skin-tagged while their living subjects remain young and unblemished. Pure mythology, of course.' Her eyes shone bright as emeralds. 'Or so most people think.'

'But it's true?' I asked, feeling my respect for the woman wane slightly. My mind was too logical, too hard-edged and scientific, to buy into fantasy and fable.

And yet . . . she really did look thirty years old.

When I examined her closely, it was the hands that gave me pause. She wore a gold cameo ring with an apricot-coloured background and a creamy female profile, with a neat brown freckle on the finger right above it. The skin was still smooth and peach-tinted, the whites of her nails like immaculate crescent moons. Hands were almost impossible to make youthful by knife alone.

Perhaps it was not surgery that preserved her beauty so perfectly.

'The Masked Painter,' Orlagh continued ardently, 'as he is known to those who encounter his mysterious powers, can capture a person with such pure light and shade that the painting gains an almost sentience. The paint itself is blended with blood and bone, almost as an anchoring. And the subjects, in the real world, are preserved *exactly* as they were the day the painting was completed. Unless marred by some brutal external force, their bodies will never change. They may cheat even death.'

A shiver ran down my spine.

Because I had just remembered my mother's warning.

Be careful.

Had she had this same conversation with Orlagh two decades earlier?

More importantly, what had come of it?

I thought of my mother's impossibly youthful glow, despite years of addiction and depression. I thought of the way she ate and ate like a wild animal and never gained an ounce. I thought of the tiny tumour doctors had found on her brain when I was a small child, and the miraculous way it had never grown or progressed.

And I wondered.

'Why are you telling me this?' I whispered, chest tight with fear – and, worst of all, an ugly kind of hope.

Orlagh ran a finger over the brass studs on the arm of the

chesterfield. 'You may have noticed that I bear a certain *youthfulness* despite my rapidly accumulating decades.' A subtle shift in her shoulders, as though she were slightly ashamed of the revelation. 'I cannot tell you the freedom this painting has gifted to me throughout my career. To be unshackled by the demands of maintaining beauty – the injections and the peels and the diets suffered by my peers – and focus solely on my *art*.'

My heart galloped in my chest, like a racehorse pounding towards some imperceptible finish line.

'Do I feel guilt for the decisions I have made?' she mused aloud. 'Sometimes, I'll admit. The patriarchy has long demonised the ageing process in women. By tying our worth to our beauty and our beauty to our youth, they ensure even the most powerful women will one day lose that status. And so should I have devoted my life to *shattering* such oppressive social structures, instead of defying them? Perhaps. But martyrdom just seems so tiresome. Why choose pain when one can choose pleasure?'

'Why are you telling me this?' I repeated, only this time there was a note of pleading in the words.

Orlagh rested her thumb on her lower lip. 'The Masked Painter has been retired for some time – his own portrait ages gracefully in some dark attic somewhere. But he is an old friend of mine. I'm sure he could be convinced to wield his paintbrush once more. If you so desired, of course.'

There. The axis tilt my fluttering pulse had somehow anticipated.

I had never bought into anything that could not be proven by science. I was as atheist as they came, and as cynical as a cantankerous old man. I scoffed at talk of astrology and manifestation, of star signs and tarot decks. My brain was a chessboard, not a book of fairy tales.

But this?

Maybe I just *wanted* to believe so badly that I would suspend all logic and reasoning.

When I spoke, it was almost a croak. 'My body would stay as it is now . . . forever? Without even trying?'

'Indeed.'

My heart bucked with longing. I could *eat*. I could eat and eat and eat, hearty stews and cheesy chips and toasties with soup, chocolate chip cookies and ice cream and pancakes dripping in syrup. I could maintain my most important currency effortlessly, as my mother did, as Orlagh did. I could stop starving, stop feeling like a brain hurling itself at the bars of its body, and open myself up to the world around me.

I could stop suffering at the altar of beauty and just be beautiful.

'And hypothetically . . . say my hair was falling out.' I swallowed hard. 'That would stop?'

Orlagh peered at me searchingly, but did not pry. 'It would. But it would also not regrow.'

A thought struck me. 'They say you have throat cancer.'

She bowed her head. 'A ruse. Too long in the spotlight was beginning to attract questions about my lack of ageing.'

Barely breathing, I asked, 'You would help me do this too? Ask the Masked Painter to paint me?'

'If it is something that might ease the burden for you.' Her expression was strange – as though she was already regretting sharing this with me, but could see how much it meant. 'I cannot say it would rid you of the desire to self-flagellate, but it may offer some level of peace. I advise you to go away and think about it, for a stretch, and –'

'I don't need to think about it,' I said quickly. 'I want to do it.'

Orlagh pursed her lips. 'There will be pain involved. Droplets of blood. A scraping of bone.'

At this I wavered, but only for a few seconds. I was already in pain. At least this would be temporary.

'I don't care.'

A long, penetrative silence. And then, 'Very well. I shall make the necessary arrangements.'

I was so impatient to make this bargain that I forgot to ask the most important question of all: *But at what cost?*

CHAPTER NINE

The Gallery of the Exquisite was indeed exquisite.

Two days after my conversation with Orlagh – a sleepy Sunday evening, for most students – she arranged for us to meet the Masked Painter in the underground gallery hidden beneath the bones of Dorian.

I had spent the whole weekend enshrined in my room, preparing my body. Because if I was to be immortalised, I had to be the most beautiful version of myself possible. I wrapped my hair in a silk turban, making sure I would not lose another strand before the sitting – it was a shame that I'd have the ten pence piece patch of bare scalp forever, but that was far preferable to a wholly bald head.

I waxed my legs, my underarms, my bikini line, gritting my teeth through the sting with the knowledge I'd never have to do it again. I tinted my lashes black, plucked and shaped my brows into perfect fluffy arches, scraped back my cuticles and tended to a small paper cut on my thumb.

I ate nothing, drank nothing. Felt my stomach shrink, my skin pulled taut over my hipbones and ribs.

Not for much longer, I promised myself. *Just one more*

day of this, and then we will be free.

Throughout it all, a twisted kind of elation settled over me. Although I knew somewhere in my chest that nothing was truly without cost, my starvation-addled mind wanted so badly to believe it that I didn't examine Orlagh's offer for traps.

I agonised over what to wear. Of course I'd be able to change my clothes whenever I wanted in real life, but for some reason it felt deeply important for the portrait to truly represent me. In the end I settled on an off-the-shoulder Alexander McQueen dress in black silk, with silver-embroidered roses at the décolletage. It was more gothic than I usually chose, but it felt fitting for the drama of the occasion.

Late on Sunday afternoon, I was to meet Orlagh outside the Basil Hallward Theatre, named for the visionary who founded the school. We entered through the stage door, which she unlocked with a large golden key, then crossed through the green room and on to the stage itself. It was the first time I'd set foot on it since my audition.

'Behold, player,' she said grandly. 'Your dais.'

Chills came over me as I looked out at the bare rows of maroon velvet chairs, imagining the heat of the spotlight on my face as I performed Lady Macbeth. Chills – but not necessarily the good kind. I thought of my ill-fated nativity audition, of the burning shame of hiding my soiled underwear, how it felt to lose that lead. How it felt knowing that my mother didn't care.

I'll show her, I thought. *One day I'll be so great she can't ignore me.*

Once the portrait was finished and my beauty sealed, I could focus all my attention on my craft, my art, on becoming great. As great as Davina. Greater, even.

And then my mother would see me. Really, truly see me.

After allowing me an indulgent moment, Orlagh strode downstage – elegant purple dress flowing silkily behind her – and crouched down to lift up a trapdoor that was used for special effects. Once it was open, she descended the first few steps leading below the stage and gestured for me to follow.

I still could not parse her expression. There was a grim stoniness to it that I didn't understand, as though she were leading me to the gallows not a gallery. Didn't she understand the immense gift she was bestowing upon me? Didn't she understand the shackles she was loosing?

She did. She knew what this meant to me. I had told her as much. And so why did she gaze at me like an executioner might?

Beneath the stage was a dim, dusty cavern filled with props, smoke machines, unplugged lights and several snarls of tangled cords. It was a low space, and anyone much taller than my five and a half feet would need to stoop. My eyes strained against the lack of light, until Orlagh pulled an honest-to-god lantern out of the folds of her skirts. It was tiny, made of brass, and a tea light flickered inside it. I had the distinct impression I'd fallen into a Victorian horror novel.

Light-headed as ever, I shuffled behind her as she strode to the far end of the space, where an almost imperceptible door was notched into the wall. Everything was wood-panelled and painted black, so the seams of the frame blended perfectly – the only thing that gave it away was a small keyhole of scuffed gold. Orlagh pulled out a delicate key from another skirt fold and slid it into the lock.

Beyond the door was a steep set of stone steps with a mildewy runner down the centre. As we crossed the threshold, cold, stale air wafted up from whatever lay below.

The steps seemed to go on forever, darker and danker and colder, until finally we hit the ground. A narrow tunnel stretched and curved out before us, and I could only see a few steps in front of us by the flickering lantern light. But this was no rabbit warren. The walls were plastered and solid, and the floor was not bare earth, but rather wooden parquet flooring worn smooth by decades of trodden feet. It was like being part of something ancient, something arcane and clandestine. Something so much bigger than myself.

'It's so cold down here,' I whispered, unsure why raising my voice felt almost disrespectful. Still my low words echoed around the tunnel.

'We're beneath Swan Lake right now,' Orlagh answered. As soon as she said it, I could almost feel the vast body of icy water pressing down on us from above, could sense the vicious swans carving lines through the glassy surface of the water. It was oppressive, and somehow frightening.

Abruptly the tunnel opened out into a much larger space, and I stifled a gasp.

It was a room the size of a hockey pitch. In the middle was propped an easel and a stool, and beyond that a maroon velvet chaise longue hastily draped in a swath of white fabric. There were few other objects – just an intricately printed screen in the far corner, behind which subjects could change in privacy. Three of the four walls were hung with portraits, but in just the dim light from the tiny lantern, I couldn't pick out any details.

'Behold,' announced Orlagh, 'the Gallery of the Exquisite.'

The dimensions of the room were wrong; too much blank space around the easel, between the chaise and the paintings. I'd always found the juxtaposition of very large things next to very small things unnerving. An ant next to a double-decker bus. A drawing pin in an empty stadium. Perhaps my great-aunt's trypophobia wasn't so absurd after all.

As Orlagh began lighting the periodic silver sconces bolted to the wall between paintings, slowly the room was illuminated, and a shiver ran down my spine.

The nearest portrait to me was of Angus Arras, a Dorian alum who had starred in several BBC dramas before making it huge in Hollywood. In real life he had barely aged at all – he was more rugged and beardy than in his youth, but his dark brown hair was streaked with only the finest silver threads. In his painting, however, all of his hair was white, his eyes wrinkled and drooping, and there was a gauntness to the hollows of his cheeks.

There were other world-class actors too. Celia Van Der Beek and Lyle Barr, who had suffered a rather public and acrimonious divorce, both looked over a hundred years old. None of the subjects looked any younger than forty or fifty – which would suggest that no new paintings had been hung in decades.

'So many famous faces,' I said, fighting the urge to run a finger over the lined brow of Lydia Fettes. She had just starred in a glossy new Shirley Jackson adaptation, her skin smooth and her eyes bright. The press had long been speculating over her date of birth, since every public record of it seemed to differ.

It felt like a veil had been lifted on one of the acting world's deepest secrets.

I also struggled to reconcile the logic of what I was seeing with my scientific and ordered world view. My brain scrambled for an explanation that did not, could not exist. Perhaps Orlagh was quite mad, and these paintings had all been recently commissioned to show how the stars might look as they aged. But standing in this eerie space below a silver-topped lake, surrounded by an esoteric chill I'd never felt before, it was as though my bones understood something my mind could not accept.

There was also a kind of tension to the paintings that didn't seem wholly natural. It wasn't that the figures moved, exactly, but nor did they seem to stay entirely still. They were not poised, elegant, but rather taut and charged with something entirely metaphysical. Looking at the portraits felt like I'd caught the subject in a vulnerable, exposed moment. It was as though I was staring at their naked forms through the crack in a curtain, and while they were very aware of my gaze, they were powerless to move away.

Then my gaze drifted over to the painting I had expected to see – but still the sight stole the breath from my lungs.

Below it, a gold plate: *Peggy Paxton, Edinburgh.*

Dazed, I sidled up to the painting, barely daring to blink or breathe. As I drew close enough to pick out the most minute details, my eyes welled with tears. Because here was my mother as she *should* have been, had she not been hung in this very gallery.

The years had not been kind. Her green eyes had dulled to a mossy grey, and the whites were shot through with red veins and a grey-pink undertone. Her face was puffy and bloated from alcohol, and the skin around her mouth sagged into low jowls hanging from the jaw. Limp, lifeless hair framed her face – not the vibrant copper I shared with her, but a straggly grey shot through with tepid ginger.

And yet while she was undeniably less beautiful, she was more real to me than the glorified mannequin I'd lived with my whole life. There was an intensity behind the eyes that was missing in reality, as though this version of my mother was capable of the depth of love I so craved. Her watery gaze almost strained against the canvas. It was as though this painted face – still, unmoving, as paintings should be – was trying desperately to communicate something to me.

But maybe I was just projecting.

'She was an incredible talent, your mother.'

Orlagh's voice behind me made me start. I hadn't realised she'd finished lighting the sconces.

I frowned. '*Is*. She's still alive.'

'Of course. I meant only that her fullest potential was not reached.' A wistful sigh. 'She could have been the best Shakespearean actor of her generation.'

It was a strange thought, so far removed from the mother I knew. She'd been intoxicated for so much of my life that I couldn't imagine her on stage, clarion-voiced and clear-minded, inhabiting some of the most complex characters ever written.

I swallowed, staring into the bloodshot eyes of who she should have been. 'Why do you think she left Dorian?' I asked, curious to see whether her answer would match my mother's own.

Orlagh rubbed thoughtfully at her chin. 'She was scouted for modelling, or so I heard. The highest compliment most young women hope to achieve. I can only assume the lure of it was too strong.'

The assertion was guarded; over-practised in the same way it was whenever I told someone *it's all I know*. I knew there was something else lurking beneath it.

'When I told my mother about our mentoring, she told me to be careful.'

Orlagh did not flinch at my directness. 'I can only assume she didn't want her daughter to make the same decision she did.'

'But why? It seems like the answer to all my prayers.'

'And such is the reason I shared it with you.' Orlagh

shrugged, then spread her arms wide, gesturing for me to look around. 'For me it has been the greatest blessing of my life, and yet not all subjects feel the same. I suppose, from her cautions, your mother is one of them.'

I pressed on, determined to unearth something more insightful about her relationship with my mother. 'You looked grim-faced as we climbed through the trapdoor.'

'My child, I think only of the hurt you're about to face.' She winced, and fear fluttered through me like insect wings. She fiddled with the apricot-gold cameo ring on her forefinger. 'It is fleeting, but intense. And the dull throb afterwards never truly leaves.'

Before I could ask anything else, behind us there was a subtle shift in the atmosphere, like the soft swish of a cloak.

Orlagh and I both turned at once, and before us was the Masked Painter.

CHAPTER TEN

Dressed all in black, the Masked Painter was tall and spindly and vaguely Gothic, like the spire of an old church.

Over his full face was a silver Venetian mask in the shape of a fox, with shimmering bronze and rose-gold details at the temples. It was impossible to tell the shape of his features beneath the mask. Perhaps he had the long, pointed nose of the fox, or perhaps a short ski-slope was tucked inside. Either way, the fox granted him absolute anonymity.

'Orlagh,' he said, his voice a tremulous purr. He lowered an enormous black briefcase to the ground with a thunk. 'It's been a long time since you brought me a subject.'

Orlagh glided over to where he stood, brushing a kiss on his masked cheek. 'It is a pleasure to see you again, old friend. I must thank you once again for the life you have afforded me.'

The statement created a prickle of curiosity – what exactly did the Masked Painter have to gain from all of this? – but nerves and a strange kind of deference kept me silent. Before me was both a living legend and an artist with power that stretched the very limits of what should be possible. Trifling questions of payment and reward seemed gauche.

The Masked Painter stilled as his eyes – almost black inside the mask – locked on to me. I shivered under his roving gaze. I'd thrown a vintage fur coat over my McQueen dress, but I was still freezing in the crypt-cold of the gallery.

'You must be Penny Paxton,' he said, voice somehow both soft and cold and *young*. 'A pleasure.'

'Thank you for meeting with me,' I replied, ashamed of the light tremor in my words.

'A pleasure,' he repeated.

A loaded silence settled over the room. Perhaps I was imagining it, but I could almost hear the domed ceiling groan and sway beneath the weight of the lake.

'Shall we begin?' Orlagh said eventually, clapping her hands together.

'How does it work?' I blurted out. 'The painting, I mean? How do you make it age instead of the real subject?'

The Masked Painter stood perfectly still, stoic as a statue. 'There is nothing that art cannot express. Most painters are limited only by the bounds of their imagination.'

My logical brain bucked with the need for a concrete explanation. 'Is it . . . magic?'

He cocked his head to one side, vulpine in his movements. 'It is alchemy, as is all art.'

'And all I have to do is let you take my blood?'

'Blood, skin and a scraping of bone.' He practically

whispered the words, and I strained to hear him. 'The visceral trinity: the life force, the largest organ and the very scaffolding our bodies hang upon.'

Orlagh winced. 'Ah. I must confess I had forgotten the skin. It has been some time.'

A hand went to her ribcage protectively, and my insides twisted at the thought of what might be about to happen to me. I stalled further.

'Is there anything I need to do?' I asked. 'Like . . . an incantation, or something?'

'There will be a test.' He talked again in feathery whispers, and I thought it perhaps more powerful than the booming Shakespearean pitch I'd become accustomed to at Dorian. 'A measure of how badly you want it. Without that intense desire, the anchor will not take.'

The vaporous dread in my lungs was solidifying. 'What kind of test?'

'All will become clear in due course. Are you ready?'

There was nothing left to ask. Swallowing the lump of fear in my throat, I said, 'I am.'

'Very well.' He reached for his briefcase. 'Let us begin.'

Orlagh pulled the swath of white fabric from the chaise longue and gestured for me to sit. When I perched on the edge, my knees sinking weakly to the frayed velvet, she shook her head.

'Lie down.'

I lay down.

The Masked Painter crossed over to the chaise, lowered the briefcase and fiddled with a combination on the top. His hands looked almost teenage in their purity, pale and smooth and slender. He must've painted his own self-portrait when he was very young, to be locked in such a youthful body forever. It would explain the soft, high voice too – it was as though the voice had been captured right on the cusp of manhood.

As the briefcase folded open, I peered over the edge of my seat and saw a vast array of oil paints and brushes of all sizes. There was also a small, polished wood box with a hole in the top, several empty glass vials, as well as what looked like a selection of silver medical scalpels. I recoiled at the sight, a kind of animalistic shudder, a feeling of *no, no, no*.

'The simplest place to perform the procedure is the ribcage,' murmured the Masked Painter. 'Would you mind lifting your dress for me? You can use the fur coat to cover up elsewhere.' He turned away, eyes fixing on the nearest portrait of Lydia Fettes.

An intense vulnerability spread over me as I shrugged out of the coat, then coaxed the silk of the dress over one jagged hipbone and up to my waist. Then I laid the fur on top of me so that just a small patch of milky-white skin was visible. Camran stood at the head of the chaise longue, gripping its arms. I felt safer for her presence.

'I'll be making an incision over the lowermost rib,' explained the Masked Painter. 'When it bleeds, I shall capture the droplets in the first vial. I will then trim the smallest sliver of skin from the opening of the wound – that's for the second vial.' His voice was like satin, as though he were reading a sonnet instead of describing how he was going to carve me up. 'Finally, the bone.' He held up a kind of razor-sharp metal scraper that looked more like a dentist's tool. 'I'll take as little as I can, but be warned, the pain can be substantial. Please try to stay still, or there's a chance I'll do more damage.'

I nodded numbly, regret washing over me, but some vague sense of pride and stubbornness kept me rooted to the chaise.

The Masked Painter crouched down beside me, his long black cloak brushing along the floor. His body didn't seem to give off any heat. If anything, the air around me grew colder at his presence. Dabbing a cotton-wool pad in rubbing alcohol, he ran a long forefinger along a patch at the bottom of my ribcage, then swiped at it with the disinfectant. The smell of it was so potent it made my eyes water, and reminded me of the time I went with my teenage best friend Samara as she got her first tattoo – the Basra skyline along the bone of her forearm.

The memory of it stung more than the tattoo likely did. I'd been madly in love with her, but she was straight as an arrow, and started ghosting me when she found out how I really felt.

Maybe if you'd been a little bit more beautiful . . . my warped mind suggested. *Maybe then she would've felt the same. Maybe then you would have been enough.*

'Now lie very still for me,' purred the Masked Painter. I saw he was wielding a narrow surgical knife and looked away. My gaze landed on the portrait of my mother, and her eyes seemed to be screaming something at me. But again, I was likely just projecting.

There was a sharp, piercing scratch in my side, and it took all my willpower not to wince, or let a single grunt of discomfort escape my lips.

A vial was pressed against the wound, capturing a few beadlets of blood. Then I felt a barbed slicing sensation, and it became harder to stay quiet.

'Very good.' He clinked the two vials back into his briefcase, and I turned around just in time to see him pull out the vicious scraper. 'We're two thirds of the way there now.'

Which meant the bone was next.

The discomfort intensified as the Masked Painter parted the skin on either side of the wound with his fingers – a stinging tug that made my teeth grit of their own accord – then the feeling of cold metal sliding between the layers of skin and flesh to the bone below. Another instrument was pushed through below the scraper, possibly to capture the bone shavings as he worked.

As steel hit bone and began to scrape, I could no longer bury the gasp. The pain was cold as ice, like a thousand nerve endings were being frozen by liquid nitrogen.

I'm sorry, came a voice in the back of my head, but I couldn't say for certain whether it was my own. All I knew is that the words appeared unbidden, as though voiced by a stranger who cared for me deeply.

It was over almost as quickly as it began, and as the metal

tools were coaxed out of the wound, the pain in the bone eased to a dull throb. There was a final ding of steel against a glass vial, then the sound of a ziplock bag as the instruments were sealed away for sterilisation.

'Well done,' said Orlagh softly, taking my hand and giving it a squeeze.

The maternal gesture made me want to cry.

The cut stung like a burn, and as the Masked Painter began to stitch it, I struggled not to gag at the feeling of needles and thread tugging through my tender skin. Relief coursed through me as he covered the wound with a wide surgical plaster and smoothed down the seal. The worst was over.

When he was finally finished, I donned my Paxton mask and said lightly, 'Would it have killed you to provide some local anaesthesia?'

The Masked Painter laughed a buttery laugh. 'The pain is an important part of it, I'm afraid.' He tucked off a pair of surgical gloves I hadn't seen him put on, dropping them into the briefcase with a snap of flimsy latex. 'Which brings us to the test.'

I sat up gingerly, pulling my dress down to retain some semblance of modesty. 'Well, it can't possibly be any worse than that.'

The Masked Painter stood abruptly, and began pacing in a way that was entirely juxtapositional with his creamy voice and elegant movements. It put me on edge at once, but I tried to focus on the cutting pain in my side instead of what might lie ahead.

'As I mentioned earlier,' he said, 'the test is a crucial display of will and intent. It is unpleasant, because what better way to display desire than to commit a wholly disagreeable act in the name of it?'

My stomach tightened. 'What is it?'

As suddenly as he'd started, the Masked Painter knelt to the ground beside the briefcase. After rearranging his peculiar array of objects in a way that didn't seem to achieve anything, he lifted out the polished wooden box with the hole in the top.

Only now I was sure I could hear movement inside it.

With a long-fingered hand, the Masked Painter turned a tiny brass key in an equally minuscule keyhole on the front of the box, then, with slow trepidation, eased open the lid.

Inside was a grey-haired mouse, nibbling on a piece of cheddar. It was apparently unconcerned by its captivity in a velvet-lined box, and didn't even glance up at the removal of the roof.

Then the Masked Painter reached for a velvet drawstring pouch, and pulled out a small hammer with a long, worn wooden handle.

A horrible kind of understanding dawned in my mind, but I held on to the slightest bit of hope that I'd misinterpreted the situation.

'What . . .?' I started, unsure how to even ask the vile question.

Angled as it was towards me, the silver fox mask looked even more angular and threatening. 'The most potent way to determine your force of will is a living sacrifice.'

I blanched. 'No.'

Silence. In that moment, I wished this arcane painter wore no mask, so that I might identify the slightest bit of emotion on his face. Remorse? Shame?

'Isn't what I just went through evidence enough of my desire?' I whispered, staring at the mouse. It had long white whiskers and tiny hands. There was a slowness to its movements – and a lack of interest in fleeing – that made me think it might have been drugged.

'One might think,' said the Masked Painter drily. 'But whenever I've painted a portrait without the living sacrifice, the anchor has not taken.'

Horror unfurled inside me like an opening rose. I'd never had the affinity for animals that a lot of my friends had. We never had pets in the house – not a cheerful family Labrador nor an aloof but affectionate cat – and I'd only ever been to the zoo once as a kid. When Samara went vegan at fifteen, I didn't really understand it, especially when she became so deeply anaemic that she had to medicate her way out of a problem a simple cheeseburger could fix. It struck me as needless martyrdom.

Maybe if I had to kill the beasts myself, I'd think twice.

I could not fathom reaching out and taking that hammer, let alone bringing it down on a defenceless being.

I shook my head vehemently, like a child trying to snap themselves out of a nightmare. 'I don't know if I can do it.'

The Masked Painter looked skyward and sighed. 'My point proven. Your will is clearly not strong enough for the portrait to work.'

'Yes, it is.' I tried to force fierceness into my tone, but the pain of the visceral trinity procedure and the week of near-starvation had left me weak and jittery. I was probably not in the least bit convincing.

The Masked Painter shrugged, as though indifferent either way, then picked up the hammer by its head and handed it to me. 'Then show me.'

I took the hammer, but didn't look down at it, just felt its heft in my palm. 'It's an innocent mouse.'

He stood to his feet and started walking in circles once more, but these steps were pensive, almost funereal, compared to the frenzied pacing of a few moments ago.

Orlagh spoke for the first time in an age. She stood behind the chaise, gripping its back with white-knuckled hands. 'Nobody is going to force you to do this, Penny. It is a decision that must be made by your own hand.'

My mind raced, a frantic hurtle, like a bluebottle slamming against a window over and over again in a desperate attempt to find another way through. But I did not find one.

And I had come this far. I had starved and preened. I had let a stranger cut into my body, let him scrape away at my bones. I could not turn away now. I could not let this all be for nothing.

Dimly, I wondered whether this was the reason the surgical elements were performed upfront. It became much harder to change your mind once you had invested tangible pain into it.

I just had to remind myself why I was doing this. So that I would not have to walk around bald and hungry. So that I could free my body and my mind from the constant pursuit of beauty. So that I could focus on my art, on Lady Macbeth, on letting my thoughts deepen and widen. So that I could chase more from life. From myself.

Sensing my indecision – or at least a turning point in my thought patterns – Orlagh went on.

'It is over very quickly. They do not suffer.'

The mouse twitched its whiskers, polishing off the last piece of cheese.

At least its final meal was a good one.

With a last self-loathing breath, I lifted the hammer and brought it down.

CHAPTER ELEVEN

I returned to the flat a little after midnight.

After witnessing how unsteady my footing was on the climb back through the stage trapdoor, Orlagh chaperoned me to the front door of Abernathy. Campus was mostly quiet but for the occasional slamming door or pop of laughter. There was the scent of woodsmoke and something earthy on the breeze. Somewhere nearby, a violin played.

'How do you feel?' asked Orlagh, a caring hand on the back of my elbow. The maternal touch only made me crave more – a hug, a hair stroke, a soothing word in my ear. I hated how desperate and young the cravings felt.

'Cold,' I answered honestly. I was frozen to the bone, and now that the adrenaline of the situation had worn off, the pain in my rib had intensified.

We stopped outside Abernathy, the white-gold light of the entrance hall spilling out of the glass-fronted double doors and on to the pavement. It illuminated every curve of Orlagh's body, made her auburn hair shine like burnished bronze, and even in my dazed and disoriented state I was mesmerised by her.

'I mean in yourself,' she said. 'Do you feel any different?'

'I do. But I can't really articulate it.'

It was as though my body had laid down roots somewhere other than where I stood. A gnawing tug towards the lake, and the gallery that lay beneath.

There had been no more pain during the painting session itself, other than the vague discomfort of sitting on the same chaise longue for hours on end. I had been surprised how little time it took for the Masked Painter to bring me to life on the canvas – part of me had been expecting multiple sessions, or to be there until the small hours of Monday morning. But the artist's hand had glided over the painting with such urgency that my form had taken shape almost immediately, and the rest of the night was spent filling in my every detail with a brush the size of an eyelash.

The whole thing made me uneasy. I'd researched beforehand how long an oil portrait should take, and the internet had told me dozens and dozens of hours were common. And yet when the Masked Painter had showed me the final portrait . . . it was as though he'd spent every waking moment of his life so far on that one piece. It was, simply put, exquisite. And it writhed with that same tension as my mother's portrait, as though my painted form was somehow sentient. To have breathed such life into a canvas in a matter of hours . . .

Whatever power the Masked Painter possessed was ungodly.

'I just hope you find the peace you deserve,' said Orlagh. She gave my elbow a final squeeze.

'Thank you.' I dimly registered that she was still wearing

only the purple gown, and the night air was bitten with autumn chill. 'Aren't *you* cold?'

'Heavens, no,' she laughed airily. 'I was warm on the night I had my portrait painted.'

The statement jarred inside me, a feeling of a missed step, a jolt of semi-realisation, but I was too sapped to examine it more closely. To look at the words head-on, and truly absorb their meaning.

Or maybe I was just afraid to.

'Get some rest,' Orlagh said. 'You have classes bright and early. *Bonne nuit, ma cherie.*'

The atrium inside Abernathy felt warm on my skin, but the sensation didn't really penetrate any further. I'd have a long, hot shower when I got to my room, I reasoned. Or would I eat first? I would probably eat first. My stomach gnawed at me, and I thought longingly of the pack of cookies in Catalina's cupboard. I was sure she wouldn't mind me devouring them if I replaced them tomorrow.

The lift to the third floor was out of order, but the promise of sugar – the rush of elation at finally being able to enjoy it guilt-free – propelled me up the stairs.

I had just reached the first mezzanine stairwell when I heard the entrance doors open and close below me, then the sound of hushed female voices and soft footsteps floated up to where I stood obscured from view.

'So why *did* you get involved with Drever?' said the first. Maisie. Which would mean the other was . . .

'I wasn't *involved* with him,' hissed Davina. 'At least not in the way you think. There was a problem with my student loan, and I couldn't afford the rent on student accommodation until next month. Drever found me sleeping in my car during the first week and said I could crash on his couch. He lives in town.'

My stomach dropped. She was innocent?

'So there was nothing romantic between you two?' asked Maisie in an excited chatter. I could practically hear her bouncing on her heels.

'Nope. Although I did try it on with him after a few nights.'

'Why?'

'I got bored, okay? I could tell he wasn't interested, and I like a challenge.'

A beat. 'Did anything happen?'

'Nah.' An incredulous scoff. 'He turned me away. Then the next day – the one your bitch flatmate captured on camera – he said he was going to talk to the accommodation office and explain my situation. Make sure I got a roof over my head at least. So I kissed him on the cheek, partly in gratitude, and partly because . . . yeah. I like the challenge.'

'So why did Drever give in to the blackmail?'

'Because he hardly looked innocent, did he? I dunno if there are cameras on his street, but if there was an investigation they'd surely show me coming and going from his flat. Coupled with the cheek-kiss photo, there's no way anyone would believe we weren't fucking.'

'Shit,' Maisie stage-whispered. 'Don't you feel bad for Drever?'

I could practically hear the glare Davina was undoubtedly levelling at Maisie. 'Do *I* feel sorry for an old privileged white dude who's never wanted for anything a day in his life?'

This seemed like an absurd oversimplification of privilege to me, but Davina seemed to wear her I-sleep-in-my-car situation like a coat of armour. Something designed to keep scrutiny bouncing off her, to shield her when she was in the wrong. In any case, the guilt waned ever so slightly. Drever may be clean-handed, but Davina was certainly not beyond reproach. She had been actively trying to seduce him, even though he'd said no. She was a predator.

Maisie's voice hitched up an octave. 'Oh no, I didn't mean –'

'Whatever.' Davina made a derogatory snort noise.

'Still, what a mess. No wonder you hate Penny.'

After a few beats, Davina said. 'Don't worry. She'll get what's coming to her.'

'Does Drever know it was her?'

'Not yet. I'm waiting for the right moment to tell him. You have to play your cards at the right time, you know? Same with Penny's revenge. It's all very well having pocket aces, but they become a lot more powerful if a third appears in the river.'

'You play poker?'

'Nah, I just know a lot of things about a lot of things. Anyway, I have to go. I'm meeting someone.'

'This late? Is it Drever?'

The near-pleading in Maisie's tone made me squirm. How could her pride allow her to beg for gossip scraps like that?

She had the air of someone who'd somehow befriended the popular girl and would do anything to keep their favour. She was worse than a gossip, I realised. She was a social climber. I just didn't understand what her ultimate aim was. Was she loyal to Davina now? Or was she just collecting rumours and secrets to use as currency?

'Bye, Maisie.' Davina's tone was pure dismissal.

I slipped the shoes off my feet and hurried up the remaining steps as silently as I could, heart pounding in my chest.

My nerves churned as I ran over their conversation in my head.

What would happen when Drever found out I'd been the one to blackmail him? Would he drop me from the production too? Or would he just keep a hateful distance?

I slipped into the flat as silently as I could. The place was quiet – Catalina's bedroom door was shut, so she was likely asleep, while Fraser was out on yet another pub crawl. The kitchen was dark but for a single pool of light over the hob.

Even the knowledge that Maisie was about to enter the flat behind me wasn't enough to curb the overwhelming hunger that propelled me to the cupboard over the kettle.

Catalina had been to the shop that day, and there were now several packets of different kinds of cookies and biscuits, as well as tins of soup and packets of crackers, dried noodle nests and cans of chickpeas, boxes of granola and jars of peanut butter, a bag of honey roasted cashews and a fully stocked wooden rack of herbs and spices engraved with the word *cocinar*. I tore into the first packet of custard creams like a rabid thing, shoving them into my mouth whole and chewing a minimal amount before swallowing and repeating.

The front door opened and closed, followed by Maisie's bedroom door, which was nearest the kitchen. The sounds barely registered.

I made it through a whole packet of biscuits, but it still hadn't touched the edges of my ravenous hunger. It took twenty minutes to feel full, I vaguely recalled from a magazine article on intermittent fasting. So I kept eating.

Tugging open the ring-pull, I held up a can of minestrone soup and drank it cold. I tore into the packet of crackers and wolfed them down too, as well as several handfuls of the cashew nuts, crunching through them with feral determination. I dimly registered a sense of guilt at devouring so much food that wasn't mine, but I'd set my alarm early and replace everything tomorrow morning before Catalina woke up. The on-campus shop didn't open until eight, but I could drive to the twenty-four hour superstore on the outskirts.

I would double up on everything, and keep it for myself. I would roll up and down the aisles with reckless abandon, scooping things into my trolley that I'd only dreamed of eating for years. I felt giddy at the thought. A soaring feeling in my chest.

As I ate, though, a sense of shame seemed to study me from

the corner of the room. A pair of searing eyes watching from the shadows. And I wondered, then, what my mother would think if she could see me now. Would she be disgusted at my gluttony? Would she be annoyed that I'd uncovered her secret – and snatched the same gift for myself? Would she be jealous, even, that I had my whole career, my whole life ahead of me?

Once I'd finished everything in the cupboard, I turned to the kitchen sink and drank straight from the tap, rivulets of cold water slicking down my chin and on to my black silk dress. Then I hauled myself up on to a bar stool, breathless, and waited for the food to hit my stomach. I waited to feel full for the first time since I was fourteen.

Twenty minutes, thirty, forty. Tiredness tugged at my eyes, but still the fist of hunger remained just below my ribs. I shivered uncontrollably, cold still gnawing at my bones. The wound in my side stung afresh.

With another disturbed fit of agitation, I yanked open Fraser's cupboard, thinking maybe I just needed more food, but found only a single tin of beans and a torn packet of ramen. Still sitting in the almost-dark, I crunched through the ramen then ate the beans cold, with a teaspoon, feeling entirely unhinged. Untethered from the world in some fundamental way.

It took an hour for the dread to finally sink in. For me to piece together everything that had been right in front of me, but which desperation had convinced me to ignore:

Aren't you cold?

Heavens, no. I was warm on the night I had my portrait painted.

Horrible understanding crept up on me like a dark ink stain. Two nights ago in Orlagh's office:

The subjects, in the real world, are preserved exactly *as they were the day the painting was completed.*

Gripping the edge of the counter, I fought the urge to vomit.

She had told me. She had *told* me. I just hadn't listened. I heard only what I wanted to hear.

Had I just doomed myself to a lifetime of dizzying hunger? Of pain in my ribs and cold in my bones?

CHAPTER TWELVE

I slept in fits and starts, waking every hour to a gnawing sensation in my stomach. A coldness unlike anything I'd ever felt. By the time my alarm went off for my supermarket dash, I was almost relieved to be up and doing something to distract me.

As I was driving home from Sainsbury's – with a car full of more food than I'd ever bought in my life – I contemplated calling my mum and confessing what I'd done. Not just the decision to sit for the portrait in the first place, but the mistakes I'd made in the execution: going to the sitting cold and hungry and afraid. Maybe there was some way around it that she'd discovered in the last twenty years, a way to unanchor certain undesirable consequences. But the notion of admitting failure – of asking for help, especially from my mother – had always felt like a sign of weakness.

Catalina surfaced around twenty minutes after I'd restocked her cupboards. Her wet hair was wrapped in a lilac silk turban, and the skin on her face was dewy with some kind of serum. She did a dorky little dance on her way over to the fridge.

'Morning,' she chirped, tying the band of her fluffy dressing gown around her waist. 'Oh, that breakfast looks *good*,' she said, appraising my plate. 'When I die, I would like to be buried in a coffin filled with jam. Or be shot out of a cannon into the ocean while someone blares flamenco music. I haven't quite decided.'

I looked down at the plate of food in front of me. Again, another jolt of failure, of shame, my warped mind telling me that partaking in this simple human experience was a sign of poor self-discipline.

Yet while I was enjoying the taste of the food, the satisfaction in the chewing, the milky sweetness of my coffee, the salty tang of butter, the juicy burst of strawberry jam, the pillowy softness of the crumpets . . . I was still left with the ache of hunger. The thought of how long I might have to endure the feeling made panic leap in my chest.

I had to make this right.

'Where were you all weekend?' Catalina asked, padding barefoot to her cupboard and pulling out a box of loose-leaf tea. She didn't seem to notice the slight discrepancy in arrangement of her food. 'I was kind of hoping to rope you into a new DnD campaign I'm starting with a few second years. Did you go home to see your mum?'

I took another sip of coffee – made the way I actually liked it, for once. A small but not insignificant pleasure. 'No, I was in my room. I had a migraine.'

'Oh, I'm sorry.' She crossed to the sink and filled the vintage tea kettle. 'You know, I recently read a pioneering research paper on migraines. My mum gets them. Apparently they've discovered this new kind of mushroom that –'

'Hi,' Maisie said coolly, appearing in the doorway with her hair in foam rollers. She went to her cupboard, slippers slapping against the tiles, and took out a cereal bar.

Catalina smiled. 'Morning!' Then, to me: 'Anyway, I'll send you that paper, Pen.'

I felt a flicker of guilt at having lied to her, but I still beamed at the nickname. Nobody had called me Pen since Samara, and though the memory of her stung, it was nice to hear Catalina say it.

Something in me glowed at the idea of having another friend. Another *best* friend, if I managed not to alienate her over the coming weeks and months. I just had to be careful not to declare my undying love, and we should be fine. Baby steps.

Fraser entered the kitchen behind Maisie, his black hair ruffled in countless directions. He grunted a hello and crossed to the fridge. There were traces of glitter scattered over his cheekbones, and black smears around his eyes, as though he'd slept in mascara. Had there been a fancy-dress event at the students' union last night?

'Morning, all,' he said, with a gruff little mock salute.

At the appearance of Fraser, Maisie stood up straighter, then cast me a knowing, self-satisfied look. 'Well, not that anyone seems to care, but I found out what Penny did to Davina. To steal the lead, that is.'

Shit.

Catalina stilled for a moment before spooning tea leaves

into a strainer. The kettle grew louder as it started to boil. 'What are you talking about?'

The smugness on Maisie's face intensified. 'I swore I wouldn't say anything. But if you want to confess, Penny, now's your chance.'

Stomach flipping, I weighed my options. Either I could stay silent on the matter, and risk losing this burgeoning friendship with Catalina, or I could tell her, and risk losing this burgeoning friendship even more.

Having not been born with a certain social skill set that most people seemed to innately possess, I didn't know how to misdirect, or feint, or lie by omission. My brain much preferred frankness, both in others and in myself. So if Catalina was probably going to hate me anyway, it might as well be over the truth.

Besides, the idea of more people knowing about Davina's shady antics gave me a small pulse of satisfaction. Let her reputation suffer over this.

'I caught Davina kissing Professor Drever and took a picture,' I said levelly, as though discussing the weather. Fraser, who'd been relatively despondent until now, looked up with bleary interest. 'Then I put the picture on his desk.'

'Davina and Drever are together?' Catalina blinked three times in quick succession beneath her owlish glasses, her hand hovering over her mug. 'That's so messed-up.'

Fraser rubbed at his forehead, a carton of full-fat milk in one hand. 'Hard yikes.'

Maisie's eyes narrowed. She obviously wasn't expecting me to so readily admit my own role in the proceedings. 'It wasn't how it looked. With Davina and Drever.'

I so badly wanted to let slip that I *knew* Davina was hitting on the professor – trying to weaken his will – but that would require confessing I'd overheard their conversation in the stairwell last night. So instead I said, 'Well, it was clearly enough to trigger a guilty reaction in him.'

'So you blackmailed Drever?' Catalina's gaze searched me.

'Yeah.' I drained the last of my coffee, letting the extra-sugary dregs coat my tongue in heady sweetness.

'Why?' she asked curiously. 'Did you want the lead that badly?'

There was so much I could say – yes, but also no, because I was terrified of actually being on stage, of being perceived in general, but I needed my mother to know I'm as much of a winner as she is, and I needed to prove to myself I had the talent to be here, and and and –

I settled on a half-truth. Part of the story, but with the other, darker half eclipsed. Two sides of the same moon.

'I didn't force him to recast *me*.' I readjusted the thick woolly scarf I was wearing in a futile attempt to warm up. 'I have a strong sense of justice, alright? I hated the thought of her sleeping her way into the role when someone else might have been overlooked because of it.'

Maisie snorted. 'Someone else being *you*.'

'As it turns out, yes.' I lifted my chin, mimicking my

mother's enigmatic smile.

Everybody loves a winner, Penny. Since arriving at Dorian, her voice seemed louder than ever in my head.

Fraser, who had lifted the carton of milk to his mouth and started drinking ravenously, wiped his mouth on the back of his hand. 'Good for you, Pen.'

Maisie glowered.

'Wow.' Catalina leaned back against the edge of the counter. 'They told me Dorian was intense, but . . .'

Self-hatred clamped around me. I wanted so badly for Catalina to like me, to respect me. To think I was a good person. I couldn't lose her friendship already.

'Maybe I shouldn't have done it,' I admitted, turning to Maisie. 'It was you who told me the rumours about Davina sleeping her way into the role, Maze.' I bolted on the cute nickname, hoping beyond hope that it would absorb some of the venom from the situation. 'I thought it was the right thing to do. But then again, I'm fundamentally not a chill person. Whenever I saw someone cheating on a test in school, I told the teacher.'

Catalina seemed to relax her shoulders a little at my light-hearted self-deprecation, but Maisie shot me a filthy look.

Stalking off towards the door, she muttered, 'All I'm saying is don't start a fight you can't finish.'

'*Bro,*' said Fraser, eyes widening at Maisie's vague threat.

Her words rekindled the flames of dread in my gut.

What *was* Davina planning to do?

CHAPTER THIRTEEN

The swan fixed its beady gaze on me. There was something unnatural about its eyes – they were wholly black but for a pale cobwebbed pattern, like glass on the brink of shattering. Its feathers had a silvery sheen, and it glided over the lake with an almost spectral smoothness. Every time its eyes met mine, I felt a peculiar pulling sensation, as though it were summoning me to my death.

Our absolutely critical and not at all pointless 'standing practice' had been moved down to the shore of Swan Lake, which curved reverently around the foot of the Great Lawn. We had all mastered the high art of standing still indoors, and so Professor Lawrie had decided a change of scenery would provide a fresh challenge.

'Root yourselves as trees,' he said, his clarion voice halfway between earthy yoga instructor and King Lear.

Behind him the Crosswoods were deckled yellow and orange with the looming arrival of autumn. A light breeze swayed through the holly. Above the canopy, little clouds drifted across the sky like ravelled skeins of glossy white silk.

'Let consciousness flow from the tips of your fingers up your arms and into your chest. Breathe it in, and breathe it out. Be where you are, and be there well.'

Everything Professor Lawrie taught us about standing still seemed to contradict itself. According to him, it is both active and passive, both easy and difficult. Stand with a low centre of gravity, let the earth pull you down, but also maintain a state of tension, with multiple countervailing powers at your waist. Feel the power drawing your body from the front, the power pulling you back from behind, the power you use to step firmly, and the power to support your body securely. You should appear to be standing still, but in fact show the audience your presence through internal strength that has nowhere to go.

Absolutely critical, and not at all pointless.

I looked around. Catalina was to my left, perfectly still and stoic, as though she'd entered a state of blissful meditation. I wondered if her brain was somewhere deep in a faerie forest, trying to break an ancient curse. Fraser looked distinctly bored – the residual make-up now scrubbed from his face – and I kept catching his eyes roving over the lines of my body.

Loathe as I was to admit it, I was struggling to stand in place. The sun beat down with unexpected vigour for the last day in September, and sweat pooled in the small of my back. I was utterly exhausted from the late night in the gallery, and terrified of the fate I might have sealed for myself.

As I tried to fix my gaze on the rotting blue boathouse, the peripheries of my vision blurred and starred, and my legs felt weak and shaky. I warred with the nausea rising in my gullet.

Pride would not allow me to vomit in front of the entire class.

I was Lady Macbeth. I was the lead. I had to act like it.

Something shifted in the corner of my eye, and I glanced back to Davina, frowning. She had taken a step towards the lake – more specifically towards the swan I had just been making eerie eye contact with. Only now, its gaze was locked on her.

Professor Lawrie, who stood with his back to the lake, held up a palm. 'Ms Burns, I advise keeping a safe distance from the swans.'

There was a small sign nailed to a wooden post beside the lake that read: NO SWIMMING – SWANS DANGEROUS.

Davina either did not hear Lawrie or did not care to heed his warning. She took another step forward, her ballet flats silent on the grassy bank.

Clearing his throat pointedly, Lawrie repeated, 'Ms Burns.'

Nairne, the nervous girl I'd helped out during auditions, shifted on her feet then whispered to the boy beside her, 'Do you think it's true that they can sense impending tragedy?' Her voice was so feather-light I almost didn't hear her. 'The swans, I mean.'

'I heard it was a sense of a star on the rise,' muttered Priyam. His tone was not so delicate, and everyone began to listen. 'Predicting who's going to be most successful.'

Lawrie shook his head tersely. 'I can assure you that the swans are just swans, but their beating wings can be ferocious. Ms *Burns*.'

Davina had taken several more steps forward, and was now submerged in the lake to her bone-white ankles. The swan was only a few feet from her, but it did not hiss or bluster – just studied her intently, as though trying to communicate something. Davina seemed utterly transfixed, unable to tear herself away, unhearing of the teacher's cautions.

A cold thrill ran up my spine, but I couldn't say for certain why.

'Didn't a swan kill a student once?' asked Nairne, now talking not only to Priyam but to the whole class. 'Like a hundred years ago?.'

'Oh yeah,' said Fraser. 'She went for a swim, right? And a swan whacked her with its wings and she sank below the surface, unconscious?'

'Please –' started Lawrie, but he had dropped the reins of our collective attention.

Nairne nodded, enthused. 'I heard that another student saw it happen from the common-room window and ran down to help, but she'd disappeared. They couldn't find the swimmer's body even after days of searching.' A meaningful pause. 'She was never seen again.'

'*Please*,' Lawrie all but shouted, clapping his hands together, and finally the chatter died. 'While I understand the appeal of ghost stories, I would caution you against spreading unnecessary fear. Ms Burns, for goodness –'

Davina was inches from the swan now, neither of them flinching, just holding that uncanny eye contact. It looked for a moment as though they might kiss.

Then the swan let out a phantasmal *hiss*, and raised its wings to full span.

In an instant the spell was broken. Davina stumbled back, and Maisie lunged forward to catch her by the elbow and haul her out of the water. The swan gave them one final glare and glided away.

Davina sat back on to the bank, staring down at her feet as though they'd betrayed her in some fundamental way. The rest of us had relaxed our soldier-straight positions, but I had to fight the urge to slump to the lakeshore myself. The dizziness was only sharpening, my eyes swirling and eddying like the ripples on the water.

Lawrie pinched the bridge of his nose. 'I understand that standing still is not, perhaps, your most titillating session. But the skill is incredibly important in your foundations as a stage actor. And your grades in this class will count towards your final degree.'

Fraser scoffed incredulously. 'We're being marked on this?'

'Indeed you are. And so I suggest you all start taking it a little more seriously.' Another thunderous clap of the hands. 'Now. Again.'

With a final flourishing swoop, my vision dived earthward, and I fainted.

*

Despite Catalina's firm insistence, I refused to seek medical attention. How was I supposed to explain to a physician what was wrong with me? How could I tell a sound-of-mind doctor that I'd tethered myself to an arcane gallery, dooming myself to perpetual hunger and fainting fits? Did they have a drug for that?

After stumbling my way through a day of classes and rehearsals, I headed back to the flat to wolf down as much food as I could physically eat. I'd bought a bunch of Chinese food from the supermarket, and scarfed six wontons, six prawn toasts, six duck pancakes, shredded beef, egg fried rice and garlic pak choi.

The crunch as I bit into a crispy spring roll reminded me of the innocent mouse's skull beneath my cruel hammer.

Then I wrapped myself in three jumpers, a pair of leggings under flared trousers, and my biggest vintage fur coat before traipsing back to Orlagh's office in Drummond.

I had to talk to her. I had to figure out how to fix this.

Campus was cast in lilac twilight, with gaggles of students wandering down to the Costumery for pints of Guinness and bowls of chunky chips. Dry yellow leaves crunched beneath my aubergine-coloured cowboy boots as I crossed the quad. The air smelled of crackling fire – the Auld Torch had been lit the previous day to signal the start of the autumn programme. A sacred Dorian ritual I had missed because I was hiding out in my room, trying to make myself perfect.

I felt a pang of sadness, but I dismissed it as best I could.

That wasn't going to be my life any more. Once I fixed this insatiable hunger situation, I would have all the freedom in the world. I smiled to myself. Maybe when I got home I'd ask Catalina if she wanted to go to the union and try the new s'mores hot chocolate they'd launched for spooky season.

As I entered Drummond, my eyes were drawn to the humongous gold-framed mirror hung over the staircase. It was larger than most houses – frankly *too* large, for a mirror – and it seemed to play strange tricks with the light. The chandelier dangling over the atrium was reflected what looked like a dozen times, in a kaleidoscope of fractured light, but the shadows looked darker than they did in real life. If I looked too closely for too long, they seemed to warp and eddy like the surface of the lake.

Just as I was about to tear my eyes away, a silhouette suddenly appeared in the forefront of the mirror.

And pressed a hand against the silvered glass.

I leaped backwards, fear bolting through me, but the human-shaped shadow disappeared as quickly as it arrived.

I'm losing my mind, I thought, heart pounding. *Hallucinating from starvation.*

Climbing the two floors to Orlagh's office was a slog, and by the time I reached it I was dizzy and panting. I knocked on the door with trembling knuckles, and waited for her to call me in.

Nothing.

I waited a few moments, and then knocked a little louder.

Still nothing.

Glancing at my gold wristwatch, I saw that I was right on time.

Had she just dozed off at her desk? We'd both been up late last night.

After a third and final knock, I tried the handle to see if it was locked. Maybe she'd just forgotten, mixed up her days. But there was a kind of shivering disquiet growing in me with every passing moment.

The handle turned all the way around, and I pushed the door open a crack.

'Hello?' I called into the room, noticing dimly how young my voice sounded.

When there was no response, instinct made me push the door the rest of the way open.

It took my eyes a few beats to process the dead body slumped over the desk.

Sunken eyes stared vacantly at the wall of portraits. The hair was long and grey, with a wispy spiderweb quality. She wore an elegant navy gown, but it hung off her skeletal frame. The hands were withered and sun-spotted, but a piece of jewellery on the forefinger made my stomach lurch.

An apricot-gold cameo ring. Next to it, a neat brown freckle. *Orlagh*.

CHAPTER FOURTEEN

Bile leaped up my throat; a hot sting of shock.

Orlagh was dead.

But she should not have been able to die.

Unless marred by some brutal external force, their bodies will never change. They may cheat even death.

Some brutal external force. Which meant . . . she had been murdered?

Every instinct screamed at me to run. To call the police. To hide far, far away. Because the killer could still be in Drummond – or this very room. But as though compelled by some greater power, I took several quaking steps towards the desk. My consciousness seemed to shimmer and detach from my body, and I floated off to the side as though watching myself as a spectator, not a participant.

I touched a hand to Orlagh's – the one wearing the cameo ring – and flinched. There were still some final vestiges of warmth. She couldn't have been dead for long. My breath shuddered in my lungs, like a ghost trying to rattle itself free.

Just as I was wondering how she'd been killed, I spotted a long purple cut slanting diagonally down her throat, disappearing into the shadows in the crook of her neck like a road disappearing into a forest. The churning in my stomach intensified.

There were similar marks all over her face too. I had only failed to spot them at first because of how severe her wrinkles were. Judging by the folds and crevasses, she must have been over a hundred years old.

Pulling back her wasted shoulder, I found what was likely the killing blow.

The fabric over the bust hung loose enough that it could not cover the stab wound over her heart.

Only . . . there was no blood. It was a dark purple gash, but the skin was not broken.

It was the same with the other marks all over her face and décolletage, from narrow puncture wounds to vicious gashes, all the same strange, untextured purple.

The contents of my stomach finally broke free, and I reached the wastebasket under the desk just in time.

I was in the same room as a dead body. And still the largest question on my mind was . . .

Why?

Why had someone murdered Orlagh?

And why now? Right after she'd commissioned the Masked Painter for the first time in years?

The same hideous, selfish core that had blackmailed Davina was most worried about what that meant for me.

Would I ever be able to track down the Masked

Painter again? If I couldn't, how could I ever reverse this horrible mistake?

Was I in danger too?

Thinking fast, I realised this might be my only chance to find the Masked Painter myself. I dimly recalled Orlagh telling me she didn't have a mobile phone, only the vintage landline on her desk. Which meant, unless she had a photographic memory, she likely had a physical stack of contacts somewhere. Could I find the Masked Painter's phone number?

There. An antique-looking Rolodex next to the phone.

I ran my fingers over it. The last contact she'd looked up was *Drever, Cameron*. This struck me as odd – wouldn't she know his extension number by now? – but I didn't have time to worry about him.

In a panic, I realised I had no idea how she would file the Masked Painter. Did she know his real name? Have her own secret code name for him?

I flipped through the *M*s and the *P*s, but found no *Painter, Masked*. I started frantically turning each card, hoping to find something that sparked recognition. Nothing.

In the corridor, there were footsteps. Multiple sets, overlapping, and the murmur of voices.

The desperation overrode my basic intelligence, because the people outside could well have been the killers. I should have hidden, but I did not. I did what I usually found so impossible.

'Help!' I shouted, feeling so weak and afraid that the thought of taking matters into my own hands was overwhelming.

At the sight of the two figures who entered the room, I didn't know whether to be relieved or horrified.

Davina and Drever.

Drever's mouth fell open at the sight of the corpse.

'It's Orlagh,' I choked out, still tasting acid at the back of my throat. 'She's dead. And she's . . . *old*. Ancient.'

I couldn't bring myself to say the word murdered. After all, my only reasoning behind the determination was something she had told me about the exquisite paintings, and I wasn't sure how much of that to give away in the heat of the moment – if ever.

It was supposed to be a secret.

And yet what if that secret had led Orlagh to her grave?

'What on earth,' Drever whispered, clapping a hand to his mouth at the sight of the withered cadaver. 'It can't be . . .'

'Look at the ring.' I pointed to the apricot-gold cameo, which was now far too big for the bony finger it hung upon. 'The freckle above it.'

Drever gripped the doorway for support, face ashen. His tie was loose, his top shirt button undone. Suspicion sprung up in my mind. What had they been doing?

'Good god,' he said, a coarseness to his tone.

'There are scars all over her face and chest.' My voice was a tremulous murmur. *Dead body, dead body, dead body*. 'But they don't look fresh. Maybe she'd been covering them up.'

My mind reeled. None of it made any sense. Had her body been yanked back to its true state the moment death befell her?

Is that why the scars looked old – because they were inflicted upon her younger body? But no. If her younger self had scars, her immortalised self would too. They had to be new.

'Why does she look like that?' croaked Drever. From his reaction, I had to guess that he had no idea about the Masked Painter. 'Are you *sure* it's her?'

'No,' I said untruthfully. 'But the ring, and the freckle . . . they're exactly the same.'

Drever nodded, patting his blazer pocket and pulling out a phone. 'I'll call an ambulance. And maybe the police.'

Davina stood stock-still in the doorway, as white and silent as a mime. She stared at Orlagh with a kind of reverent horror, and all at once I realised that she had likely been mentored by her as well, before I'd blackmailed Drever.

Was she *still* being mentored? Or had that opportunity been torn from her too?

Had Orlagh also told her about the Masked Painter?

I didn't see Davina's portrait in the Gallery of the Exquisite, but then I hadn't looked at all of them in great detail.

The potential realisation unsteadied my footing even further.

'Are you alright?' I asked her, as Drever slipped into the hallway to make the call. It was hardly a peace offering, but it seemed like the right thing to say in the moment.

'We should get out of here,' she replied, and her tone chilled me. It was like ice, emotionless, and a thought so painfully obvious struck me that I wanted to kick myself for not realising it earlier.

What if *she* was the killer?

At first I'd been partly relieved at the sight of her, a familiar figure with whom to share the burden of the discovery, but didn't it make *sense* that she might have had something to do with this?

Hell, maybe they both did.

I thought of Davina's hand curled around my ponytail, the vicious sting of a loosed lock, the peculiar satisfaction on her face when she held it up to the light. The subtle violence to her, written all over the sharp ridges of her face.

And it *fit*.

Maybe Camran had caught them in the throes of passion. Maybe there was a confrontation, in which she threatened to go to the dean. Maybe the two of them knew they would lose everything if that happened – Davina her future, and Drever his reputation.

The last contact open on the Rolodex had been *Drever, Cameron*.

Had Orlagh called him to confront him?

Had it all gone sour after that?

Davina had put on a good show, when she first walked in – the way her mouth fell open, her eyebrows shot up, the little start of shock like an electrode pressed against her skin. But we were here as budding actors, and she was better than most. Drever too had enjoyed a decent level of stage success before the work dried up.

If anyone could feign innocence, it was them.

'You're right,' I said finally, carefully, laying down the wastebasket on the parquet flooring. I was suddenly deathly afraid. 'We should get out of here.'

Though my pulse hadn't truly recovered from the shock of finding Orlagh, it kicked up once more, a frantic skittering, a rush of blood to my temples. If they had killed her, they had the exact same reasons for killing me too – I knew enough about their affair to blackmail Drever with it. What was to stop them from murdering me right now?

I started walking towards Davina, and she moved to block the doorway. As I drew close, I smelt that familiar tobacco-breath, the musky rose perfume, and something altogether headier. There was a kind of carnal intoxication to her dilated stare, a rumpledness to her outfit, and I wondered whether she had finally won Drever over.

When she stuffed a hand in the pocket of her leather jacket, my heart lurched.

A knife? The same knife wielded against Orlagh?

'What are you doing?' I asked, trying to keep myself steady despite the tremor in my legs and the quiver in my voice. 'You just said we should leave.'

I can't be about to die. I can't be.

And yet if she wanted to murder me, there was realistically nothing I could do to stop her. I was frail, malnourished, the muscles in my limbs atrophied from starvation, my vision dizzy with hunger. I didn't stand a chance. There was a flicker of intellectual thought in the back of my head, a kind of flinty understanding of *why* a patriarchy might want its women to feel like this, but I was too caught up in the perilous moment to pluck it from the sand and examine it in more detail.

Davina pulled the object out of her pocket. Not a knife, but a lighter.

'You don't fool me, you know.' She flicked the flame up and down, a compulsive habit turned implied threat, and I felt like the room was twisting and spiralling, a spinning top about to teeter earthward.

'What?' I croaked, a sense of doom cascading around me from all sides, a sense that one decision to capture a private moment on camera was on the brink of unravelling everything.

'The act you put on,' Davina said. Flick, flame, flick, flame. 'Playing up to that innocent beauty. I know it's not who you are. I know there's a darkness inside you.' Her zombie-pale eyes, until now locked on to the gold glint of the lighter, snapped up to me. 'And I want you to know that no matter what hideous things you may have done –' her gaze flitted to Orlagh and then back again – 'I am not afraid of you.'

Fear and confusion warred inside me.

Was she threatening me? It felt as such, and yet she had a way of talking that slithered and crept around the edges of my understanding, nothing concrete enough to grab with both hands, a spectral shadow that shifted under too fierce a gaze. Did she do it on purpose, to wrong-foot me? Somehow I suspected not. It was just the way she was, enigmatic and recondite – and potentially a cold-blooded murderer.

Not for the first time in my life, I wished that other people thought and communicated the way I did, in columns and rows, clear and orderly, easy to parse and easier still to evaluate.

Perhaps it was just my imagination, but the room had begun to fill with the stench of decay.

A cold, animal rot.

'Let me go,' I said, gathering up all the scraps of conviction I had left.

She smiled, broad and mean, and then stepped aside. 'With pleasure.'

The relief of breaking free was cut short when I remembered what she'd said to Maisie in the atrium of Abernathy.

You have to play your cards at the right time, you know? Same with Penny's revenge. It's all very well having pocket aces, but they become a lot more powerful if a third appears in the river.

She was just biding her time.

CHAPTER FIFTEEN

The texture of the world was wrong.

An ambulance crew arrived in the atrium of Drummond as I was descending the staircase, my hand gripped to the swooping bannister like a claw. The red and blue lights outside flashed and swirled through the arched glass windows, refracted countless times in the grand mirror of the entrance hall. It illuminated the myriad portraits, and in doing so made the backgrounds of the paintings seem off, somehow. They shifted and stirred in unnatural ways, as though a torch was being shone into the den of a mythical beast and awaking it from a long slumber.

I remembered the strange silhouette that had appeared in the mirror on the way to Orlagh's office. I'd dismissed it as delusion, and yet I *knew* there was something fundamentally wrong about the portraits of Dorian – my own painting was proof enough.

Why too couldn't the mirrors be haunted? What would it mean if they were?

My mind felt like it was spinning off the edge of the world.

Looking around the vast hall at each portrait in turn, they

didn't seem to be entirely static. The figures in them didn't move, as such, but nor were they still. I remembered my mother's painting in the Gallery of the Exquisite, the way she almost seemed to be straining against the canvas. A subtle bulge of the eye, as though desperately trying to communicate something.

I wondered how Orlagh's looked now she was dead.

Then the terrible understanding struck me.

What if Orlagh had not been stabbed in person?

What if somebody had destroyed her painting? And in doing so, they had destroyed her too?

It would explain the lack of blood, the unbroken skin around otherwise fatal wounds.

Smooth purple cuts, like the echoes of a wound rather than the wounds themselves.

Was it even possible? Would taking a knife to a painting have the power to kill its subject?

My knees were on the brink of buckling, but sheer adrenaline held me steady as I took the last few stairs and headed for the exit.

Darkness had descended on the quad, but quiet had not. A knot of students were performing an impromptu rendition of *The Two Gentlemen of Verona*, with a tall third year cross-dressed as a man and a flamboyant-haired classmate on all fours, wagging an imaginary tail in his role of Crab. A small crowd had gathered to watch, unaware of the ambulance parked up on the other side of Drummond. I couldn't imagine the paramedics had employed their sirens – Orlagh was already dead, after all. The pops of actors were blissfully ignorant to the ravaged body of an icon slumped just a few hundred yards away.

Tucking my chin to my chest, I wrapped my fur coat tighter around me and headed straight for the Basil Hallward Theatre.

A low, urgent voice in the back of my head told me to heed caution. If my suspicions were correct and Orlagh had been murdered through her painting, there was every chance the killer was still on campus. Still in the very gallery I was heading towards. Of course, if it *had* been Davina and Drever, I knew they were in Drummond right now, talking to the paramedics. But if I was wrong . . .

And yet risk be damned, I had to *know*.

I had to know what Orlagh's painting looked like right at this second.

More pressing still, I needed to find out whether Davina hung there too.

If she didn't, I could rule her out as the killer.

If she did . . .

Well, I didn't know what I would do next. I had to gather the pearls of information before I could string them into a necklace.

When I got to the stage door and tried the handle, however, it was locked. I remembered Orlagh opening it with a large golden key and inwardly despaired. I hadn't been here long enough to understand how these things worked – was the theatre only used as a rehearsal space under supervision? Students could come and go as they pleased in the other buildings, but was the Basil Hallward Theatre off limits to preserve its immaculate facade?

I wrapped around to the front of the building, to the box office that looked over the Great Lawn and down to the lake and the Crosswoods. This time, luck was on my side. The grand entrance doors, corniced with palatial gold, swung open into a cool, deserted lobby. The space was lit only by two small green bankers' lamps on a table scattered with old programmes. The cold air smelled of hairspray, dusty costumes and freshly polished floors.

When I pushed through the 'stalls A–J' doors to the auditorium, however, the hope died in my chest. There were a dozen second years mid-flow on stage, rehearsing *Much Ado About Nothing* with exaggerated gusto.

At the sight of the roadblock, it took everything I had not to slump to the floor. How was I going to get down to the gallery any time soon?

And if the killer wasn't Davina or Drever, how were they going to get out?

Was a nefarious figure crouched beneath the stage as we spoke? Or had Orlagh's murder been committed hours before these students took to the stage? No. She had still carried traces of warmth. She couldn't have been dead long.

So many questions, popping up in my mind like the whack-a-mole machine in the arcade Samara and I used to spend our weekends in. Either way, all I could do was wait. I took a seat in the very back row, the adrenaline leaving me in defeated waves. I tucked my feet up on to the edge of the maroon velvet chair and wrapped my arms around my knees, folding my whole body around the grinding pit of hunger in my stomach.

As I sat and gathered my breath, a sense of desolation settled over me like dense fog. No matter how or why or who or what or when, the simple, inescapable fact was that my mentor was dead. A vault of knowledge – on the world, on society, on my body and on the Masked Painter – forever locked to me.

Cavernous despair opened up in my chest, along with a feeling of helpless entrapment. I had built myself a cage of hunger, and Orlagh's death had locked the door.

Unless, of course, my mother knew something. Her portrait hung in the gallery too, after all. But the thought of confessing all I had done to her was excruciating. A last resort I hoped never to need.

The student actor playing Don Pedro boomed:

'Why, what's the matter, / that you have such a February face, / so full of frost, of storm and cloudiness?'

Act V. They were near the end. I wouldn't have to wait much longer.

Once my heart rate had simmered down somewhat, I pulled my phone out of my pocket. There was a text from Catalina in the flatmate group chat:

fancy meeting at the costumery later? i think there's a trivia quiz or something, could be fun! :)

Fraser had left her hanging, but Maisie had replied:

i'm with Davina, sorry

I frowned. The message was sent fifteen minutes ago – around the exact time I was with Davina and Drever in Orlagh's office. Was Maisie lying to get out of spending time with us? Or was there something more sinister there – had Davina asked Maisie to cover for her? An alibi?

All of this was pointing one way.

I decided not to reply just yet. Catalina would soon hear about Orlagh's death, and she could hardly be angry at me for not texting back right after finding a body.

Instead, I opened up the chat with my mother. The last thing I'd said was:

so I've been assigned an essay on the subject 'what is an audience' and my overly literal brain is struggling not to just write 'a group gathered to watch a play' haha. any tips on how to impress keddie without driving myself mad??

She had not replied.

I started typing with a shaking hand:

orlagh camran is dead

My thumb hovered over the full stop button for far too long before deleting the message unsent.

Just then I heard the pompous Shakespearean tenors relax into casual student chatter. The second years had finished their rehearsals, and were scooping up backpacks and messy scripts covered in highlighter strips. A short dark-haired girl with French plaits and no bra giggled falsely, grabbing the elbow of a dark-skinned guy in skinny cigarette trousers. His discomfort was obvious, even to me, but she continued to shamelessly flirt with him as they clambered down from the stage and strolled up the aisles.

As they drew level with the back row, I held my breath in case any of them questioned why I was spying on their rehearsals, but none of them batted an eyelid. They banged out of the stalls door into the lobby in a wave of sweet perfume and fresh sweat. A few moments later, the theatre fell into silence as they left the building.

Instead of heading straight towards the stage, however, I crouched down in my row – ankle and knee joints clicking and moaning as I did – and peered around the edge of the outermost seat.

If the killer had been waiting for their chance to escape, now they had it.

Heart thumping, I pictured them holed up beneath the stage, biding their time until the theatre emptied. Would they give it another few minutes, waiting for everyone to filter out for certain? Afraid of being caught by any stragglers?

But when the moments rolled into minutes and nobody appeared, yet again the situation pointed to Davina and Drever.

Then the doubts started to appear. Had I jumped to conclusions? Was it possible Orlagh hadn't been murdered at all, but rather died of natural causes?

No. *Unless marred by some brutal external force, their bodies will never change. They may cheat even death.*

There had to be a brutal external force.

First, I would figure out the how, and then the who and the why.

Who could have wanted to kill Orlagh? To what end?

And what did it mean for me?

When nothing happened for at least a quarter of an hour, I decided the coast must be clear. I climbed inelegantly to my feet, riding out the intense head rush, and strode purposefully towards the stage before I could talk myself out of it.

Descending through the trapdoor, the air beneath the stage felt cold and stagnant. I stepped carefully over the electrical cords and discarded props and crossed to the door leading to the tunnel.

I tried the handle.

Locked.

I inwardly kicked myself. I should have searched Orlagh's body for the key while I had the chance, instead of wasting my time on the Rolodex. Now it was too late. The ambulance had descended. To the morgue she went.

No matter how badly I burned for answers, I would not be finding them tonight.

CHAPTER SIXTEEN

'I can't believe it.'

Catalina stared at the open news page on her iPad, which was propped up on a pale wooden cookbook stand. Sunlight spilled through the window in golden swathes, illuminating her curls with a burnished warmth. It felt wrong, somehow. Shouldn't it be dark and dreary outside? Shakespeare was a big fan of pathetic fallacy.

I glanced at her screen and swallowed hard:

Actor and Philanthropist Orlagh Camran Found Dead

'Didn't you have a mentoring session with her last night?' she asked, cupping both hands around a steaming mug of cardamom tea.

Maisie's ears visibly pricked up. She was sitting on the sofa in the living area, her laptop on her knee as she typed up Keddie's audience essay at the last minute. I dimly remembered my own draft was still raw and unedited.

Nodding to Catalina, I padded over to the fridge. 'I was the one who found her.'

I stifled a yawn. I'd slept terribly, for obvious reasons.

'Oh my god, that's so traumatic.' Catalina turned the radio on, catching the tail end of an eighties rock banger. It felt almost comically incongruous with the situation. 'Are you okay?'

I stared at the contents of the fridge. Despite the deep crater of hunger in my stomach, none of the food held any appeal. Not the creamy strawberry yoghurts, nor the smoked bacon and sausages, nor the perfectly ripe avocados with tiny cherry tomatoes. I *wanted* to eat it all, wanted to savour each and every mouthful, and yet something guilt-shaped was stopping me. I tried to tell myself it was the sight of Camran's corpse, but deep down I worried that the demon in my brain had an even tighter hold on me than I feared.

Catalina sipped at her tea with a sigh. 'Was she . . . did she –'

'How did it happen?' Maisie asked, clearly dismissing any dislike she had for me in the search of first-hand gossip.

Despite everything that had happened, I was still hurt about the way she'd spoken to me back in the Costumery. I'd tried so hard to make her feel included, to be warm towards her, to make sure she never had to feel as alienated as I so often did. But instead she'd essentially called me a talentless shrew and swanned off to befriend my mortal enemy.

I had to be careful around her. I had to be prepared that whatever I said in front of her would likely make it straight back to Davina.

'I really don't know,' I replied vaguely.

'Suicide?' One of her pointed red nails was poised over the space bar.

'I don't think so.'

'It's so sad.' Catalina would have made a good priest, I thought. Her tone was the perfect pitch of reverent and elegiac. 'She was such a queen.'

'She really was,' I agreed, my voice seeming far away. My nerves were frayed, my thoughts frenetic, an undercurrent of fear coursing through me. Using the past tense to talk about Orlagh already felt wrong.

Catalina scrolled down the news article with her forefinger, scanning the text with a well-practised scholarly speed. 'I dunno, though. The vibes are a little off with all this. Like, it's kind of weird how nobody knows how old she actually was.'

'She was adopted, apparently,' said Maisie. 'Her birth certificate had been lost, and she had no living relatives. Her agent was her next of kin, I heard. That's who announced it to the press.'

I was barely listening. *Just choose something to eat*, I inwardly screamed at myself. In the light of everything that had just happened, what did it even matter?

Yet the demon did not loose its grip for something as petty as perspective.

Orlagh's words echoed in my mind.

And so it is about control – and punishment.

Was she right? Was this exercise in needless self-discipline the vice I leaned on when everything else spiralled out of control?

Coffee. I'd start with coffee. Coffee was safe.

I closed the fridge. There was a note stuck to the outside of the fridge, handwritten in block capitals on a torn-out sheet of lined paper: PLEASE STOP DRINKING MY OAT MILK!! Maisie was the only one who drank oat milk. I couldn't imagine carnivore Fraser taking a cheeky swig, nor could I imagine Catalina stealing literally anything from anyone. Unless I'd been sleep-drinking, which was a distinct possibility, Maisie was simply hallucinating drama.

'Just so sad,' Catalina murmured again. 'All that money and fame, but nobody beside you when you pass.'

'She seemed happy enough,' I replied, filling the pale turquoise kettle over the sink.

'On the outside, maybe. But you can never really know how lonely a person is.'

'Sometimes I think I could never see another living soul again and I'd be perfectly happy,' I said, but I sensed as I said it that there was an element of performance to the statement. 'No offence,' I added with a smile. 'I'm just good alone. I like my own company.'

Catalina nodded, looking out of the window and over the Great Lawn. The grass shone with dew. 'For me, happiness is only real when it's shared. But everyone's different, I guess. Did you have fun with Davina last night, Maisie?'

'Yeah, what did you get up to?' I asked, suddenly remembering through my hunger-daze the fact that she'd lied about being with Davina.

Maisie stilled, almost imperceptibly, then slurped iced coffee from a metallic straw that clinked on her teeth. 'I helped her unpack.' She didn't look up at us, only the computer screen. 'She's only just got into her student flat.'

'How long were you out for?' I tried to keep my tone as casual as possible, but I felt mentally alert as a hawk. If I could add some specificity to the lie, I could determine just how suspicious it was.

'Erm, pretty much the whole night? Like five till midnight. Why?'

My heart pounded at the trap I'd set. I was with Davina in Orlagh's office just after seven.

'Just wondering.' I smiled, but she was now furiously focused on her laptop, the slightest spots of pink appearing on her cheekbones.

I didn't understand Maisie's swift and unshakeable loyalty to Davina. If it were any of us, she'd be gleefully gossiping about how we'd asked her to cover for us – and speculating about what dark deeds we were committing instead. Yet Davina had a kind of cruel magnetism to her, like a cult leader you wanted so badly to impress. I could hardly blame Maisie for being sucked in.

'Do you want to invite Davina to have lunch with us?' Catalina asked.

Fraser, who had entered the kitchen with a sleepy stretch, yawned.

'Are we talking about Davina Burns? Man, she'd *get* it.'

Maisie's gaze snapped up. Fraser wore only a pair of grey

cotton striped pyjama bottoms, and was otherwise shirtless. She flushed even further at the sight of his bare, muscled torso, before rolling her eyes.

'That's beautiful, Fraser. Is it Shakespeare?'

I couldn't help it. I chuckled at her joke.

Fraser swished a carton of cloudy apple juice, then swigged it straight from the top. 'Shame about Camran,' he said, nodding towards Catalina's screen. '"Golden lads and girls all must, As chimney-sweepers, come to dust." Happy now, Maze?'

'Ecstatic,' Maisie said drily, but there was a light glow to her. Was it the nickname? The fact I'd laughed at her joke? Or simply Fraser's naked torso?

Speaking of which, his chest looked recently waxed, and there was a subtle sheen to his skin, like the remnants of body glitter. And his lips were stained slightly darker than usual, as though he'd scrubbed hard at lipstick that wouldn't shift. Surely there hadn't been two fancy-dress nights in a row?

'What did you get up to last night, Fraser?' I asked, genuinely curious.

'Oh, erm . . . I was in the library.' He looked a little shifty. 'Studying. Obviously.'

Catalina looked up from the new fantasy map she had started sketching on a loose piece of printer paper. 'Were you? I was there all night. I didn't see you.'

Why were two thirds of my flatmates lying about their whereabouts?

'It's a big library, hey.' Fraser tossed the empty apple juice carton at the recycling bin and missed entirely. He didn't bother picking it up, just made one of his trademark mock salutes. 'Anyway. Bye.'

He left the kitchen a little faster than he usually would.

Strange happenings upon strange happenings.

Draining my coffee in one ravenous go, I took a seat at the breakfast bar opposite Catalina. She looked up briefly before doodling some coastal islands off her main continent. But a few seconds later, she frowned and glanced back up at me again, as though just registering what she'd seen.

'What's that on your neck, Penny?'

My hand went to the spot on my throat she was staring at. 'I don't know, what is it?'

'It's like . . . a purple mark. It looks like a cut, almost.'

A cool kind of dread twisted in my guts long before my brain caught up.

Wordlessly I leaped down from the stool and sprinted back to my bedroom, starry-eyed and terrified.

My bedroom door banged shut behind me as I stood in front of the mirror over my sink, praying that what I was seeing was not really what I was seeing.

But it was.

An inch-long smooth purple wound, a hair's breadth away from my jugular.

The exact same hue and texture as the marks I had found all over Orlagh.

No.

It felt like the walls of my life were crumbling to the ground.

The faceless hand had marred me too. As if to say: *I could've killed you, but I didn't.*

My heart slammed in my ribcage as I tapped my phone screen.

A dozen missed calls from my mum. She'd obviously seen the news.

I called her back, but she didn't pick up.

As her voicemail kicked in, I blurted out:

'Mum? I'm coming home. We need to talk.'

CHAPTER SEVENTEEN

Driving in the strange combination of blue skies and eldritch fog, the vanishing roads could've been anywhere.

Hunger clawed at me, a feral thing, a beast with spectral wings and a blackened heart.

I didn't check my rear-view mirror once.

I couldn't bear to see that mark, purple and sinister, threatening as a dark spot on a brain scan, as a glint of gunmetal from the bushes, as the smell of a stranger's perfume in your house.

What did it mean?

Was it a warning? A shot across the bow?

When had it first appeared? At the same time as Orlagh's? Had I just been so pumped with adrenaline that I didn't notice the sting of pain?

Either way, the message seemed to be this: *I could have killed you, but I didn't.*

And there was only one person I knew of who wanted to hurt me. Who had even told me as much.

You're going to regret fucking with me. Maybe not today. Maybe not this week. But sooner or later, I will come for you. When you least expect it.

Then, in the lobby, with Maisie: *Don't worry. She'll get what's coming to her.*

A dark picture of the situation was emerging. Davina had reason to silence Orlagh. Davina had reason to hurt me. Davina even had Maisie lie about her whereabouts last night.

But I'd watched enough procedural dramas to know this evidence was all circumstantial. I needed proof if I wanted to bring her to justice. But how? And what would I even do if I managed to find it? I doubted the police would take any of this seriously. Especially if the portraits really were the murder weapon.

I felt entirely unmoored from reality, as though I'd suddenly learned that the laws of physics were a lie. That gravity was only reliable half the time. That the sky was the ground, and vice versa.

As I pulled up outside our townhouse in the Old Town, I tried to settle my breathing. Maybe this throat cut was a one-off. Maybe Davina would consider it vengeance enough to scar me for life. To instil a deep, writhing fear in me. To let me know she could kill me whenever she damn pleased. To affirm her power over me, over the situation.

I had to find a way to untether myself from that painting. To remove the threat first and foremost. Then I could work on compiling enough evidence to take Davina down.

And if Orlagh could no longer help me track down the Masked Painter, maybe my own flesh and blood could.

As I climbed out of the car, I winced at the lance of pain in my ribs, shivering inside my countless layers of wool and cashmere. I was almost bent double around the snare of hunger in my stomach.

I raised my hand and rapped the silver gargoyle knocker on the polished black door. There was a handmade autumn wreath hanging over the door number – sprays of red berries, clusters of orange leaves and miniature glass pumpkins painted gold – which undoubtedly came from my aunt Polly. My mother would rather slice off her own eyebrows with a butter knife than do crafts.

When there was no answer, the sense of unease grew. Come to think of it, Mum had never actually replied to my voicemail. After calling me a dozen times, she'd simply dropped off the face of the planet.

The vague sense of dread sharpened into a jagged point.

Had something bad happened to her too?

With a dizzy swoop, I had the horrifying thought that maybe her own portrait had been destroyed by the same blade as Orlagh's. As an act of revenge it was fairly extreme, but I didn't put anything past Davina.

Was I about to walk in on my own mother's corpse?

So blindingly frightened that I was almost numb, I turned my key in the lock and let myself in. The scent of white lilies and black coffee filled the hallway.

My fears were immediately dispersed. There were low female voices coming from the kitchen. When no calls came out, I assumed they hadn't heard me enter. Slipping my shoes shakily off, I strained my ears to hear what they were saying.

'. . . can't understand why anyone would do this to Orlagh.' It was Mum, her voice laced with urgency. 'She had a heart of gold. Me, I could understand, but . . .'

'You think she was definitely killed?' My aunt Polly's accent was far broader than mine or Mum's, since she'd never left Edinburgh for the bright lights of the Big Smoke. Its familiarity warmed me. My aunt had been a saving grace while Mum was in rehab. All six times.

'There's no other way she could've died,' replied Mum. 'The portraits make one immune to natural death.'

At this, I faltered. She'd told Aunt Polly about the Gallery of the Exquisite? I supposed Camran had never explicitly told me to keep it a secret, but I felt brittlely ashamed at the thought of anyone knowing what I'd done. What I'd slavishly sacrificed at the altar of something so fickle as beauty.

'But it's not being reported as a murder,' said Aunt Polly.

'Maybe the police are trying to keep it under wraps.'

The air inside the house was no warmer than it was outside, and I shivered uncontrollably despite my hat, scarf and long leather gloves. The thought that I might never be warm again was torturous.

'Surely it would've leaked by now.' I heard a kettle switch being flicked, and knew my listening time was almost up – I wouldn't be able to hear them over the boil. 'Dorian would've been crawling with detectives, and it'd only take one student to talk to the press.'

When the kettle grew loud enough to drown them out, I padded through the living-dining space and into the big, faux-industrial kitchen.

'Hi, Mum,' I said, and she jumped at my voice. 'Hey, Aunt Polly.'

'Jesus, Penny!' Mum clutched her hand to her beige cashmere jumper. 'I didn't hear you come in.'

'Hi, sweet girl.' Aunt Polly climbed down from the high stool at the marble island and threw her arms around me. She smelled of toast and Imperial Leather soap. 'How are you?'

'I'm alright thanks,' I said weakly, but I felt anything but.

She pulled away and looked me up and down, disapproval eminent on her face. She was a GP at a small practice in East Lothian, though she only worked a couple of days a week these days. 'You're thinner. Too thin.'

The horrible demon in my mind glowed.

Aunt Polly was the antithesis of me and my mum. Her copper hair was duller, muddier, and pulled back in a practical crocodile clip. She was short and round – the approximate shape of a pigeon – and wore plain, well-worn clothes that she mended instead of replaced. Her wire-framed glasses were non-designer, even though Mum made sure she never wanted for money, and her features weren't as sculpted. She loved crafts of all kinds – card making and crochet, homemade candles and dried flower arrangements. She was wonderful, warm, maternal. I had spent a not-insignificant portion of my adolescence wishing she was my mother instead.

When Aunt Polly had my cousin Pippa, I was eleven or twelve, and just beginning to truly understand how emotionally absent my own mother was compared to everyone else's. Aunt Polly had always been amazing with me, taking me on day trips and buying me ice cream, getting me my first library card and buddy-reading the Percy Jackson books so we could chat about them over peppermint hot chocolates. Then Pippa came along, and all that maternal energy was channelled towards her own child. It wasn't that she suddenly didn't care about me – it was more that whenever she visited us without the baby, she wanted adult conversation, not to mother someone else's kid.

I felt bereft, and more alone than ever.

There was one day when Pippa was a toddler, still breast-feeding, and she grew drowsy and sleepy on my aunt's nipple. Polly gazed down at her, full of love, stroking her cheek and cooing that she was *a good girl, such a good girl*, as Pippa's eyes drifted carelessly shut. I left the room in floods of tears, not really possessing the emotional maturity to understand why it upset me so much. I thought I was just evil, for resenting my sweet innocent cousin, for wishing she had never been born.

'Shouldn't you be in rehearsals?' asked my mum now, something wary and suspicious on her face.

Irritation prickled beneath my skin like sunburn. *She* had called *me* countless times. And now she was being stand-offish that I'd come to see her? She was maddening.

'Drever gave me the afternoon off after the shock of what happened last night.' I fixed a pointed look in her direction. 'I found her. Orlagh.'

The peach-pink colour in her cheeks faded to a pallid taupe. 'Oh.'

I turned to Aunt Polly, who was clattering around to find a third mug. 'So you know about the Masked Painter too, then.'

That finally got a proper reaction from my mum. 'How do *you* know – oh, Penny. You didn't. Oh, I *warned* you to be careful.'

As twisted as it was, her lukewarm concern felt good.

I took a seat next to her at the island, staring at the wilting lilies in the goldfish-bowl vase. Several red stamen littered the white marble. 'Right, well you could've been a bit more specific, couldn't you?'

Mum rubbed at her face, but not hard enough to disguise the jitters in her hands. 'I thought if I started harping on about immortal paintings before you even met Orlagh, you'd just chalk it up to my creeping insanity.'

'You have a point,' I replied. Aunt Polly laid a cup of tea in front of me, and I took a sip straight away. It scalded my throat, and I could almost feel tiny blisters forming on my tongue, but I was glad of the sting. It gave me another sensation to focus on rather than the cramping hunger and the gnawing cold. 'Do you have any biscuits?'

Mum shook her head absently, but Polly pulled a packet of Borders all-butter shortbread out of her plain leather handbag.

I dunked each piece in the tea until it was soft and sweet, trying to ignore the feeling of failure as I ate – the sense that I was losing a battle with myself that I couldn't remember ever deciding to wage. But at least Aunt Polly looked pleased that I was feeding myself.

'I just don't understand how . . . I don't understand.' As Mum spoke mistily, her teeth were almost chattering. I looked at her face properly for the first time in years, at the impossibly smooth skin and the plump, youthful lips, at the utter lack of ageing *anywhere* on her body. Even her neck and chest were free of crêpe-like texture. Her hands were almost identical to mine. 'It's impossible, or so I thought. I suppose that's why I let you go to Dorian in the first place – because it should've been impossible. So how? Unless . . .'

'Mum, what are you on about?' I interrupted, trembling with cold despite my fur coat.

She picked up her cup of tea, but didn't drink. She looked somehow both haunted and frantic. 'I suppose – well, look at it this way.' She seemed to be having a conversation with herself. It was unnerving to watch. 'You were always going to do it anyway, that's the heart of the matter. But *how* could . . .?'

At this I bristled. 'What makes you say I was always going to do it anyway?'

A shrug, as though offending me was the least of her problems. 'Very few young women would have the integrity to say no to such a thing.'

Aunt Polly scoffed indignantly. 'I'd say no.'

'Well, quite,' said Mum drily. 'Your looks are hardly worth preserving.'

'Cow,' muttered Aunt Polly, but she didn't seem too wounded by it. Her own lack of societally accepted beauty never seemed to bother her, and I wondered what her secret was. Did she truly not care? How could she not? I was, in many ways, jealous of her.

Yanking my attention back to the problem I came to discuss, I wiped the crumbs off my flared corduroy trousers and said, 'I messed up, though. I went into the sitting hungry and panicked and cold, and now no matter what I do, I stay hungry and panicked and cold. I feel like I'm going mad.'

Mum stiffened beside me. She still hadn't taken a sip of tea. 'An easy mistake to make,' she murmured. 'I went into it deeply depressed, and look how that turned out.'

I was struck with a sudden and terrible understanding.

'That's why you're so . . .'

A brief, sharp pain darted across her face. 'That's why I'm *so.*'

'The addiction,' I said quietly. 'The partying. All of it.'

Aunt Polly looked down at her hands, criss-crossed with veins and wrinkles. As they should be.

'I just wanted to *feel* something.' Mum's voice was, to the average onlooker, devoid of emotion. But I was so well versed in its cadence that I picked up on the minuscule cracks and crevices below the surface, like the juddering together of two tectonic plates. 'And I haven't for – god, for nearly two decades, no matter how many highs I chased. No amount of rehab can fix what's broken inside me.'

The statement was a whip-wound across my heart. I was born eighteen years ago.

She hadn't felt anything then? *Anything?*

Yet the harshness with which I perceived my mum's flaws flickered and shifted. She wasn't just born flighty, neglectful, shallow. Cold. There was a far more sinister driving force behind it than I ever could've imagined.

The portrait.

And I was heading down the same path.

The silence that descended on the room was weighted, charged, and I hoped one of them would break it first. But when nothing was said for several moments, I cleared my throat. I had to tell them the whole story.

'My theory is that Orlagh was killed through her painting.'

Mum's gaze snapped to me, and I loathed the hard-edged suspicion on her face. 'What makes you say that?'

'There was no blood. No police. I haven't been asked any questions, and considering I was the one who found the body, it must mean they're not investigating the death as suspicious. They must believe her to have died of natural causes, even if they can't explain how much older she looked in death.'

Aunt Polly nodded. 'Okay . . .'

I shivered again. It felt as though the cold was expanding in my bones. 'But like you said earlier, she shouldn't have been able to die at all. She said to me: "Unless marred by some brutal external force, they may cheat even death." So what if that brutal external force was applied not to her body, but to her portrait? Her face and throat were covered in marks that looked like healed wounds.' My stomach clenched at the memory.

'You're right,' Mum said, but there was a caution to her tone, a guardedness that I didn't understand. 'That's exactly how it works. But who would –'

'I made an enemy.' I swallowed hard. 'A ruthless one.'

Mum and Aunt Polly listened in horrified silence as I filled them in on the auditions, on catching Davina and Drever in his car. I cringed with shame as I described how I'd blackmailed my way into the lead, but they had to know. They had to understand why I suspected Davina so strongly. I told them about how she'd torn the hair from my head, how she'd lashed me with threats, how Maisie had lied about her whereabouts at the exact time Orlagh was killed. How the last contact open on the Rolodex was *Drever, Cameron*. My theory about Orlagh finding out about the affair and confronting them. The swift silencing – whether from Davina alone or them as a pair.

'And then . . . I found this.'

I unravelled the scarf from my neck and pointed at the purplish wound.

At the sight of it, Aunt Polly gasped and cupped her hands to her face. Even Mum looked terrified by it – she gripped the edge of the counter for support, as though she was about to faint.

'I don't know what it means.' I wrapped the scarf back around me, desperate for the slightest scrap of warmth.

'Whether it's a warning not to investigate Orlagh's death, or pure revenge. And I don't know whether she'd do it again. Keep toying with me. But I'm scared.'

The last three syllables were torturous to utter – an admission of weakness so at odds with the Paxton women.

'Oh, Penny . . .'

Aunt Polly's words wobbled, and it rocked me. She was usually as steadfast as a farmer, stoic in the face of trauma. She'd had decades of practice caring for my mum, after all. She'd delivered countless terminal diagnoses to her patients. She'd examined young children with horrifying symptoms, known deep in her bones that they were in trouble. But now, fear seemed to have robbed her of the ability to speak.

I studied Mum carefully. Her pupils darted back and forth like a gambler counting cards, brain whirring with the intensity of the mental load. But still she didn't say a word. No sage counsel, no gentle affirmations that we'd get through this together. Just frenzied calculations, formulae that could never balance, paranoid propellers spinning frantically off the face of the earth.

Except . . . her paranoia wasn't unfounded, was it? There had always been this dark secret to hide.

'What do I do?' I whispered. 'Please. Tell me what I should do. Can we track down the Masked Painter somehow? Surely there's a way to undo these . . . *anchors*, whatever they are. There has to be a way. We just have to find him.'

The colour still had not returned to my mother's face.

She shook her head, stiff as a rag doll. 'We won't find the Masked Painter.'

'Why not?'

Her knuckles were ivory as she clung on to her mug.

'Because the Masked Painter is dead.'

CHAPTER EIGHTEEN

'He's dead?' I frowned, confused, but a cloying dread coated my throat like soot in a chimney. 'He can't be. I saw him two days ago.'

'That's what I can't figure out.' Mum laid the mug down abruptly, climbed down from the stool and crossed over to the fridge. Her legs were as unsteady as a newborn foal's. 'I know for a fact that the Masked Painter died a long time ago. And so how . . .?'

This revelation rattled me.

Had Orlagh known this was a different artist to the one who'd painted her?

I had the distinct sense of tugging at a single thread and the whole world unravelling.

'Okay, well there must be another painter, then,' I said fiercely, mind whirring. 'Another artist with the same powers. Maybe a whole guild. We just have to find the Masked Painter that did my portrait, right?'

Mum opened the fridge with a perfectly manicured hand – round-tipped nails a dusty-rose pink, the same as mine – and peered inside. 'Right. But I already asked *my* Masked Painter, many years ago, and he told me the anchors were permanent. I'm sorry, Penny. I should've warned you better. I just assumed that because he was dead, you were out of danger.'

She closed the fridge, and Polly and I both realised at once what she'd gone to get.

A bottle of Sauvignon Blanc.

'No, Peggy,' said Polly fiercely. She stood up to her full five foot two and stood before my mum, hands on hips. 'I won't allow it.'

Mum smirked, but there was no humour behind it, just a grim expression of defeat. 'You won't allow it? Truly, I would like to see you try and stop me.'

Without pause, Polly slapped my mum right across the face.

In the split second it took my mum to recover – clasping a hand to her blotched-red cheek – Polly grabbed the bottle from her other grip and stuffed it inside her bag. 'Any more gauntlets you'd like to throw down?'

I fought the absurd urge to laugh.

Mum glared at Polly, still rubbing her face, but there didn't seem to be any fight left in her.

Still, an acute foreboding coiled inside me. Polly wouldn't be around Mum at all times. The second my aunt left, my mum would open another bottle.

Why was the wine even in the fridge to begin with? Had she gone out first thing this morning to buy some, as soon as she'd heard the news? The thought made me impossibly sad. At the very same time I was scooping food into my trolley like a deranged wolf, my mother was doing the same with her own vice.

Two years of sobriety, shredded by Orlagh's death.

Orlagh's *murder*.

The little girl at the heart of me wanted to throw herself down at her mother's ankles and beg her to stay strong, but I had long since learned it didn't work like that. My love alone could not save her – particularly because, in her own words, my love didn't make her feel anything at all.

And could I blame her? I felt half demented after less than two days trapped inside my eternal cold and hunger. How must it feel to live over seven *thousand* days under the mercy of this self-made curse? What did that kind of suffering do to a person? Depression was bad enough in itself, but to know beyond all doubt there was no way out of it? To know you would feel so empty every day for the rest of your life? The burden must have been unbearable.

'We still have to try and find him,' I argued, fighting the urge to hug my mum. She hated physical affection. 'We have to believe there's a way out of this. We can't just live our lives sad and hungry and cold and scared and *empty*. And now that Orlagh is dead, and I seem to be a target . . . we have to break free. As soon as we can. Or I might be next.'

'Alright,' said Mum, sullen as a teenager as she slumped back into her stool. Defeat weighed on her shoulders like a stack of bricks. 'Do you have a plan?'

Such an innocuous question, and yet something inside me

flared up at it; the sense of frustration that I was more of a parent than she was. The insatiable wish for her to step up and care for me, to take the reins, to tell me everything was going to be okay. But she just wasn't wired that way – because she'd always be twenty years old at heart. Twenty years old and hopelessly lost.

The myriad emotions of the situation mingled in my mind, but I wrenched myself back into focus. I tapped a forefinger on the counter in a rhythmic *pah–pah–pah*.

But as I thought through the situation from every angle, I realised my mum was right. All of my ideas for finding the artist stemmed from some kind of technological tracing – finding a hacker to break down Orlagh's phone calls, emails, text messages, trying to figure out when and how she contacted the Masked Painter. Yet she was a digital ghost. No mobile phone, no computer that I saw. She famously wrote all student feedback by hand. Her only means of communication were just an analogue phone and a pair of well-heeled feet.

And if she'd gone to visit the Masked Painter to ask for his help in person, how would I ever trace those movements? Normal people couldn't just tap CCTV footage.

There was the possibility that a phone bill sent to the university would list her outgoing calls, but how was I supposed to get my hands on that? Another student with more gumption might break into the administration office, try and find some physical evidence. But it was likely a paperless bill, and in any case, this month's calls wouldn't show up until next month's bill. It was too long to wait. I might be dead before the bill ever arrived.

'I think we have to go to the police,' I said slowly, the realisation solidifying in my head. 'Only they have the necessary resources to actually track him down. And if we go to them, we can tell them all about Davina too. Maybe they can protect me from –'

Mum jumped as though a burglar had leaped from behind a curtain. 'No police. I *mean* it, Penny.' Her tone was ferocious.

Polly blinked at her, baffled by the heated outburst. 'Why on earth not?'

'Bad things have happened in that gallery.' Her eyes were carnival pinwheels. 'What we have done – *no*. None of this can ever come to light. *Never*.'

'What's the alternative?' I snapped. 'We let Davina keep terrorising me? I just . . . walk around with a bullseye on my back, hoping the next hit won't be a fatal one? That's better than this secret coming out?'

'No. Police.' Mum's words were two gavel strikes.

But anger was rising in me now, mercury shooting up a thermometer, and I could not temper it. 'Seriously? The thought of me getting hurt – or *dying* – is somehow less horrifying than the world knowing your enduring beauty came at a price?'

'That's not what I –'

'No, it is. That's exactly what you're saying.'

'Penny's right,' murmured Aunt Polly. She looked deathly

afraid. 'We need the police for this, Peggy. It's got out of hand. And who knows, maybe with the general public searching for the new Masked Painter, we might –'

'If you go to the police,' Mum snarled, 'I will kill myself. I'll kill myself, Polly. And it'll be your fault. You'll have to live with that knowledge forever. That you killed your own sister.'

What followed was a silence as harsh and absolute as a salt plain.

Mum had always been immature, irrational, emotionally manipulative.

But nothing as stunningly horrific as this.

Aunt Polly took on the calm, level tone of a hostage negotiator. 'You don't mean that, Peg.'

An adolescent upward tilt of the chin. 'Try me. I dare you.'

That moment, that singular, awful moment, was the final straw.

I never wanted to see my mum again.

I wanted to sever myself from this broken family forever.

I turned towards the door and stormed out.

I hate her. I hate her I hate her I hate her.

Tears of fury stung at my eyes, blurring the beige-white-cream furnishings into one. The blood was roaring so loudly in my ears that I didn't hear the footsteps following me out the front door. Didn't notice that it never slammed shut behind me.

Aunt Polly caught up with me as I was fumbling with my car keys.

A hand on my elbow. 'Penny, she didn't –'

'She did, though.' I swung to face her, feeling half wild with the deluge of emotions thrashing through me. 'She did mean it. And I'm done. I don't want anything more to do with her. She can drink herself into oblivion for all I care.'

'I understand.' Aunt Polly wept silently, making no effort to wipe away the tears. 'Believe me, Penny. I understand more than anyone else ever will. And you're allowed, alright? You're allowed to cut her out of your life. If that's what's best for you, I will support you to the ends of the earth. Just don't disappear on me, alright? Please. I love you so much.'

All at once, the emotions dragged me below the surface. I erupted into tears, planting my face on Polly's shoulder, and I sobbed. I sobbed like a little girl. I sobbed like I might never stop.

'Shh, shh,' cooed Aunt Polly. 'It's okay. You're okay. I'm here.'

And it was so fucked up, all of it, because part of me was glad this was happening, that Aunt Polly was caring for me the same way she'd held Pippa to her chest as a baby.

You're a good girl, such a good girl.

'I wish you were my mum,' I whispered, the words muffled into her cardigan.

She didn't say anything – she might not have heard me – but her hand stroking my hair felt better than anything.

Eventually, even though I wanted to feel this comfort forever, I pulled away.

Furious intensity burned in Polly's eyes as she cupped my face in her hands. 'It's up to you whether or not you go to the police. Whatever happens with your mum . . . leave her to me, alright? I can't watch her every minute of every day, but I can try to do damage control. And promise me you'll stay away from this Davina girl, Penny. Promise me you won't provoke her any more.'

I turned to my car, disquiet swirling in my gut. 'I promise.'

And I kept that promise – until the next cut appeared.

CHAPTER NINETEEN

A few days later, I awoke in the middle of the night to a sharp scratching sensation on my neck, and I *knew*.

The apple tree outside Abernathy scraped at the window again. I flicked on my bedside lamp, dread curling through my lungs like whorls of cigarette smoke. As I stumbled over to the mirror nailed to the wall, my worst fears were confirmed.

It was on the other side of my throat, perfectly symmetrical with the first. A few millimetres longer, perhaps, though I didn't take a tape measure to it.

This one was no simple deterrent. I hadn't been near the gallery since the night of Orlagh's death. I hadn't investigated for a single moment. There was nothing to warn me *against*.

No, this wound was not carved with the intention of deterring me.

It was for sport, plain and simple. A cat toying with its prey, relishing the moments before the killing blow.

Then – something appeared in the mirror.

A set of eyes. Arctic blue. Cold as glaciers.

Davina's eyes.

They vanished as quickly as they'd appeared, and I rubbed at my own eyes fiercely, trying to shift the unsettling image.

Was I hallucinating again, the way I had imagined the darkened silhouette in Drummond?

Did it even matter, when my very life was in danger?

Forehead pressed to the cool glass of the mirror, I began to weigh my options in earnest.

Was it worth calling my mother's bluff and going to the police anyway?

Would she really follow through on her threat? Would her life really not be worth living if the world knew her secret?

Could I live with myself if she died over this?

I still hated her. Every time I thought about that moment with Aunt Polly in the kitchen, I wanted to smash something. I wanted to scream at the top of my lungs and never stop. I wanted to claw my own skin off, tear away the need to be loved so that her words and actions no longer hurt so much.

And yet when I pictured myself standing graveside at her funeral, knowing beyond all doubt that it was my fault she was in the ground . . .

I couldn't do it. I couldn't take that risk.

As I lay awake for the rest of the night, I started to realise that confronting Davina – making amends once and for all – was the only way to keep myself safe. Neutralising the threat. Begging her forgiveness. Praying, beyond all prayer, that she was not the cruel monster I believed her to be. That she had the capacity to forgive.

Unfortunately, Davina fell off the face of the earth for two whole weeks after Orlagh's body was found.

She wasn't in seminars, learning about research for performance with Catalina's enthusiastic commentary, nor was she practising dialects with Professor Ó Broin. She wasn't in rehearsals for *Macbeth*, of course, nor was she seen talking to Maisie about me in darkened alcoves. Her absence filled me with a profound foreboding. I didn't know exactly what it could mean for me, but I doubted it was anything good.

It made me think of how, in horror movies, the Big Evil was more terrifying before you saw or understood it. That sense of the unknown, a shadow where there should be none. Constant glances over your shoulder. The fear of falling asleep.

The days crunched on in fits of mind-bending cold and hunger and exhaustion, until Davina finally re-emerged.

Content that we had all mastered the art of standing still, Professor Lawrie arranged a first-year field trip to Edinburgh Zoo. We'd all been sent mysterious envelopes with a purple wax seal, hand-delivered to our flats with only our names on the front. Inside each was a single word – an animal we'd been assigned to 'embody' for the rest of the semester. We were supposed to study it, observe it, *become* it.

I had been assigned a tarantula, which was fantastic news for an arachnophobe, but the thought of watching a spider move for hours on end was not the worst part. It was that I already felt mortified at the idea of crawling around on the floor in front of my peers. Shame smeared my cheeks whenever I remembered I'd have to do it. But Catalina, Maisie and

Fraser – a frog, a chimp and a meerkat respectively – seemed to find it hilarious, not humiliating. Maybe they were made of stronger stuff.

In any case, Davina finally showed up just as the bus was about to depart from Dorian. She wore a black beanie hat, blood-red lipstick, black leather jacket and skinny jeans. Over her ballet flats she wore thick knitted legwarmers, and her legs above the fluffy material were twig-thin, with delicate cords of muscle around the calves. It made me twinge with envy – or at least something with a similar texture to jealousy.

She and Maisie talked in hushed voices the whole way there, and while I'd been hoping to chat to Catalina, she was reading a postgraduate research paper with a furrowed expression on her face. I plugged in my headphones and listened to Phoebe Bridgers as the countryside rolled into cityscape.

The zoo was far quieter than it had been the last time I came with Aunt Polly and Pippa. It was a weekday in mid October, so tourist season was very much in its twilight for the year, and there were no shrieking schoolkids to be seen. A light, pattering rain fell in half-hearted sheets as we entered the grounds and dispersed to perform our studies.

The tarantulas lived in a dark hothouse for insects and reptiles. They crawled too slowly over the moss and dirt in their tanks, like the disembodied hands of mindless zombies. And yet the more I observed them, the more keenly I felt a sense of solidarity with them, with the way they shrank shyly away from the glass separating us as though the weight of being perceived was too much to bear. I was unused to being on this side of that particular power dynamic, and somehow it felt just as wrong as the reverse. The urge came over me to avert my gaze, to lend the poor creatures some privacy.

It was hot and humid inside the insect house, but I still felt chilled to my bones, as though I'd been left outside in the snow as a baby and never quite recovered.

Just as I was wondering how I might execute my plan with Davina, she wandered into the insect house alone. With a jolt, I initially panicked that she was here to confront me, to intimidate me, but there was an aimlessness to her gait that made me think otherwise. A kind of deep, lonely boredom.

An opportunity had just been handed to me on a plate.

She didn't see me, at first. The spiders were around a slight bend from the entrance, and the house was dark and blurred with shadows. Her spiky hair and all-black outfit disappeared into the gloom, leaving her ghost-white face floating through thin air.

Swallowing the nerves climbing up my gullet like fire ants, I stepped out from behind the corner and approached.

'Davina,' I said, and the word came out as a question.

If she was surprised to hear my voice, she didn't show it, and it struck me that maybe she *had* come in here to see me. Maybe the careless stroll was all an act.

Still, she didn't respond, just looked over at me disdainfully.

Did she spend an extra second studying my exposed neck? Or was I imagining it?

I steeled myself, growing armour like a beetle. 'We need to talk.'

A muscle rippled on her jaw. 'No, we don't.'

'I want to make things right between us.' I tried not to betray my fear – tried to be genuine, rather than apologetic for the sake of saving my own skin. 'I'm really sorry for what happened. What I did with the blackmail. It was a mistake.'

She said nothing, but there was the slightest quirk at the corner of her mouth.

She was enjoying this. She knew I was afraid, and she liked it. She fed on it like a leech, a parasite.

'What can I do to fix it?' I asked. 'I can give you back the lead. Stand down from the whole production.' It would be a small price to pay to remove the target on my back.

'Damage is done.' Her words were stone cold. 'Drever wouldn't risk giving it back to me.'

I swallowed. 'Have you told him yet? That it was me?'

I remembered what she told Maisie: *You have to play your cards at the right time. It's all very well having pocket aces, but they become a lot more powerful if a third appears in the river.*

She shrugged. 'Not yet.'

What was she waiting for? The knowledge that she kept this card close was deeply unsettling. It made me think she had some grand finale in mind – that the cuts on my throat were just a warm-up.

'Okay.' My voice sounded much calmer than I felt. 'So what do I have to do to get you to stop?'

'Stop what?' Her eyes were fixed on the electric-blue frogs inside the nearest tank. They hopped morosely, like circus animals performing a joviality they didn't truly feel.

'The cuts. Please, Davina. Please stop.'

But Davina just stared into the tank – or perhaps at the half reflection of her own face in the glass. As I stepped closer, I noticed her lips were chapped. Her posture was rod-straight, but unnaturally so. Strained, like she'd been tied to a lamppost.

Frustration began to creep in at her utter lack of response. This spineless pleading wasn't working.

Time to stop pulling punches. To let her know that I *knew*. To show her that I had as many cards to use against her as she did me.

I blackmailed her out of the lead. Maybe I could blackmail her into ceasing fire.

'Davina, I know about Orlagh,' I said, urgency creeping into my tone. 'I know what you did.'

She turned to face me, and I shivered involuntarily. Meeting eyes with Davina was like staring into the abyss, and having the abyss stare back – with bared teeth.

Still she said nothing. And I hated it, this subtle exercise in control over the situation. The way it made me want to shake her and shake her until she finally spoke.

'What were you and Drever doing in his office after hours?' I pressed on. 'The Rolodex was flipped open on his number. She found out, didn't she?'

A kind of wicked grin spread across her face, her lips so dark they were almost purple. I remembered how carnal she had looked in Orlagh's office, the way Drever's shirt was loose and rumpled.

I sighed and dropped my balled-up hands to my side. 'Why Drever? You could have anyone in the world, yet you threw your future away for him.'

Something shifted behind her eyes, and finally she spoke. 'I could have anyone in the world?'

'You know what I mean.' Heat prickled across my cheeks at the insinuation.

She snorted. 'Don't worry. My future is far from thrown away.' With her hand curled into a panther-like claw, she examined her fingernails. 'He's been pulling strings for me, to make up for dropping me from Macbeth. I've had a bunch of real-life auditions in the last week that I wouldn't have got without his contacts. I'm down to the last two for a recurring role in a soap.'

Anger simmered in me like a hot spring. Or was it jealousy, that she was already making headway towards acting fame? While I toiled away on a student production that was never going to be a big break? Everything about her made me feel so small, so pathetic.

'I could go to the police, you know.' Rage was causing my vision to vignette at the edges. 'With the picture of you and him. How it links to Orlagh.'

'So why haven't you? Because you know it proves nothing?'

Her voice was staccato, like gunfire. 'Yeah. Good luck framing me over this.'

I frowned. 'Framing you? It's not framing if you did it.'

'Leave me the fuck alone, Penny.' The curse carried an emphatic weight. 'Don't make this worse for yourself. You do not want me as your enemy.'

'I know.' I tried to lower my temper, to remind myself why I'd approached her in the first place. 'Believe it or not, I wasn't trying to make things worse.'

'Okay, so what exactly *was* the purpose of throwing around ridiculous accusations?'

I frowned inwardly. I was so sure Davina was the killer, but she was refuting the accusations pretty staunchly. Most normal people would do such a thing, in case I was recording the conversation, but Davina didn't operate like normal people. The Davina I knew would've found a way to throw a slanted confession into her rebuttals, to maximise my fear, to reinforce that she could kill me in a heartbeat, if she so chose to. That she was not above wounding and maiming me to keep me silent and complicit.

Yet she was doing none of that.

But still . . . who else would want Orlagh dead *and* want to hurt me at the same time?

How could I figure out for certain that it really was her?

My mind whirring, I realised that in order for her to feasibly be the killer, she had to know about the gallery. And for her to know about the gallery, she had to have been painted herself.

An idea came to me, then. It would not yield proof, as such, but it would be a thick notch in the guilty column.

'I'm sorry, Davina,' I said, softening my voice into something almost affectionate. Romantic, even, with a sultry gaze. I'd seen my mum do it, and it was intoxicating. The Paxton mask at full force. 'I want to make it up to you.'

I took a careful step towards her, then another.

When we were just inches apart, she leaned towards me the smallest sliver. The gentlest of tilts. A subtle dilation of her pupils. An almost imperceptible shift in the power dynamic, the scales tipping ever so slightly in my favour. The Paxton superpower working on her at last.

And with a deep, visceral thrill, I knew I had her.

Before she could react, before I could talk myself out of it, I grabbed the raw hem of her black jumper and yanked it upwards.

Snatching her clothes away from me, Davina took a livid step backwards. 'What the fuck –'

But she wasn't fast enough.

I saw it.

Right there on her rib: a small, fresh cut, recently scabbed over.

She planted her palms on my collarbones and shoved back. Hard.

I stumbled but didn't fall, reeling from the confirmation that she too hung in the Gallery of the Exquisite.

I was right. It was her. It *had* to be.

'Don't you *ever* fucking touch me again,' she hissed, and this time the venom in her voice was real; a coiled viper ready to spring. And the lick of fear in my throat was real too.

She breathed raggedly, fists clenching and unclenching at her sides. I held up my palms like a criminal surrendering.

Then a third figure appeared in the doorway in a plaid pink coat.

Maisie's voice was a jarring trill as she surveyed the scene.

'Is Penny bothering you?' she sniped, glaring at me.

'No,' replied Davina, without even turning around. Her eyes still fixed unrelentingly on me, her chest rising and falling unevenly. 'You can go.'

Maisie was visibly wounded by the dismissal, but she didn't turn to leave. Instead she said, 'Whatever. I just came to tell you the news.'

She held up her phone on a bold black headline.

At the sight of the headline, fear bleached the world white:

Divorced Actors Celia Van Der Beek and Lyle Barr Found Dead In Separate Homes

Van Der Beek and Barr, who met as students at Dorian Drama Academy and married soon after, were found dead hundreds of miles apart . . .

[SUBSCRIBE TO READ FULL ARTICLE]

The ground pitched below me.

Two more faces from the Gallery of the Exquisite were dead.

Which meant Orlagh was not a one-off, a lone wolf acting on a personal grudge.

Three deaths made this a serial killer.

CHAPTER TWENTY

The new deaths sparked a fresh wave of press attention around Dorian.

Reporters fluttered around campus like moths devouring cashmere, and no matter how many pleas the dean issued, they would not dispel. It was a free country, after all, and that freedom hinged upon the efficacy of the fourth estate. Upon the rights of the press to expose ugly truths.

Autopsies had deduced, as they had with Orlagh, that the glittering alumni had died of natural causes. But a medical examiner had leaked the fact that they were covered in the same strange, faded marks, and it had caused a surge in conspiracy theories.

None I read were remotely close to the truth – what person of reasonable intelligence would suspect a haunted gallery? – but there were some especially outlandish ideas being published. Tales of cruel hazing practices at Dorian, bodies tied to posts and whipped senseless, the scars enduring for decades after. Hypotheses about sinister cults and satanic rituals. Fresh spotlights cast on the faculty, and on the campus itself.

The whole of Dorian seemed to be suspended on a held

breath, anticipating police investigations and widespread questioning. But the obituaries were published, and the weeping funerals were held, and neither ever came.

And I was no closer to knowing for certain whether Davina was behind it all.

Yes, I'd confirmed that she too hung in the gallery, and she knew the power of the paintings. She had enough of a vendetta against me to justify the spiteful cuts on my throat. And if Drever had been hooking her up with auditions she had no hope of booking otherwise, she had a very real reason to want to silence Orlagh about their affair. Drever was her golden ticket, and she was the kind of person who would stop at nothing to keep it that way.

But she had no motive that I could find for the last two murders, unless she really did just love the sport of it all. The sense of power, of control, of being in the driving seat. Seeing me squirm.

Of course, she was with me when the news about Lyle and Celia broke, but that didn't prove anything. It could have taken a while for the bodies to be found – she'd been missing in action for weeks, after all.

The cold, raw fear I felt around her was pure gut instinct. Something ancient and evolutionary. It had to mean something.

Another cut had appeared on my throat that night, once again jolting me from sleep. It was tiny, a pinprick, right beneath my chin. Which meant that whoever killed Celia and Lyle had gone *back* not long afterwards. Just to toy with me.

Another compass pointing towards Davina. I'd pissed her off, and sustained a fresh wound mere hours later.

Over the next week, more cuts started to appear over my chest – nicks along my collarbone, a thin crescent carving over the top of my breast. Controlled and precise, designed not to seriously hurt but to torment. It worked. With every fresh scar, a new wave of panic crested. That feeling, once again, of a jungle cat batting around a mouse before finally putting it out of its misery.

While Davina no longer fit perfectly as the perpetrator, she was still the only suspect I had. I couldn't think of anyone else who would want to hurt me like this, nor could I discern a clear pattern between Orlagh and the other victims. There were no other leads to follow but her, and so follow her I would.

I formed a tentative plan to tail Davina as closely as I could, trying to find any evidence I could to prove my theory correct. I wasn't sure what I'd do once I *did* uncover proof, but it seemed like something I should have regardless. So that if things escalated and I was forced into going to the police, they could act quickly against her. They could bring me to safety.

But once again, Davina vanished from class.

Was she attending more auditions? Booking her first real roles? It was the only reason I could think of that she'd willingly compromise the place at Dorian she'd worked so hard for. She didn't seem the type to value education for education's sake, like Catalina. This programme was a means to an end, and if she was already successful without it . . . why stick around?

That's not to say I never saw her on campus. I caught occasional glimpses of her talking to Maisie in shaded corners; brief licks of her tongue-pink ballet slippers in the crowded Costumery. From the quad, I saw a fleeting glimmer of her in Drever's office window before the blinds were snapped shut. Every time I came remotely close to her, though, she disappeared like a swallow swooping and diving around a net. Like a mirage, or a shadow, or a ghost.

One pattern did emerge, though: every time I caught sight of her at Dorian, a fresh cut would appear. Was that her only reason for returning between auditions? To torment me? Did she really loathe me that much?

My mother had been calling me fifteen times a day since the fresh murders. I never picked up, though the sad little girl inside me liked feeling pursued, for once. Even if Mum was likely just calling to remind me what she would do if I went to the police.

In truth, the idea of going to the police grew more appealing by the day. The stack of dead bodies was mounting, and I was being slowly but surely maimed. And yet the thought of standing in a cemetery, watching my only parent's coffin being lowered into the earth . . .

I couldn't risk it. I would have to solve this myself.

The Masked Painter was a dead end, and Davina was impossible to capture, so I decided to pursue the next best thing: Maisie.

She had grown close with Davina, and while her loyalty

almost certainly lay with my nemesis, my flatmate was also a notorious gossip. If she knew something strange or suspicious about Davina – that she had been sneaking around in the dark of the night with a dagger in her purse – she might not be able to help herself. She might tell me just for the thrill of it.

Worth a try.

One morning after class, she disappeared in the direction of the library instead of hitting the Costumery for lunch with the rest of us. Giving my apologies to Catalina and Fraser, I told them I'd see them in rehearsals and followed suit.

The campus was aflame with autumn leaves: sprays of brilliant orange and red yellow popping against the red-brick buildings. On my stroll through the quad, not one but two separate improv troupes tried to rope me into their elaborate performances – a bank heist and a divorce hearing – but I shook my head and tried to look amused instead of irritated.

Have a day off, will you? I muttered to myself, feeling rather acutely that I could not fit in less if I tried.

I found Maisie alone in a small library nook, poring over a volume I didn't recognise from the course reading list. She didn't see me, at first, and I had the chance to observe her in her natural habitat, like a curious wildlife species. She carried herself differently when she was alone, and therefore not trying to impress people. Her hair was tossed up in a messy bun, and she was biting her nails rather fiercely. Shoulders relaxed, even a little hunched. Her headphones played something that sounded suspiciously like country music, the quality tinny through the speakers.

I pulled out a chair, its legs squeaking over the chequerboard tiles, and said, 'Mind if I sit?'

She jumped ever so slightly, before yanking out her headphones and slamming the book on the table shut. I caught a glimpse of the cover before she stuffed it under her handbag: *RSPB Handbook of Scottish Birds: Second Edition.*

I smiled as warmly as I could, disguising the grunt of discomfort as my bony legs pressed into the stiff wooden chair. I could feel every protruding nobble on my backside. 'What are you reading?'

'Nothing.' Two perfectly round spots of pink had appeared on her cheeks, like a china doll. 'It's for the animal studies class.'

I frowned. 'I thought you were a chimp.'

The pink spots burned redder, but Maisie just shrugged.

'Don't be embarrassed,' I chuckled, in a way I hoped was reassuring instead of patronising. 'Birds are cool. And hey, I have my fair share of nerdy interests too.'

Maisie scoffed, but not in a cruel way. 'Oh yeah? Like high fashion and starring in plays? So nerdy.'

'Nope. Like chess.' I beamed at her, trying my best to win her over. 'I know all the main lines of every single chess opening there is. If you want a detailed rundown of the Icelandic Gambit, I'm your girl.'

The corners of her mouth lifted despite her best efforts. She pulled the bird book back out from under the handbag, then ran a thumb over its cover. 'I think I saw a capercaillie in the Crosswoods yesterday. I wanted to make sure it really was before I told my grandpa.' A sheepish smile. 'Birds are kind of our thing.' There was a subtle Geordie twang to her accent when she talked about her family.

'That's adorable. Why are you trying to hide it?'

She shot me a defiant look. 'Same reason you don't talk about chess, I'd imagine. We're all just playing a part, right?'

'Speaking of which . . .'

I was reluctant to break the fragile kinship between us, but the wounds on my throat and chest seemed to burn and throb whenever I thought about them. I needed to stop this.

I swallowed hard. 'Is Davina okay? I haven't seen her in class recently.'

I could tell immediately this was the wrong tactic.

Maisie shook her head, clenching her jaw. 'Is that why you're really here? To talk about Davina?'

Shame coiled inside me like a spring. I scrambled to regain the ground I'd just lost. 'I just feel bad about everything that's happened. I want us all to be friends.'

She raised a single eyebrow, and I envied how naturally expressive her face was. 'You want to be able to blackmail someone, steal what's rightfully theirs, and then sit around a campfire and sing "Kumbaya"?'

I chewed the inside of my cheek. There was a thick web of scar tissue from where I'd bitten into it during the night, when the most recent scar appeared. 'I offered her the lead back. She wouldn't take it. I fucked up, okay?'

'I'm not your messenger.' She shook her head again, a lock of hair falling out of her bun and into her face, then picked up her headphones.

Panic surged in me like a rush of river water. 'No, wait. Please, Maisie. This is important.'

She didn't respond, but her hand stilled.

There were so many things I wanted to say, but I had no idea which would be most likely to glean a response.

Where has Davina been?

Has she been acting strangely to you too?

Do you think that darkness inside her has the capacity to kill?

Do you think she might kill me?

No. I couldn't ask something solely about Davina. I needed her to feel relevant, like a critical cog in the story.

'The night Orlagh died,' I started, throat suddenly arid. 'You said you were with Davina, but you weren't. I saw her with Drever in Orlagh's office. Why did you lie? Did she ask you to?'

Maisie looked over her shoulder suddenly, as though expecting someone to jump out on her. Davina? Was she secretly as afraid of the cruel-mouthed ballerina as I was?

'Maisie,' I whispered. 'It's okay. Please, just say yes or no.'

Seconds sprawled into minutes sprawled into hours – or so it felt – until finally she said, 'I was birdwatching at an observatory in Musselburgh. It was me who lied, not Davina.'

Then the headphones went back on, and I knew the conversation was over.

*

A few days later, I was walking to rehearsals with Catalina when my whole world was pulled out from under me.

'Why are you at Dorian?' I was in the middle of asking her, genuinely curious. She didn't seem to crave fame and adoration the way the rest of us did.

We had been spending a lot of time together lately. With Fraser always out and about and Maisie off hunting hawks, the two of us were often alone in the flat. We studied together, watched Netflix true-crime documentaries together, drank tea and ran lines together. I had begun to associate Catalina with the feeling of *home*.

And in truth, it frightened me. The last time I'd felt like this was with Samara, who had been my best friend in the world. When she cut me out of her life for developing feelings, it was so deeply painful. I had to guard my heart around Catalina. I had to make a real effort not to sink too deeply into the friendship.

Yet I found myself endlessly fascinated by her. Every question I asked yielded a thoughtful, interesting response.

'What do you mean?' She was folding a piece of lined notebook paper in her hands, every crease neat and elaborate, concentration etched around her brows and temples. She'd recently dyed blue streaks into the front of her hair, and it made her bronze eyes shine brighter than ever.

'You just don't seem like the typical self-obsessed thespian. And I've never heard you talk about what you want to do after this. Do you want to be on stage? Screen?'

'I don't know, in all honesty. I'll go and audition, of course, and whatever happens, happens.' She adjusted her mustard-yellow bobble hat. 'But I would equally love to teach. I can totally see myself in a little office filled with books, getting paid to do nothing but sit and read and ponder. Such a vibe. And I'd play an indecent amount of Dungeons & Dragons, of course. Teach a course on its academic merits, maybe. What about you?'

'West End,' I replied automatically. 'I want people to come from far and wide to see me perform. I want standing ovations and adoration. Your typical narcissistic bullshit.' I laughed in self-deprecation, hoping she didn't try and psychoanalyse this desire any further. 'You'd really be content with a small office and pretending to be an orc?'

'First of all, my character is an astral elf, so let's get that straight.' She shrugged, her breath fogging in front of her. 'And yeah, I would. Standing ovations are wonderful, but . . . I don't know. Big joy and small joy are the same, right? I get as much happiness out of my first tea of the day as I do out of landing a big part in a play. Paper is the perfect example.' She held up an origami lion and offered it to me. 'Something so ordinary can be something so beautiful, if you look at it the right way. God, I sound like a fortune cookie.'

Endlessly fascinating.

The paper was warm from the brush of her fingers. I tucked the lion into the deep, satin-lined pocket of my fur coat, careful not to crush its intricate folds. I had the strange desire to take it out once I got back to my own room and pore over its every detail.

As we were crossing the quad, a tall, dark-skinned journalist with white-grey stubble and a navy wool coat approached me, dictaphone outheld.

'Ms Paxton –'

'I have nothing to say about the deaths,' I said, staring at a fixed point just over his shoulder. It wasn't the first time I'd been approached in the past week, and my patience for it was wearing thin.

'That wasn't what I was going to ask you about.' His voice was a gravelly tenor, the words raking over pebbled earth.

Spiked fear opened inside me, like a hedgehog unrolling barb by barb. I couldn't say for certain what I was afraid of.

I stopped walking abruptly. A few paces ahead, Catalina followed suit, frowning over her rounded shoulder at me.

'Okay,' I said, frozen in place.

His heels twitched forward, eager, and he pushed his gold-rimmed glasses up his broad nose. 'Do you have any comment on the contents of your mother's book?'

I felt a flicker of surprise, as though I'd pulled back the corner of a duvet expecting to see a monster beneath the bed and found only a lumpy pillow.

Of course. My mum's book came out today.

'What? Oh.' Relief ebbed tentatively at my shores. 'No. No comment.'

The journalist quirked a brow, equal parts playful and provoking. 'Not even the new revelations about your father?'

Another missed-step plummet in my gut. I knew my mother's publicist had been drumming up interest based on the promise of new information, but I thought she'd just put a clever media twist on stale old stories. Had there actually been anything of substance?

'What new revelations?' I asked quietly, like a child who'd been offered candy by a stranger's hand and was afraid to trust it.

The journalist wore the expression of a fisherman who'd landed the biggest salmon in the river. 'The three new facts revealed in the book: that they met at Dorian, that he was an artist, and that he is no longer with us.'

All the air was sucked from my lungs.

Terrible understanding struck me across the face, harsh and true.

The Masked Painter was my father.

CHAPTER TWENTY-ONE

After running from the journalist, running and running and running until I was hunched over by the lake and struggling to breathe, I called my mother ten, eleven, twelve times, but still she did not answer.

It felt at once incredibly obvious and utterly impossible.

The Masked Painter was my father.

Or at least, the original had been. The one who had painted my mother two decades ago.

And according to my mother, he was dead.

I hadn't seen it. I hadn't seen how clearly the dots connected. Her fear of the police, her assertion that bad things happened in that gallery, her certainty that he was gone. The paranoia that had ravaged her for as long as I could remember.

All at once, the truth hit me.

She had killed him.

The secret she didn't want getting out was not the cost of her beauty.

It was the fact she was a murderer.

My father was dead. I would never know him.

It shouldn't hurt, but it did. It hurt so much, the certainty of it, the crushing permanence.

A vast, gnawing part of me had always hoped to meet my father one day. I had spent so much of my childhood and adolescence fantasising about the love that would pass so freely between us. He would be wonderful and warm and kind, caring in a way my mother would never be. Maybe he would take me to football matches on Saturdays, and I wouldn't care at all about the outcome but I'd just be so happy to be there with him, chanting and cheering in our team's ugly striped scarves, and he'd throw his arms around me whenever we scored. When my car broke down, he would take it apart in our garage, wiping black oil from his hands with an old rag, animatedly teaching me how to use a socket wrench to tighten the . . . something.

I was keenly aware that this was a facsimile of fatherhood constructed from careful study of pop culture, but I had no other reference point beyond lazy stereotyping of what a family man should be.

One of my favourite fantasies was based around the holidays. He'd take me gift shopping on Christmas Eve, and it would be hurried and stressful because we'd left it so late and there was no bloody wrapping paper left anywhere, but then it would start snowing and Princes Street would be all twinkling lights and carol singers, like a scene from *Love Actually*, and we'd laugh and laugh and laugh because we'd realised all that really mattered was that we were together as a family.

I had wanted him so badly. He would open up a whole new world for me.

Except now he never would.

He was part of this whole twisted nightmare.

A swan glided over to where I crouched on the lakeshore. Its movements were too silent; a shadow of the thing rather than the thing itself. Then there were those eyes, coal black and frosted with cobweb wisp, something unnatural in their empty stare.

My father was dead.

My mother had killed him.

My thoughts whirred faster and faster in my head, a steel ball running the opposite way around a spinning roulette wheel, never finding a notch in which to settle.

A hand cupped my elbow, and I jumped. I hadn't heard anyone approach.

'Oh, Penny.' Catalina's soft voice. 'I take it you didn't know your father had died?'

So cold I felt on the brink of death, I shook my head, the movement stiff and jarring.

She squeezed my arm. 'Come on, let's get you inside.'

'What about class?' I asked. The words were hollow as a well.

'We can catch up.' An astonishing suggestion from her – nothing meant more to her than her studies. 'I think right now the greatest importance is soup and blankets.'

There was a clenching sensation in my chest, like a fist gripping my heart, and I struggled to breathe.

I'd had a few panic attacks before. I knew the signs.

I tried to do the long, slow inhale, the controlled exhale, but the breaths hitched in my throat, high-pitched and sob-like.

My father was dead, my mother was a murderer, and I was in danger. My portrait hung in an arcane gallery, the subjects from which were being gradually executed. I felt terrified and small and alone. I felt like I was in a room whose walls were gradually closing in, and sooner or later, I would be crushed. I wanted to run, to scream, to hide. I wanted to break free of the prison of my body. I wanted to escape.

Catalina lifted me to my feet, and as we walked up to the dorm, I decided to tell her everything.

Everything.

I don't know what made me do it: shock, or fear, or desperation. Maybe the unexpected tide of grief shook it loose, like the waning sea dragging pebbles back from the shore. Perhaps it was all of those things, in part, but deep down I think I wanted to vocalise it to convince myself I wasn't going mad. I needed a calm, rational mind to talk it through with. To make it exist outside my own absurd experiences. Because maybe, to an outside ear, it was all exceedingly obvious – who was doing this, and why, and what on earth I could do about it.

Or maybe I just wanted so badly not to be alone.

Catalina listened as we squelched back up the rain-slicked lawn, as we squeaked wetly over the foyer in our halls, as we slipped into the kitchen with a swift flick of the kettle. She listened as I told her about Orlagh's offer, and my sitting with the Masked Painter, and about all the famous faces hanging in the Gallery of the Exquisite. She listened as I described Orlagh's strangely marked corpse, and of how it fitted into the medical examiner's leaked story about the bodies of Celia Van Der Beek and Lyle Barr. She listened as I told her my theory – that I believed Davina was using the paintings to kill off Dorian alumni – and my fears that I would be next.

She listened as I told her I was certain the original Masked Painter was my father – though I left out my suspicions over who killed him.

She listened as I told her that my mother had threatened to take her own life if I went to the police.

She listened even though everything I said sounded like the twisted nightmare of a confused child.

As I talked, I sank on to the squashy sofa in the living area, and she laid a bobbly knitted blanket over my legs. It was hideously ugly, this blanket, every colour of wool under the sun, with wonky crocheted flowers stitched all over it, but even though it was incapable of warming me up, it spread over me an indescribable sense of comfort. As though it had magical properties, and not the dark and twisted kind I was becoming accustomed to at Dorian.

She didn't coddle me as tears slicked down my face, nor did she coo or fuss when I described the cold and the hunger I feared might never leave me. She just . . . *listened*. She started chopping vegetables, soaking lentils for soup, little acts of love that came so effortlessly to her.

I don't deserve it, said a miserable voice inside my head.

Why not? asked a far younger one.

'Firstly, thank you for trusting me with all of this,' she said, once I'd finally finished talking. 'I can't even imagine how you must be feeling right now. Like you've fallen into a horror movie, I guess.'

'You believe me?' I stared at her in a very out of character manner. 'About the paintings being somehow . . . *magic*?'

She simply shrugged, brushing a lock of hair out of her face with the back of her hand, still clutching the kitchen knife. 'I mean, first of all, I'm quite used to my hippie mother's tarot readings and Ouija boards. She taught seances as part of her homeschool curriculum. And secondly, yeah. I believe in magic.'

'You do? But you're so . . . smart.'

Catalina cackled, rich and earthy, the kind of laugh that made you smile just to hear it. 'That's *why* I believe. You really think the only real things in this world are the ones we can see? The stuff we can measure with a yardstick or a barometer or a pie chart? The absolute arrogance!'

'I don't know what to do.' I tucked my feet under myself, pulling the blanket up to my chin. It carried Catalina's scent: cardamom tea and incense and honeysuckle fabric softener. 'It's like a maze where every passage is a dead end. Where all the walls are mirrors.'

'You're sure it's Davina? You think she could really do something like that?'

'As sure as I can be without proof. She's threatened me

to my face. And she had reason to silence Orlagh.'

'What about Celia and Lyle?'

'That, I haven't figured out.'

There was, of course, the chance I was wrong. That my suspicions about Davina were simply confirmation bias; my mind looking for evidence to back-up the innate fear I felt around her. But there were no other immediate suspects, no other apparent connections between the wounds on my body and the tally of corpses.

'And you can't go to the police, because your mum said she would . . .' Her eyes – slicked with warm copper eyeshadow – narrowed. 'Why do you think she wants so badly to avoid the cops?'

I had to lie, even though it bristled against every fibre of my being. 'I think she just doesn't want the truth about her beauty to leak.'

Catalina looked at me then, searingly, not the cold vulpine iciness of Davina but something altogether softer, brighter.

'Why did you do it, Penny?' she asked, laying down the knife and wiping her hands on a vintage floral tea towel.

I averted my gaze from the fierce search of hers. There was a fuchsia pink feather boa slung over the back of the sofa – stolen from the Costumery, perhaps – and I focused on its garish plumage.

'Do what?'

'Say yes to Orlagh's offer.' A quiet beat. 'It's so unbearably sad.'

Sad.

That's not the word I ever expected her to use. Stupid, selfish, shallow . . . but not sad.

And yet there was such precision to it. She hadn't chosen that word by accident.

Somehow, it made me feel sad too; aching in a place I tried so very hard to ignore. It brought to mind that voice in the back of my head right before the Masked Painter cut into me: *I'm sorry.*

'I don't know why,' I answered, although it wasn't the whole truth. It was simply that the whole truth was too complicated and messy for even me to comprehend. 'It's just . . . being beautiful is so important to me. To the world. And I don't know why that is. I don't know why I would value it over my life.'

She resumed chopping, dicing potatoes with a chef's deftness. 'A lot of scholars link it to finding a mate – we're wired to be obsessed with procreation, right? Survival of the species? Getting railed is our first priority.'

Just as Orlagh had said. I laughed, but it was brittle. 'Even for us gays?'

Catalina beamed. 'Even for us gays.'

With a sharp, bright jolt, I registered the fact she was gay too. It felt like the sun appearing from behind a cloud.

Stop it. Not this again. Remember Samara.

But the way the cool autumn light was hitting her face . . . the way she made me feel so safe and warm. It was hard to ignore.

'I think . . . I think there's more to it, though.' I took another sip of tea. 'The self-starvation thing. Because logically I know that being a bag of skin and bones is hardly beautiful.' I pressed my thumb against my bottom lip, feeling the soft brush of my cashmere jumper on my skin. 'Orlagh thought it was about control.'

'And I get that. What young woman *doesn't* want to feel like they actually have control over something? Maybe it's why I like DnD so much. Master of my own fate, yada yada.'

Another strike of the tuning fork. I thought of all the miniature rules and challenges I set for myself – *make it to eleven and you can have a coffee, an apple at three, a Diet Coke at four* – and the surge of satisfaction when I met them.

Something, something was in my control, no matter how small. A stark contrast to the rest of my childhood, pushed and pulled along on the whims and pitfalls of my mother's addiction, like a piece of driftwood at sea. The control over my own body was the smallest of anchors.

'You feel it too?' I asked, a lump bobbing in my throat now. Catalina's keen intelligence always seemed to cut right to the heart of the matter, and it left me breathless. 'That need for control?'

'Of course.' She filled the kettle, then crumbled two stock cubes into a measuring jug. 'You know, when I was thirteen my parents decided to quit their corporate jobs in Madrid, sell our house and all our belongings, and move into a converted van. They said they were going to homeschool me and my sister, and that we were going to travel all over Europe instead of living a conventional life.' Something bitter passed over her usually gentle face. 'Over the course of a single weekend, I felt like I lost everything. My school, my friends, my home. My privacy.'

'They didn't ask if you even wanted to?'

'They did. They just ignored the answer. Said I'd change my mind once I saw how free we could be.' She pressed her hands on the edge of the counter, bent at the waist as though momentarily winded. 'Then they started posting *everything* about van life on social media, as though it was this idyllic, nomadic lifestyle. But in reality, we'd just pull into beauty spots, take photos and videos of the view, then spend the rest of the day trying to find somewhere with actual facilities. I resented them so much. And my sister and I fought *all* the time, because we'd gone from having separate bedrooms to sharing a bunk bed over the driver's seat. I used to dream about her getting sucked away with the sewage.' A bright peal of laughter.

She stood back up and flicked the light on the gas stove. 'And yeah, I just felt like I'd lost all the control over my own life. I started restricting for a few years, because if I couldn't control my world at least I could control my body. Then came the diabetes diagnosis, and I had to start eating properly again. If I didn't want to die, of course.'

'Was the diabetes . . . linked? Caused by –'

'No.' She shook her head. 'It's type one, which means it's a genetic autoimmune disease. Nothing I could've done to prevent it.'

'How do you feel now?' I asked. 'About your body, I mean. Which is, as far as bodies go, a fucking astounding one.'

I realised too late how brazen the comment was, wishing I could yank it back.

Catalina blushed furiously, but a smile worked at her lips. 'Thanks. I dunno, it's hard. I think I look great. And as long as my sugars are under control, I feel pretty great too. It's just hard, sometimes, when the world equates thinness and beauty. I have to be pretty vigilant with my thoughts. Make sure I don't buy into that shit again.'

I gazed out of the window to the Crosswoods as a breeze whirled through the branches. I noticed that, despite the terrible revelations of the morning, I felt less anxious and frightened than I had in weeks. Catalina's presence was so easy that even my bucking heart, doomed to palpitate forever, seemed to calm.

'It's all so messed-up,' I said. Now that we'd started talking about it, I found myself not wanting to stop. I'd kept it locked inside me for so long. 'It's like I told Orlagh – I don't know who I am without my looks.'

'So maybe it's not that you want beauty,' Catalina said thoughtfully. 'It's that you want identity. Everyone wants to feel like someone, and beauty is a short cut to that.'

A tuning fork chimed in my chest; a visceral reaction of *yes, yes, that's it*.

She was so right it stole the breath from my lungs. I'd spent my whole life in my mother's shadow, a poor imitation of her, without ever having a true sense of who I really was. 'Beautiful' was just an easy shorthand.

Once the pan of soup had started to bubble, Catalina placed a lid over the top and started scraping peelings into the bin. 'Can I ask you something?'

'Of course.'

'What did you love doing as a kid?'

'As a kid, I was pretty much obsessed with gaining my mother's love, by any means necessary.' I fiddled with the hem of my jumper. 'I'd do fashion shows up and down the hallway, thinking that's what she wanted from me. But when I was at school, and I could kind of forget about her for those hours every day . . . I loved chess.'

Catalina's smiled broadened. There was the slightest gap between her front teeth. 'That's not what I thought you were going to say.'

I shrugged. 'It made sense to me. I've always found other people's thoughts and feelings and emotions so hard to navigate, but there's not really any of that on the chessboard.'

'Why did you stop playing?'

'We moved from London to Edinburgh, and my new school was so much smaller than my last one. There was no chess club, and to be honest I was too self-conscious to try and start one. I played a bit online, but it wasn't the same, really.'

Catalina clapped her hands together. 'Would you like to play with me?'

A flicker of childish excitement flared in my tummy; a

pleasant change from hollow hunger. 'You'd do that?'

'Sure. My dad played a lot of street chess in Madrid. He taught me and my sister when we were kids.'

'I only have a tiny travel set,' I warned her.

'That's okay. I have good glasses.'

After I'd retrieved the chess set from the back of my wardrobe – stuffed there hastily the day I arrived, as though hiding a dark secret – we sat on opposite sides of the breakfast bar. I was still wrapped in my thick fur coat, bone-cold, but my skin could tell that the room was warm and cosy. The windows were steamed up from the soup. The lid rattled on top of the pan.

We set up the board, and my fingertips almost fizzed with anticipation.

Catalina took the white pieces. She pushed her queen's pawn forward two squares. I moved my king's pawn forward two; an invitation, and an attack.

'The Scandinavian Defence,' she said, nodding pensively. 'Nice. Aggressive.'

'You know the names of the openings too?' I asked in surprise.

'Sure. Doesn't necessarily mean I know how to play them, though.'

She took my pawn with hers, and I captured back with my queen – meaning all other pieces were still in place, with the exception of my dominant queen in the centre. She did the obvious thing of pushing my queen away with her knight, but

I swung it out to the side of the board and she couldn't touch it for a few more moves.

I used the time wisely, getting all my minor pieces into developed positions, castling queenside ready for an aggressive pawn rush on her king. I thought I'd be rusty, but the beautiful thing about chess was that it never changed. I slipped back into the rhythm of it, calculating and intuiting and strategising. Catalina never made any glaring mistakes, but I was able to capitalise on some of the minor inaccuracies she made.

As I played, I found that all other thoughts left my head, since I needed all my brainpower for the complex positions I was processing. I found a calmness, a rhythm, that I hadn't felt in a long time. Something almost resembling peace.

I pushed and pushed, relentless in the forward thrust of my attack. She countered as best she could, but after ten minutes, I had mate in three, and she had nothing to defend with.

She stared down at the board. 'My god, Penny.'

Glowing beneath her admiration, I couldn't help the unsportsmanlike grin spreading across my face. It was an unfamiliar feeling, to smile so widely. 'I forgot how good that feels.'

'There you go – a new identity for you. Frighteningly gifted chess player.' She shook her head, then laughed, then studied me with those burnished bronze eyes.

I nodded sincerely. 'Have I told you I'm also a fairly decent fencer?'

A serious expression fixed on my face, I climbed to my feet

and mimed out my best moves. Fencing had been a brief but furious passion when I was eleven, before I realised how uncool it was. How unbefitting it was for the daughter of an icon.

Catalina collapsed with laughter. 'I'll bear that in mind next time I need a swordswoman.' She gazed up at me with an impenetrable look on her sunny face. 'I think you might be the most interesting person I've ever met. You make me want to peel back the layers of you to see what I might find next.'

Everything in me sang. And for the first time in a long time, I realised this was what I wanted. I wanted joy and softness, laughter and kinship, games and food and *love*. I didn't want to be a husk of a person any more.

Catalina . . . she made me want to be better. She made me want it more than I ever had.

And – also for the first time – she made it feel genuinely possible.

*

Later that night, I awoke to a hot, sharp pain on my face.

Gasping, I sat bolt upright, limbs white-hot with adrenaline. It felt as though a blade had been dragged across my cheek, the pain searing bright. I half expected to see a hulking silhouette in my room, but there was no one there. When I held my palm to my stinging cheek, there was no warm ooze of blood.

I lay back against the pillow, steadying my breath, reining in my bucking heartbeat. Just a dream, I told myself. One of those awful, sentient dreams where the pain follows you out of it.

Switching on the bedside lamp with a trembling hand, I picked up my phone from the bedside table and opened the front-facing camera.

No. Please, no.

A stark red-purple mark bisected my jutting cheekbone.

CHAPTER TWENTY-TWO

I stumbled into the hallway and towards the front door, my limbs clumsy and weak from terror. Like a baby deer running from a hunter's crosshairs.

Whoever carved this mark on my face was in the Gallery of the Exquisite right now. They could kill me at any moment, and I was powerless to stop it. I pictured a disembodied hand hovering a blade over my chest, a fraction of a second from plunging.

This one felt different. It was so brazen, so *big*. So . . . final, somehow. A twisted murderer reaching their crescendo.

There was a gun to my head, and nowhere to run.

Nowhere to run except home.

It was time to confront my mother. Because I was going to the police, with or without her approval. I had to get Davina behind bars, before she could land the killing blow.

But first I had to know exactly what I was condemning my mother to.

Had she really killed my father? Could she have ever been that cruel?

Part of me already knew the answer.

Grabbing my car keys, I ran from the flat, down the stairs and into the atrium, and then outside in my bare feet, not feeling the frozen graze of the ground shred my tender skin. and I ran to my car and piled myself into the front seat and I *drove*.

I hurtled out of the Dorian grounds and on to the main road into the city.

I pushed the pedal to the floor, balls of my feet stinging, until the fear of my speed outweighed the fear of everything else.

Classical music played on the radio this time.

Vivaldi. The delicate piano, the swoops and soars.

Tears streamed down my stinging face, and I could barely see. The rain-slicked road was mercifully deserted; my car clock read 3.14 a.m. I kept driving into the city, still crying uncontrollably, until dual carriageways became low, sprawling suburbs. Leafy neighbourhoods became tall Georgian townhouses. I half mounted the curb as I hastily slammed on my handbrake outside the front door.

It was unlocked. A wall of staleness hit me as soon as I walked in.

Mum was slumped on the leather sofa in the living room, all lights off except the flickering television illuminating her face in unnatural colours. The room smelled acidic, stagnant. Three empty bottles of wine lay discarded on the floor like a child's unwanted toys, and her hand clutched a wine glass. The thin stem of it had snapped in her grip, like a broken swan's neck, but she was snoring too loudly to notice. There was a small, perfectly round patch of drool on the velvet cushion.

Emotions warred in the battleground of my chest. An infantile sadness, a simmering anger, a pseudo-parental need to protect her. Something with the same silhouette as shame. It wasn't my fault, but it felt like it might be. It had always felt like that – some failing of mine, that I wasn't enough to keep my mother sober.

I wasn't *enough*. No matter how much Catalina made me feel otherwise.

'Mum,' I said into the miserable room, barely recognising my own voice. It wasn't choked with tears, as it should be, but rather a clarion pitch.

But when she didn't even stir, everything in me splintered.

I bent down and picked up one of the empty wine bottles, and for a second I worried I might never stand up again, but rage pulled me to my feet.

'MUM!' I roared, and then I hurled the bottle with all my strength at the wall furthest from her.

It shattered into a thousand glittering pieces, falling to the ground like icy hail in a car's stark headlights. And for a searing moment, I imagined what Catalina would think if she saw me now. The shame burned even hotter in my chest.

With a dazed jolt, Mum shuddered awake, peeling her eyes open one at a time and looking up at me blankly.

'What?' she slurred, a single unfeeling syllable.

She looked at me like she might look at a burglar who'd broken into her house in the night; a burglar who held a gun to her head, and she didn't have the energy to protest. Complete and utter apathy.

And even though I now understood more than ever why she was like this, it still carved me open.

It was too much to bear.

'My dad,' I hissed. 'What happened to my dad?'

She didn't even have the good grace to look ashamed.

'All my life I begged for scraps of information, and you refused.' I was trembling from the maelstrom of emotions. 'Then you sold it all to the highest publishing bidder? I don't understand you. I don't understand how you can have so little regard for me. Did it even cross your mind, how I might take this? Was I an afterthought? Was I even a thought at all?'

Still she said nothing, and the urge to grab her by the narrow shoulders and shake until her brain bled out her ears was almost too strong.

'I hate you!' I screamed, crouching to pick up another wine bottle. 'I fucking hate you!' Hurl, thunk, shattering glass. 'You've ruined my life and you don't even fucking *care*!' On the last syllable, the echo of the smashed bottle dissipated.

Nothing resembling sadness or shame crossed her face – she didn't even have the decency to raise her voice, to show some kind of depth of emotion.

'Oh, because I've been such a terrible mother?' she said flatly, still slumped over the sofa as though all her bones had melted. She hiccuped, and her eyes drifted in different directions. 'I might not shower you with hugs and kisses every minute of every day, but I've given you things most people can only ever dream of.'

She buried a hand into the crease of the sofa, pulled out her phone and tapped the screen.

That single second of casual phone-checking was a heeled boot in my gut.

'You think most people have a house like this?' she continued, once she'd ascertained nobody more important had messaged. 'You think most people go to the kind of school you went to? You have the best of everything, the designer clothes, the nice car, the –'

'Did you kill my father?' I yelled, not even caring who heard me.

She just stared blankly at a spot over my shoulder, dropping her phone back to the floor.

'Tell me, Mum.' My voice was a hot snap, like an elastic band pulled taut for a decade and finally released. 'Tell me everything, right now. Or I'll go to the police myself.'

That got her attention. 'You wouldn't. You know what I'll –'

'I'll dial nine nine nine right in front of you, if you don't believe me.' I pulled my phone out of my back pocket.

She held up her hands in defeat. 'Fine. Fine, alright?'

Everything in me stilled, hardly daring to believe I might finally peel back the curtain on my own haunted past.

'It all started with him. With the Masked Painter.' All the inebriation ebbed out of her voice, like this conversation was a leech draining the alcohol from her blood. 'He was your father. And yes, I killed him.'

Somehow the confirmation felt worse than I could ever have imagined. My mind was a house on fire, flames licking out of every window.

'Why?' Such an absurdly narrow word for the moment.

Silence.

'MUM!' I yelled. 'For fuck's sake!'

She didn't flinch, but she did start talking – a distant drone. 'We had sex the night he painted my portrait. I was the only subject he ever invited back to his own home – a cabin in the woods – and he paid for that mistake with his life.'

'You killed him that night?' My chest was tight and heavy, like a corpse lay directly on top of it.

'No. I had no reason to. But a few months later, I began to realise the true toll of the portrait. The things I usually did to combat depressive episodes no longer worked. I couldn't eat, couldn't get out of bed, couldn't see the point in anything. All the important friendships in my life slowly fell away, because of how miserable I was, how difficult to be around. I wanted to die. The veil of darkness could not be lifted, and I eventually realised it was because the painting preserved me *exactly as I was* in that moment in time. Just as Orlagh said.

'So I went back to the Masked Painter's cabin, and I begged him to undo it, to destroy the painting, whatever it took. No matter how much I wanted to preserve my looks, it wasn't worth the excruciating cost. But he told me there was no reversal, and that destroying the painting would destroy me too. Such was the nature of the anchor.' She swallowed a dry lump in her throat. 'We fought, then, viciously. I screamed at him for not warning me, I screamed and screamed that he was evil, that he was preying on women's insecurities for his own twisted ends, that this was all just some way to wield power over us.'

True. It was all true. The thing I couldn't quite understand – what he stood to gain. No money changed hands, and there was no fame or adoration to be garnered from a gallery deep underground, far away from the general public.

'Did he tell you why he did it?' I asked.

'He said that he'd been born with this impossible gift, and that he wanted to use it to shape the world.' Mum scoffed with disdain. 'To make gods of mortals.'

I waited for her to continue, but her uneven gaze had parted again. Her head swayed slightly, but didn't seem to realise she was doing so.

She still hadn't noticed the blighted mark on my face.

A small reminder that she did not, in any meaningful way, see me.

'So you fought with the painter,' I prompted. 'Did you know you were pregnant at the time?'

'No. I was hysterical, and started slapping him, and he grabbed my wrists to stop me. I yanked them free and shoved him backwards, and he lost his balance. He fell. His temple hit the corner of the coffee table, and he was dead before he hit the ground.' A strange physiological response clapped through her, and she shuddered once – a puppet-like jolt.

'The body was found a few weeks later,' she went on, voice murky. 'Some hikers smelled something awful coming from the cabin. But as far as I know, there was no real murder investigation. No signs of forced entry to the house, no evidence of foul play on the body – my futile slaps hadn't left a mark. I think the police must have chalked it up to a bad fall.'

Suddenly noticing the snapped wine glass in her hand, she let it fall absently to the ground, splintering into more despondent shards. 'I wasn't even relieved to be let off the hook. To be honest, I wasn't really thinking about the fact I'd killed someone. I was thinking about how I was trapped inside the black cloud of depression for the rest of my life, unable to feel anything at all. Another month later, I realised I hadn't had a period in a while. I thought maybe it was because of the portrait, somehow, since I wasn't menstruating when I sat for the painting. But then came the positive pregnancy test.'

Which you felt nothing for, I thought miserably. *You've never felt anything for me at all.*

'How was it possible?' I asked, focusing on the logistics so I didn't have to process this very specific pain. 'To get pregnant, I mean. If the painting preserved you exactly as you were –'

'That, I don't understand.' She shrugged. 'But I know plenty of the Gallery's alumni have gone on to bear children. One of them is even in the *Guinness Book of World Records* as the oldest mother in history.'

'So that's why you really left Dorian. You were pregnant.'

'Indeed.' She rubbed her hands over her face. 'Yes, there was the depression, the model scouting luring me away, but the heart of it was the baby in my belly. I hid it for long enough to do a few high-profile shoots, then disappeared to birth you in private.'

Why had I never done this maths before? It should have been so obvious that she'd left Dorian because of me, but I'd never thought to lay down the timeline. To ask her how old she was when she joined Dorian – and when she'd left.

'You kept me.' My voice was hoarse.

'Pardon?'

'When you found out you were pregnant. You didn't get rid of me. Why?'

A long, agonised silence. And then, in a tiny voice, 'I thought you might fix me. I thought you might break through the fog of depression.'

But I didn't.

'Of course, it doesn't work like that.' She gave a bitter little laugh, sharp and acidic. 'I couldn't fix my mother, and you couldn't fix me. You know, your grandmother was as beautiful as us. A farmer's daughter, a carpenter's wife, a homemaker. She measured herself with a pink dressmaker's tape every single morning, and she wrote down the numbers in a little red notebook. "I'm the same size now as the day I was married," she'd say, so proudly, as though if that were all she ever achieved with her life it would be enough.' A deep swallow. 'Maybe that's why I made the decision I did. Maybe it's why you did too. The family curse.'

A lot of the fight or flight had left my limbs, and I crumpled into a stiff loveseat, bending myself around the pit of agonising hunger. My cheek still stung like a hot whip.

'Aren't you going to ask what happened to my face?' I asked quietly, pettily.

'What happened to your face?' she muttered immediately. She didn't need to look at me to know what I meant – so she *had* registered it earlier, but hadn't cared enough to ask.

I looked down at the last unsmashed wine bottle, feeling the dim desire to hurl it at a wall, but I was too bone-tired to rise to my feet.

'I'm still being carved up. Cuts all over my neck and chest. And now this.' I gritted my jaw. 'I'm going to the police, Mum. About Davina. I'm going to die otherwise.'

I hated the pleading notes underpinning my voice. It felt like asking for mercy.

Why wouldn't my mother do *anything* to protect me, the way mothers in stories always did?

'I'll kill myself.' The words were so plain, which somehow made them feel even crueller.

'Mum,' I pleaded, just a girl, just a little girl at the heart of myself. 'What other choice do I have?'

She shrugged. 'You could take care of this Davina character yourself.'

I stared at her in horror for several moments – this ghoul of a woman I had mirrored for so long – before storming out of the house once more.

I was dimly aware that it might be the last time I ever saw her alive.

The drive back to Dorian was an erratic spiral of blaring headlights and corkscrew thoughts. Classical music, a starry sky, the feeling of being stuck on a merry-go-round I could not get off.

CHAPTER TWENTY-THREE

Over the next few days I mulled over what to do, turning over every possible stone until the facts themselves seemed warped – the way a word repeated too often loses its meaning, becoming a mere fumbling of the tongue over teeth.

My life hung in the balance, yet still I was plagued by indecision.

Because what should you do? What should you do when your only choices are risking your mother's death, or somehow incapacitating the most fearless person you know?

Classes and rehearsals went on as normal, but Davina still didn't attend them.

After one session ironing out the kinks in Act IV, I approached Drever after everyone else had filtered out of the rehearsal space.

'Where's Davina?' I asked without preamble. I was shaking so profoundly that it was miraculous he didn't notice.

He looked up from the script he was scribbling on in red Sharpie, visibly surprised. 'She booked a small TV role. It's filming in Mallorca this week. The dean granted her special dispensation.'

I stared at him for a few seconds too long, the temptation of telling him that I knew *everything* almost too strong to resist, but I still didn't want him to know it was me who blackmailed him at the start of the semester. And so I left the room without another word.

Striding to the library to meet Catalina, realisation dawned. If Davina was out of the country all week and the cuts suddenly stopped appearing on my body . . . there was a high chance she was the perpetrator. This was an opportunity to add further evidence to my growing dossier.

As for the large facial scar, I found myself less bothered by the aesthetic appearance of it than I should have been. For someone who had dedicated her whole life to the pursuit of physical perfection, such disfigurement should have been the most traumatic thing that could happen to me. A permanent and irreversible defeat.

But in reality, it was oddly exhilarating.

Freeing.

Because now I would never be perfect, no matter how hard I tried.

As I studied the beet-purple hue in my dorm's fogged-up mirror, tracing the ragged edges with an icy fingertip, that quote from *East of Eden* played on a loop in my mind: 'Now that you don't have to be perfect, you can be good.'

The wound felt, in a way, like permission. Like a long, slow exhale. Like dropping out of a race I couldn't remember actively choosing to run.

Being born beautiful had carried with it a sense of obligation. It was a gift I had been granted, and was honour-bound to take great care of this thing that so many people coveted. I'd often felt as though remarkable beauty was the universe's way of marking me for greatness, and I had a crushing sense of responsibility to make the most of it. Whatever that meant.

But now the worst had happened – my greatest currency had been compromised – and the overriding emotion was not devastation but relief.

Now I would have to find another race to run. And the thought was quietly exciting.

There was still the fear, of course, of what it meant. A final brutal swipe before the killing blow came. But at the sight of my own reflection, I felt a perverse kind of satisfaction. A dark smile played across my face like a silent movie. My pupils dilated to their fullest, swallowing the green of my irises with blackness. A blackness without a bottom. I frowned at the hue – I'd never seen a black quite like that before.

Then –

No.

My eyes were playing tricks on me.

I lifted my finger to the wound –

In the mirror, my fingers reached up to touch smooth, blank skin.

In my reflection, the wound was on the wrong side.

I turned away from the mirror, chest pounding, a dizziness yanking the floor out from under me.

When I turned back, the image had righted itself. The mirror wound matched my face wound.

Shuddering, I turned away. There was something not right with the mirrors in this place.

I covered up the scar as best I could with stage-quality make-up before heading to classes and rehearsals. Just because it gave me a peculiar thrill didn't mean I wanted to invite questions from outside parties.

A week wore on without a single sighting of Davina – and without a single new mark appearing on my body.

For every morning I woke up unblemished, I felt even more grimly certain that the most obvious answer was the right one: Davina was the killer. But why Celia and Lyle? Did the two famous actors have something to do with her immediate auditioning success, or was it pure and simple bloodlust?

To both my horror and exhilaration, Davina finally resurfaced the day of the master and subject class.

Morning sessions had become increasingly embarrassing – the day before, Lawrie had us embody the four elements for hours on end – in order to slowly erode our egos. To make us more comfortable around each other, so that we might act together without inhibition. It was all building to this one game: master and subject. The game that had made Dorian infamous when stories of it hit the news a few decades ago. A rite of passage at a prestigious institution. One I had been dreading ever since I arrived.

The sight of Davina lounging in a wooden chair, leather

jacket slung over the back, was an electric jolt. A battering ram straight to the chest, all the breath slammed out of my lungs.

Suppressing the urge to cower away, I watched her carefully as Catalina and I walked past her to seats a few rows behind.

Davina's gaze snapped up to mine like a band of elastic.

And she stared.

Not just at my face, but at my throat, my chest, my collarbones. All the places I was criss-crossed with esoteric scars. I wore a thick cream turtleneck jumper, so she couldn't see a thing. But the way she looked . . . it was as though the fabric didn't exist at all.

She was so *brazen*. Was she trying to make me feel threatened? To spark fresh dread at her return, and what that might mean for me?

Hatred sank deep into my stomach like a stone in a well.

She was enjoying this.

Catalina, however, was not. We slid into two chairs near the back of the room, and she reached out across the aisle and squeezed my hand. 'Are you okay? That was intense.'

Her touch was like cotton: warm and comforting and charged, somehow. I didn't want her to pull away.

'I'm okay,' I lied. I felt anything but.

Catalina nodded fiercely. 'I've got your back, okay? Whenever you need me, I'm here. Just say the word and I'll smother her with a pillow.'

Despite everything, I *laughed*, feeling so glad I'd confided in her about everything. At the sight of the fresh facial wound – shown to her in a bedroom adorned with fantasy maps and Funko Pops – she had made me sleep in her bed for the night, so that if anything else happened, she was there. She had curled up on the floor in a bed made of cardigans and blankets, and though I found it impossible to drift off, the sound of her breathing had been a soft, steady anchor, hypnotic as the sound of gentle waves lapping a shore.

Come morning, she had been ready to hunt Davina down herself. I talked her out of it, of course. The last thing I wanted was an innocent girl getting hurt just to protect me. No matter how good that protection might feel.

Davina was my problem to deal with. I just had to figure out how.

'Think of the most disturbing movie you've ever watched,' boomed Drever, once class had begun in earnest. He leaned back against his desk, his shirt unbuttoned at the collar and the sleeves rolled up to his elbows. Thick veins wormed all over his forearms beneath coarse grey-black hair. 'Whether it's as physically abominable as *The Human Centipede* or something altogether more psychological, remember that actors had to perform it. They likely had to perform it again and again and again, over many takes, from many different angles. It's important that you become well acquainted with distress and humiliation, with vulnerability and shame, with exposing yourself in all the ways it is possible to do so.'

Discomfort churned in my gut like the contents of a witch's

cauldron. A raven sat on the windowsill, watching our human folly with vague disinterest.

'When Tom Six was casting *The Human Centipede*, many actors found themselves too shaken to enact, even fully clothed, what happened to those victims. They would read the lines, and the chemistry would be there, but when it came time to crouch on hands and knees, mouths agape, they found they could not do it. They fled.

'Few auditions are likely to invoke such strong revolt in you, and yet it's important to be prepared. To be exposed to even a fraction of that degradation here, now, the way a vaccine works with a microdose. Because in truth, opening yourself to horror of the mind and body will create countless paths into the film industry. Let's face it – not all of you are going to play Hamlet. Not all of you are going to capture hearts as Romeo or Juliet. Most of you will have to find other doors to crank open with a crowbar. Most of you are going to have to force your way in.

'And look, there will always be weird, niche indie movies looking for up-and-comers. As voyeurs, we're endlessly compelled by disturbing things happening to the human body.' My hand went to my cheek without thinking. 'High-profile actors rarely want to take on such roles. For that they need newbies. For that they need you. And you need to be ready.'

The witch's cauldron bubbled over, and immense dread spilled into my veins and arteries. Not just at the hideous premise of that film, but at the idea of having to perform it, any of it, anything that went beyond the relatively safe confines of

Shakespeare. Hell, the auditioning process was fraught enough for me as it was – I always felt vulnerable, exposed, self-conscious to the point of paralysis.

Maybe Drever was right – that needed to be beaten out of me by whatever means necessary.

'This is how it will go.' He clapped his hands together, and it made me jump. 'You'll be paired up with one of your classmates, and you will each take a turn to be master and subject. For ten whole minutes, the subject must do anything the master tells them to do. *Anything*. And then the tables will turn. The subjects will become the masters, and the power will be theirs.'

'Can you give us some examples of things people have done in the past?' asked Nairne, nervously plaiting and unplaiting the end of her thick blonde ponytail.

'Certainly.' Drever raised a bushy brow, white and ginger like a fox's tail. 'There has been a lot of nudity, as I'm sure you can imagine. Things always seem to develop sexual undertones. You're all young, I suppose, and rampant with certain hormones.' A parental chuckle, so at odds with what he was doing with Davina behind closed doors. 'Last year one of my finest students was slapped in the face by his friend's . . . *appendage*. Another had her subject suck all of her toes one by one.'

Dominic snorted. 'That's messed-up.' The tone was jock-ish, unbothered, but there was a twitchiness to his movements that made me think he was quietly nervous.

'What happens if subjects refuse to do something?' asked Davina, and beside her Maisie smirked.

Drever looked at her almost too carefully, consciously, and it seemed so *blatant* that there was something between them. I didn't understand how nobody else could see it. Then again, was I really parsing subtext and body language when I already knew what to look for? When these actions had a fully formed meaning already ascribed?

'Then they will know, in themselves, that they lack fortitude,' he answered seriously. 'And *I* will know they lack fortitude. Future roles will be cast with that knowledge in mind.'

Allow yourselves to be humiliated and degraded, or success will be snatched away like a child's favourite toy.

How was this any better than the blackmail I'd snared Davina with?

At the interviews, they'd warned us Dorian was a constant exercise in breaking down in order to build back up. We would be made to act out animals defecating, all shame and embarrassment left at the door. Lead roles would be given, only to be snatched away on opening night, to steel against rejection. I'd even heard rumours of students forced to audition naked, back in the sixties, before even my mum's time, before the Office for Students caught wind of it. All in the name of greatness.

'And there won't be any consequences?' asked Fraser. 'For what we have our subjects do? Or . . . say?' He seemed nervous too.

'So long as it's within the confines of the law, yes.'

'Slapping a dick in someone's face isn't legal,' said Catalina indignantly.

'You're right. It isn't.' Drever fixed us all with a meaningful stare. Was he implying that pretty much anything goes? Were we about to go full *Purge*? 'I'm about to read out your pairings. If your name is called out first, you're the master first. Catalina, you'll be mastering Fraser.' Fraser's shoulders visibly sank with relief. 'Dominic mastering Erin. Nairne, Maisie. Penny –'

I held my breath so tight in my chest it became painful.

'– Davina.'

Of course. Of *course* it was Davina.

Had she convinced Drever to pair us up just so she could humiliate me? Had she asked to be the master second, so she could take whatever I'd made her do and boomerang it ten times worse?

As Davina crossed over to me, fear wrapped around my lungs like a leather belt, stiff and unyielding.

I'd spent the last few weeks wondering if the girl now standing in front of me was a murderer. Wondering whether she was about to murder *me*.

Now we were about to dive into a vicious mind game, and I didn't know if I had the strength to win.

All the tables and chairs had been pushed to the side of the high-ceilinged classroom, creating a kind of arena in the centre. Weak morning light washed through the bay windows, silvered by winter clouds. Davina wore legwarmers and ballet slippers with silent soles, gliding over the slatted wooden floorboards like the swans over the lake.

She stared at the spot on my face where the wound was almost perfectly disguised.

The twin pillars of anger and fear rose in my chest. She didn't care that I knew it was her. She *wanted* me to know, without ever truly knowing.

Around us, fellow students began merrily barking commands at their subjects. Most of them sounded fairly tame: *Play the air piano. Jump up and down like a frog. Cock your leg and pretend to pee like a dog.* Boundary testing. I heard Catalina, ever the innocent soul, order Fraser to sing a nursery rhyme of his choosing. Soon the room was filled with off-pitch 'Twinkle Twinkle' and other generalised tomfoolery.

Yet I couldn't move.

Davina stood a few feet in front of me and stared. Those pale eyes, like an Arctic fox, bore into me – daring me to do something, say something, flip a figurative table. And yet terror rooted me to the ground, as though dark vines had risen from the earth and wrapped around my ankles.

Over her shoulder, Dominic watched gleefully as Erin tied her red plaid scarf around her eyes as a blindfold. A subtle exercise in domination, beginning to be pulled along on a sexual undertow.

'Aren't you going to master me?' Davina said, cool and clipped and composed.

I was torn. If I was truly honest with myself, I wanted to

embarrass her, to make her feel as small as she so often made me feel. But I was also afraid of angering her further, given the gash on my cheek, the power she had over me. I didn't want to give her reason to end my life with a final carve through the canvas.

And yet I *hated* that I was afraid of her, because that meant she was winning. The marking of my face had been intended to terrify me, and I couldn't bear to give her the satisfaction.

'Go and kiss Drever,' I muttered, low and fast as an incantation cast before common sense could prevail. A sinister thrill tore through me like a gunshot. 'Tell him you've been thinking about him.'

Rather than looking angry, Davina's expression was one of gratification. She'd *wanted* me to make her do something messed-up. So she could justify what she was about to do to me?

Her tongue-pink ballet slippers glided over the wooden floorboards as she crossed to where Drever stood, arms folded, against his desk. Rather than under-baking the task, she cupped his jaw in her dainty hand and planted a passionate kiss on his lips. Other students turned to watch, gleeful entertainment written in their grins.

Davina ran her hand over his chest, his torso, his waistband, then purred, 'I've been thinking about you.' Every word dripped with fearless seduction.

I thought it would give me a lick of satisfaction to see her openly perform their affair for the class, and yet nobody seemed to take it in the least bit seriously. They thought it was all part of the game.

If anything, the line-crossing seemed to embolden my peers. Within minutes there was more kissing, more over-the-clothes fondling, some recreations of sexual positions. Subjects mounted each other like stallions. A sense of nauseous disorientation came over me, as though I'd taken some kind of hallucinogenic and couldn't escape the sickening phantasmagoria.

'Anything else?' Davina asked me sweetly, wiping her mouth on the back of her hand.

There was so much I wanted to make her do. I wanted her to smack herself in the face over and over, as hard as she could. I wanted her to run full tilt at the bay windows and smash right through. I wanted to hurt her, to make her a vessel for all the anger and shame and guilt I'd felt over the last weeks and months and years. I craved the release more than I'd ever craved anything.

Yet I couldn't do it. Call it a conscience, call it cowardice, but I simply couldn't do it.

'Time's up,' called Drever, before I could sling a final command in her direction. The hesitation felt like failure. 'Now the fun really begins. Subjects, it's time for revenge.'

'Take off your clothes,' Davina said instantly, as though she wasn't going to waste a single second of this power, and I hated her unfaltering assurance.

But not as much as I hated the command.

Nobody had ever seen me in my underwear before. At least not in recent memory – I had to assume my mother had bathed and changed me as an infant. She'd refused to get a nanny out of sheer paranoia, so convinced was she that any interloper in our home would leak all of her little secrets to the press. And even when I was at my closest with Samara, we never got undressed in front of each other. She was prudish, private, but then again maybe she already suspected I had developed the wrong kind of feelings for her.

I had always thought that this moment would be special. Choosing a person I loved and trusted enough to share my bare body with, watching their eyes light up as I unwrapped myself like a present, both of us fizzing and giddy with the anticipation. The lighting would be soft golden pools, lamps and candles and closed curtains, not sharp squares of grey daylight in a crowded classroom. It would be private and lovely. It was an image I held close to my chest, right up against my heartbeat.

And Davina had just stolen it from me. The promise of that first.

Because no matter how much I abhorred this command, I could not let her win.

My fur coat came first, then my jumper. My long-sleeved tee, then the thermal vest. The floral-embroidered jeans, and the fleece-lined leggings beneath. My Chelsea boots and childish socks – Piglet, from *Winnie-the-Pooh*. A gift from Samara, before she shut me out of her life.

I was colder than the surface of Mars, but I burned with quiet shame.

I couldn't look down. I couldn't bear to see my milky-white skin, my jutting bones, the gnawing wound in my ribs. The freckled plane of my stomach; the outie belly button. The scar on my knee from when I fell off the monkey bars in primary school. The private map of my body, all of it in the public domain.

Several sets of eyes lingered on me, the heat of them like spotlights. Normally I was an ornament on a top shelf, perpetually out of reach. An art exhibition for which nobody could afford the entry fee. But now I was a free-for-all.

What did they think of the cuts on my chest and collarbones? Did they think I'd done it to myself? The tortured daughter of an icon with her own dark secret?

Davina's gaze had brightened keenly, and I knew then that it would always be like this between us, a cruel push-pull, a constant attempt to conquer the other, the broken pieces of ourselves sharpened against the whetstones of our hatred.

Yet she still did not look below my collarbone. It was as though the most satisfying thing for her was the vulnerability, not the almost-nudity itself. Did she just *want* everyone to see what she'd done to me?

She studied each mark as though she were seeing it for the first time. I suppose, in a sense, she was. She'd only ever seen them on my portrait.

My portrait.

A thought struck me, diamond-clear.

How was she getting into the gallery in the first place? Did she have a key?

Maybe that's how I'd get her. I'd hide out in the Basil Hallward Theatre every single night until she showed up again, climbing beneath the stage as the rest of the campus slept.

And then . . . I wasn't sure what I'd do next. My mother's suggestion repeated in my head like the reverberations of a church bell. Could I restrain her, somehow?

'Now your underwear,' said Davina, yanking me back to the horrifying present moment.

Everything in me sharpened to a singular point of dread.

No.

I wouldn't do that.

I couldn't.

My mother had a famous full-frontal scene in a spy movie – the kind of iconic moment watched over and over by teenage boys in dark bedrooms around the world. I'd never seen it, but I'd always sworn it was a hard line I would never cross myself. Once those images are out there, they're out there forever. You can never take it back.

I couldn't quite describe exactly why the thought of total exposure filled me with tar-like horror. It just felt like a violation. Was it so wrong to want to keep parts of you to yourself?

Bodies are just bodies, but they're also *not*. Bodies are sex and power and identity.

Davina watched the emotions play out over my face. 'If you

don't, you will lose. You will know you don't have the stones to be here.' She nodded her head in Drever's direction. 'And the professor will know too. If you don't play the game, Lady Macbeth will be your first and last lead.'

Catalina was watching over Davina's shoulder, absolute fury on her usually bright face.

But I was a piece on a chessboard, and Davina had trapped me. A queen pinned to the king; I couldn't move in any direction without losing the game on the spot. And yet by staying where I was, I would be destroyed.

There was no way I could obey the command. And yet by not obeying the command, my future at Dorian would be in tatters.

Davina had won.

I grabbed my clothes in a hasty bundle and fled.

CHAPTER TWENTY-FOUR

All I wanted to do was run into the Crosswoods and hide forever.

I wanted to quit Dorian on the spot. I wanted to pack my bags and go home, except was home really a home at all? What else would I even *do*? The last half decade of my life had been pointed towards Dorian – a constant compass guiding me north.

And besides, my portrait would be left behind. An open wound that could be probed whenever a certain twisted hand so chose. A permanent executioner's axe hanging above it by a single thread.

I was trapped in every way.

That's where all bad decisions laid their seed, I realised. When the walls were closing in, and there were no better options, and survival instinct managed to convince you to save yourself first.

And so I don't know what I was thinking when I decided to confront Davina once more. I don't think I was *thinking* at all. It was a primal decision, not a cognitive one. A desperate animalistic urge to make sure she never dominated me again.

My mother's words echoed in my head unbidden.

You could take care of this Davina character yourself.

I hated that maybe she was right. That maybe this was my only option.

After the bell sounded for the end of the lesson, I stormed out of the bathroom stall I was hiding in and snuck back to the corridor in Drummond. I waited around the corner by a trickling silver water fountain, watching as the rest of the students filed out into the corridor and down to the atrium.

But Davina never came out.

Had she stayed behind to talk to Drever?

Before I could talk myself out of it, I crept down the now-deserted corridor and positioned myself just beyond the door, which stood ajar.

Their voices were clear as crystal.

'You took it too far, Davina. I *asked* you to go easy on her before I partnered you up. What the hell were you thinking?' Anger gave his voice a coarse quality. I recognised the timbre from one of his famous performances as King Lear. 'In what world was that going easy? She's already a flight risk. I can't lose another female lead.'

The words were a ridiculous sting of embarrassment.

'Penny doesn't need your protection,' Davina snapped. A long, loaded pause. '*She's* the one who blackmailed you.'

Well, there it was. An ace card played at the perfect moment.

Give Davina her dues, she was a great poker player.

'She was?' Drever sounded stunned by the revelation. 'How do you know?'

'I just do.'

'Compelling evidence.'

'Go to the library and see what she's printed out with her student ID if you don't believe me.'

A livid sigh. 'So that's what your little stunt was about. Revenge.'

'Surprisingly, no, despite the fact I eat revenge for breakfast.' A taut beat. 'You know those little cuts that keep appearing on my body? I wanted to see if she had them too.'

The revelation was a lurch.

She had the cuts as well?

But how . . .? Why?

'Okay,' replied Drever slowly. 'And asking her to remove her underwear . . .?'

A bitter laugh. 'Maybe that was for revenge. I knew she wouldn't do it. She's too uptight.'

Another whip of shame. I was beginning to regret listening in. And yet I needed to know more about what she meant – more about these supposed matching marks on her own body.

'So, hang on,' said Drever. 'Why did you think Penny would have the same mysterious markings as you?'

'A hunch.'

My mind juddered over the conversation.

If this was true, and she was also being maimed . . .

It would surely mean she was not the perpetrator.

But then again, maybe she was treating this all like a giant game of poker. Careful lies and sleight of hand, trying to coax certain information out of certain people. And somehow I didn't think she was above giving herself some tame little scratches to cover her own back.

Look, it couldn't have been me. I'm hurt too.

Did the logic work? I could no longer tell.

One thing I couldn't quite figure out was how much Drever knew, if anything, about the Gallery of the Exquisite. He'd seemed genuinely astonished by the state of Camran's corpse all those weeks ago. A total lack of understanding at how someone could look so much older in death. The disbelief that it was even her at all. But there was a chance Davina had since told him the truth about the twisted secret connecting us.

Would she have played that card yet?

'I'm worried about you,' Drever said softly, and the tenderness in his voice gave me whiplash.

'I know,' Davina replied, but her tone was cooler.

The romantic undertones raised another question: how did Drever know about the marks on her body? Were they now sleeping together – had she won him over at last? Or had she confided in him about the wounds in a moment of fear? Or a combination of the two – she was using her pain to manipulate his male instincts into protecting her?

'I should go,' Davina said. 'But I'll come over when you're done with rehearsals? There's something I need to talk to you about.'

Haring down the corridor before she found me lurking, I tried to process all of this, but there was too much material.

Every passing day raised more questions, and my brain was burning on fumes.

After skipping lunch to regroup in the library – in which I received approximately eight thousand messages from Catalina asking if I was okay – I walked into the rehearsal space several minutes late. All eyes snapped to me. There was a ripple of whispering, like wind through river rushes. I fixed my gaze on the floor and hurried over to a row of seats to dump my bag. I tried desperately hard not to think about the fact they'd all seen me mostly naked.

The saving grace was Davina's absence from rehearsals. At least I wouldn't have to face her victorious smirk.

'Just when you're ready, Ms Paxton,' said Drever coolly. Disdain was plain on his face.

He knows, I thought miserably. *It finally came back to bite me. And I deserve it.*

Dominic and Nairne – Banquo and Fleance – launched into Act II, Scene 1, and before long Fraser took the stage as Macbeth. I used the extra few minutes to skim over my lines for the next scene. We were supposed to be off-book by now, and yet the highlighted words swooped and dived on the page like moths I couldn't catch. Concentration was impossible when all I could think about was the conversation I'd just overheard.

Soon it was my turn to take the stage – in this case a series of electrical tape markings on the wooden floor, with lines and crosses mapping out where the various sets and sceneries would stand come showtime.

I forced my posture into something resembling dignity. "'That which hath made them drunk hath made me bold; / What hath quenched them hath given me fire. Hark –'"

Drever held up an irritable hand. 'I don't think there could be any *less* fire in that performance if you tried. We need emotional intensity, but you're stiff as a grandfather clock.'

Apparently there was no discernible difference between dignity and rigidity.

'I'm sorry,' I said.

'I don't care about sorry. I just need *more* from you.' His jaw was grinding, like a cow chewing cud. 'This is a pivotal scene in which we begin to understand the Lady's brutality and lack of conscience. She should be almost *giddy* from violence, with fleeting flickers of paranoia to foreshadow her eventual madness. It's the beginning of her unmooring.' He gesticulated wildly. 'As the scene goes on, she should scorn her husband's perceived cowardice, but there are layers of irony there too – for he has done something she could never do herself, and deep down she knows this. It requires a nuanced performance within a performance.' His hands fell to his sides. 'Are you sure you're up to the task?'

No.

'Yes.'

'Okay. Keep going.'

Fraser's Macbeth was robust, masculine, but with something vulnerable beneath it. "'And one cried 'murder' that they did wake each other. / I stood and heard them, but they did say their prayers / and address them again to sleep.'"

I tilted my head to the side ever so slightly while wringing my hands, aiming for that nuance, remembering how Davina had embodied the Lady in her audition without uttering a word. '"There are two lodged together?"'

'"One cried –"'

'Stop.' Drever's command was an executioner's axe come down. 'It's like a mountain and a molehill up there. Penny, you're being completely washed away by Fraser.' Fraser had the good grace not to look too pleased with himself. Instead he listened too intently to Drever's lecture, as though it were for both our benefits, and I felt enormously grateful to him for it. 'We should be beginning to understood that the Lady is formidable, a tour de force in her own right, someone to fear and respect as much as her male counterpart. And yet you play her as a shrinking violet. Where is the rough intensity you found in your audition? It's like watching another actor entirely.'

Forcing more acid into my performance, I proclaimed, '"These deeds must not be thought / After these ways so, it will make us mad."'

Drever pinched the bridge of his nose. 'Now you're overacting. If I wanted am-dram, I'd go down to the community theatre.' My cheeks burned. '*Nuance*, remember? Make it dimensional. Use all the colours in your palette.'

I knew, without him articulating it as such, that he was comparing me to Davina. This should have been her – the girl whose performance brought grown men to tears. Not some overblown amateur with a pretty face and no depth. An overblown amateur who'd snaked her way into a lead she didn't deserve.

Hunger grabbed my stomach in its fist, and naked shame rattled at my ribs, and I wanted to collapse to the ground and sob. But I needed to redeem some of the pride I'd lost today – to gather at least a few scraps of respect.

Focus. You can do this.

I tried to relinquish my obsession with nailing the iambic pentameter and just focus on the emotions of the scene. The veneer of superiority Lady Macbeth was trying desperately to convey, despite feeling like a scared little girl inside. That wasn't exactly hard to relate to.

"'Give me the daggers: the sleeping and the dead / Are but as pictures. 'Tis the eye of childhood that fears a painted devil.'" At the words, my concentration lapsed. The imagery chimed in my mind; there was an obvious similarity to current events. I dismissed it as coincidence, and tried to continue. "'If he do bleed, I'll . . .'"

I trailed off, all memory of the next line vanished from my brain. Drever, who had his thumb pressed to his lips in intense concentration, looked up, expectant. When I didn't continue, he made a rotating gesture with his hand: *get on with it.*

'I need a cue,' I muttered, loathing the meekness in my own voice.

Drever tossed his own script to the ground, then kicked over an empty paper coffee cup. 'This is beyond help. Take a break.' He stormed towards the exit. 'Take the fucking day. It won't make a difference.'

My ears rang with shame, the failures of the day clanging like bells.

I shouldn't be here, said the overriding voice in my head.

The stares from my classmates were, if possible, even more dogged than they had been at my half-naked body. What were they thinking? Did they pity me? Did they resent me, for bagging the lead when I so clearly didn't have the chops? Did they hate me, for spoiling a whole rehearsal? Which would be worse?

Slowly, like dazed fawns, the other students packed up their bags and filtered out – Maisie shot me a gleeful look as she passed, her pleasure at my downfall impossible to contain – until the only person left was Catalina. She'd taken Drever's seat in the director's chair, and was folding a page of her script into what looked like a lotus flower.

I felt immense relief at the sight of her, like I was a ship that had been thrashed by a storm and finally found a lighthouse. She was a reminder that not everything was cruel and bleak. I wanted to be around her all the time – and that in itself was terrifying. Being too hungry for love only ever pushed people away.

'Well, that could have gone better,' I said as I approached, trying to imbue some self-deprecating levity into the joke. In actuality, it just came out strangled. 'Someone could've drowned me in pig blood, for example.'

'Oh, Pen.' She stood up and gave me a sympathetic smile. 'Firstly, Drever is an absolute motherfucker, so there's that.'

I laughed from the sheer shock of hearing her curse. She rarely did. 'The motherfucker to end all motherfuckers.'

She nodded sagely. 'Lord of the Motherfuckers. The lesser-known Tolkien masterpiece.' She took a step closer to me. 'Are you okay? Does your face hurt?'

I shook my head. It was the truth. Other than the initial brutal sting of the wound, it had faded quickly to nothing. It behaved differently to normal cuts, somehow.

'You've done a good job of covering it. Although now I know it's there . . .'

She lifted a finger to my cheek, running it softly down the length of the gash. I shivered involuntarily, and for a moment I forgot to breathe.

'I'm scared for you,' she whispered.

Tears pricked at my eyes, warm and sharp. 'I'm scared for me too.'

In more ways than one.

CHAPTER TWENTY-FIVE

I awoke in the hour before dawn to a piercing scream.

A full moon hung low over the mirrored surface of the lake, round and silver as a ten pence piece, and a darkened figure knelt on the shore, shrieking like a wounded animal.

Blinking sleep from my eyes, I squinted through the arched window in my dorm room. With a sickening lurch, I recognised the long, spidery limbs and the short black hair.

Davina.

After what she'd done in the master and subject class, I should have felt a surge of joy, of satisfaction, at the sound of her guttural cries. But they cleaved right through me like a butcher's knife, and I threw myself out of bed.

Something was badly wrong.

Stuffing my feet into sheepskin boots, I tossed a trench coat over my pyjamas and hurtled out of the flat. The night air was so cold it felt solid, and the Great Lawn was slicked with dew as I sprinted down towards the lake.

Maybe she wasn't lying about her wounds, I thought fearfully. *Maybe she really is being maimed too.*

Which would mean she isn't the killer.

And I've misjudged everything.

A low mist gathered in the Crosswoods beyond, swirling with moonlight to cast a spectral glow over the grounds. Everything smelled of frost and silt.

As I grew closer, Davina's howls ebbed to a low sob, and somehow that was worse.

Breathless, I skidded to a halt beside her. Her head was in her hands, narrow shoulders shaking violently inside her leather jacket. Her knees pressed into the wet lakeshore, and damp was spreading up her black legwarmers – she must have been freezing.

'Davina,' I said, torn between softness and ferocity, the words coming out somewhere in between.

She stilled at the sound of my voice. 'Leave me alone, Penny.'

'No.' I pulled my coat tighter around me, teeth chattering. 'Are you hurt?'

Please don't be hurt.

Her hands clasped her face with a kind of fierce desperation, as though trying to hold her features in place. 'Just fuck off.'

'No.'

I wanted to drown her in the lake and hug her tight in equal measure. I didn't understand the latter instinct at all. I still burned with shame over the almost nudity she'd enforced on me. I still *loathed* her for making me lose the game. For tossing my entire future at Dorian into the gutter with a task she knew I'd forfeit. And yet the brokenness in her called to the brokenness in me, and the desire to share the burden was almost overwhelming.

Now Davina began hyperventilating, rollicking gasps wracking her whole body as she tried to take in air. Then she said something else, but it was so obscured by her laboured wheezes that I didn't catch it.

'What?' I asked. I'd been crouching beside her, but had to give in to my trembling muscles and lower my knees to the ground. The cold wet earth turned my silk pyjamas into ice in an instant.

Slowly, silently, Davina lowered her hands from her face, turning to face me.

My stomach heaved, and I fought the urge to cry out.

Her left eye was *gone*.

But there was no blood. The socket was simply welded shut, bisected by a ragged gash from the arch of her brow to the ridge of her cheekbone. Even in the silvery moonlight, it was clear the scar was a faded purple, as though the wound was weeks or even months old.

Planting a palm on the ground, I stared at the earth and fought to keep from fainting. My vision blurred, shimmering like mist and silk and shadows.

'Oh my god,' I whispered, bile stinging the back of my tongue.

I looked up at her again, dizzy and disoriented, the feeling of landing into a parallel world where everything was *wrong*.

Davina was shaking uncontrollably now. 'It's real, then. Not a nightmare.'

Pull it together, I told myself. *This isn't about you.*

Except it was.

I'd been so convinced it was *her* wielding the knife. So convinced that she was the villain. But I was wrong. Wrong about . . . almost everything. She hadn't killed anyone. She hadn't laid a finger on me.

'I'm so sorry,' I all but moaned. Blood thundered in my ears. 'I'm so fucking sorry.'

She covered her face once more, and my heart broke for her. She started murmuring lowly, urgently, like a litany. 'Not my eye. Please, not my eye, I – it can't be gone. No, no, *no*. I'll do anything.'

My skin prickled with vicarious dread. 'Does it hurt?'

A frantic sob. 'I felt the blade, I – it doesn't make sense, there was no real knife to my face. How can – *arghhhhhhh*.' She drove her fingers through her black pixie-cropped hair, grabbing desperate fistfuls of it.

'Were you awake?'

She shook her head fiercely. 'The pain woke me up pretty quickly.'

'And you came here?' My stomach was gripped in a vice, threatening to empty at any moment.

'I don't know why I was compelled to.' She dropped her bone-white hands into her lap and stared out to the eerily still water. The swans barely caused a ripple as they circled hypnotically. 'It was like my feet dragged me of their own accord.'

I thought of the ghost story whispered in Lawrie's standing lesson, back when the September heat shimmered on the water. A student out swimming, back in the late nineteenth century. Beaten unconscious by swan wings, sinking to the bottom of the lake. By the time help arrived, her body was nowhere to be found.

Whether it was true or not, there was something badly wrong with this place.

'I didn't even scream, at first. I thought it was a dream.' Her whispering voice rose an octave. 'It *has* to be a dream, Penny. It has to.' I'd never heard her sound so young.

A strange kind of protectiveness came over me. I grabbed her by the shoulders, looking at her straight on, not flinching at the sight of the wound even though I so badly wanted to. 'We're going to find who did this.'

Because she was a victim too. We were on the same terrible side of this. We had both made the same ill-fated decision, and we both bore the wounds of that catastrophic error in judgement.

But she wasn't in the right place for a rally cry, a plan of action. That devastated disbelief had descended on her once again, and the trembling intensified. She once again began praying to a faceless deity. 'No, no, no, *please*, please don't be real, please –'

'Davina . . .'

Then she fully loosed her emotions, let the pain and anguish and fear roll out of her in visceral screams. She dug her fingers into the earth, dragging deep claw marks along the shore. 'No, no, no, no . . .'

A new breed of terror sank into my bones. Somehow, the fact that Davina wasn't the murderer felt a thousand times scarier than when I'd believed she was. Better the devil you know than the devil you don't.

The ghostly swans on the lake watched with funereal ambivalence. Fear gripped me by the ribs as I ran a finger over my own savage warning scar.

The message was clear: if we didn't find the killer soon, we would be next.

But why? Who hated both Davina and me enough to want us dead?

CHAPTER TWENTY-SIX

Maisie and Fraser walked into the kitchen to find Davina, Catalina and me sipping coffee and whispering in low voices. By the look on Maisie's face, she might as well have walked in on Beelzebub nibbling cucumber sandwiches at a teddy bear's picnic.

The early morning was sharp and sunny, the Great Lawn frosted with a glittering layer of ice like a festive cookie. In the cold light of day, Davina's missing eye was even more abjectly terrifying: a sunken socket, that awful gash. Catalina had fashioned a makeshift eye patch out of a long strip of cotton torn from a pyjama top.

'What's going on?' Maisie asked from the doorway, still as a buzzard hunting prey.

'Nothing.' Davina was visibly shaking, and trying too hard to stop, so her whole body was rigid with tension. 'We're just talking everything through.'

'What happened to your eye?'

'We got in a fight.' Davina gestured stiffly to the brutal mark on my face, which I hadn't bothered painting over this morning.

In reality, I'd taken Davina by the arm and ushered her up to Catalina's room just after midnight. I trusted my flatmate not to panic, not to scream at the missing eye, just to offer care and comfort. That's exactly what Catalina had done. She had laid down her earlier anger towards Davina, talking so softly and soothingly that it almost brought tears to my eyes. Yet as I watched her rub Davina's ridged back, murmuring that it was going to be okay, I hated myself for the jealousy I felt. It felt too much like watching my aunt Polly coo over baby Pippa.

Catalina had also tried to insist we go to the hospital, but Davina had refused. It wouldn't make the slightest bit of difference. The eye was gone. And how on earth would she explain how it happened?

Eventually Davina's distraught wails had ebbed to feeble whimpers, and with every passing second, the debauchery of the master and subject class became less and less important. Because really, all she had ever done to me was yank out a lock of hair and dare me to take my clothes off. That was it – the only concrete acts of antagonism I could think of. Everything else had been smoke and mirrors. Confirmation bias, on my part. Once I had decided she was evil, I had arranged all the pieces of the story to fit my theory.

But I was wrong.

The real killer was still out there.

And we were both in the crosshairs.

Maisie took a few steps into the kitchen, retying the fluffy belt of her dressing gown. 'What were you fighting about?'

Davina shifted on her stool. The tap dripped behind her. 'Nothing you need to worry about.' There was a note of dismissal to her tone, as though Maisie had ceased being of value. 'Now kindly piss off, won't you?'

The words were a shock of fire, so needlessly cruel that for a second I felt vindicated for how much I hated her.

Fraser took a few steps forward, like he was shielding Maisie. 'Alright, bro. We're not having you coming into our flat just to shit on people. Maze was just making sure everyone was okay.'

Davina rolled her eye. 'That tracks. She's always got her nose in other people's business.'

She seemed at once like a cult leader, toying with her subjects' emotions for the sport of it – a way of asserting her authority, of cementing her position as doyenne. Still, there was something endlessly compelling about her, in the same way horror movies and serial-killer documentaries were compelling. Equal parts grotesque and fascinating. The theatre of cruelty personified. I felt lightly electrified that she was here in our kitchen, no matter how grim the circumstances.

Yet I still felt horrible for Maisie. I pictured her birdwatching in a wild garden with her grandfather, asking excitedly about the different types of sparrows. We were all still just kids. *We're all playing a part*, as she'd said in the library. She didn't deserve this.

Thankfully, Fraser had her back. 'Nah, we're not having this. You're leaving. Now.'

Davina fixed him with a cruel glare. Then in a low, cutting voice, she snarled, 'I know where you were last night.'

Fraser stilled for a moment, a breath hitching in his chest, then turned on his barefoot heel and stormed out of the kitchen.

Maisie shot Davina a filthy look then tailed off after him, saying, 'Fraze? Fraze. Are you okay?' His bedroom door – the one nearest the kitchen – banged shut.

Something in my gut twisted at the fresh poker card Davina had played. Even Fraser was hiding something?

'That was slightly unnecessary,' said Catalina, sipping her tea.

Davina scoffed. 'Oh yeah, I'm just the Wicked Witch of the West, aren't I?'

A protective instinct bucked inside me.

Say something mean to Catalina, I growled inwardly. *I fucking dare you*.

But she didn't. She clearly wanted to save her other eye.

'What do you know about Fraser?' I asked her. I was reluctant to give her the satisfaction, but I had to know whether our flatmate was someone we should be worried about.

Fraser kept strange hours. He was out most nights, and while it could have been that he was always partying, he didn't stink of stale booze the way he had during the first couple of weeks. He napped for a few hours in the evenings after rehearsals before heading out with an oversized sports bag over his shoulder, despite not playing for any of the Dorian teams. I sometimes heard him return around three or four in the morning. And yet during the day, he didn't seem to have a discernible group of friends outside of us. He ate lunch with us in the Costumery, and studied in the library alone.

'I'm keeping that card close to my chest for now,' Davina said coolly.

I frowned. 'But if he's out every night . . . couldn't *he* have something to do with the gallery? With the murders? Your eye? You've clearly antagonised him.'

She shook her head. 'He doesn't. Just leave it, Penny.'

'I still think you both should go to the police,' Catalina said quietly. Tiredness clung around her eyes. Her cardigan had slipped off her shoulder, and I made out a handwritten tattoo snaking over her collarbone. *Haz el bien y no mires a quién.* I didn't know what it meant, and that embarrassed me more than it should. 'This is all so dangerous, and you're victims.'

Davina lifted a shaking hand to the makeshift eye patch, as though confirming to herself that it had really happened. She'd been doing it all morning. 'What detective in their right mind would believe us about what's happening?'

'And my mum . . .' I trailed off, but Catalina winced in understanding.

'Your mum what?' Davina prodded. It was strange, having her show an interest in my life.

'My mum's worried about all of this getting out,' I said quickly, before Catalina could tell her the truth about my mother's suicide threats. 'Her portrait is down there too.'

Catalina chewed the inside of her cheek. 'I don't know what else you *can* do, though, other than go to the police.'

'Find the fucker ourselves.' Davina drained the last of her coffee.

'How?' I asked.

'We go down to the gallery, night after night, until they resurface to strike again.' Her skin was ghost-pale, almost blueish, in stark contrast with her red-rimmed eye. 'We catch them in the act. Maybe we can hide somewhere and film it, so the police *have* to believe us about how this is happening. Or we take them down ourselves. Self-defence, isn't it?'

I shook my head. 'Even if we were willing to put ourselves in danger –'

'– I'm pretty handy with a knife.' Davina's hand went to the pocket of her leather jacket, patting the surface. 'We'll be fine.'

'Of course you are.' I gave her a tight smile. 'But that aside, we don't have a key to the gallery.'

'Oh, I have a key,' said Davina matter-of-factly.

'How?'

'Stole it from Camran's office.' Her knee bounced up and down, powered by fraught energy. 'When Drever was calling the ambulance, and you left the room. It was in the top drawer of her desk.'

Residual suspicion prickled in my mind like a nettle sting. 'Why did you take it?'

'I suspected that her death was because of the portraits, and knew I might need access to that gallery in order to save myself.'

Catalina studied Davina cautiously now. 'Have you used it?'

'Not yet.'

Something occurred to me, then, as I thought back to that night in Camran's office.

'Davina . . .' I said slowly.

'What?' she snapped, almost automatically, like an impulse she couldn't control.

I fought the ridiculous urge to laugh. She wasn't an evil murderer. She was just kind of a bitch.

'How much does Drever know?' I asked. 'About the Gallery of the Exquisite. The Masked Painter.'

She shrugged. 'Nothing. There was no reason to tell him.'

'Did you see him last night?' I was careful to phrase it as a question – she couldn't know I'd been listening in on their conversation.

Her remaining eye narrowed. 'I did. Why?'

'Did anything . . . happen?'

I wanted to know what exactly they'd talked about. Because I had a theory.

Her gaze drifted out of the window, to where the swans glided over the ice-blue lake. 'I ended things, actually. He'd served his purpose.'

My heart started to beat a little faster. 'How'd he take it?'

'He was angry. Said I'd ruined his life for nothing.' She shrugged again, as though none of it mattered at all, as though people were just games to win or lose. 'He'd fallen in love with me.'

Ruined his life seemed a stretch.

The thought I'd had on the edge of the moon-dappled lake came back to me: who hated both Davina and me enough to want to hurt us?

'Did you ever tell him it was me who blackmailed him?' I asked slowly. Of course I knew she'd told him yesterday, but I had to hear it from her.

'Yeah. After he lectured me for going after you in the master and subject class.'

'And there's no way he could have known earlier? And just not told you?'

She shrugged. 'I mean, he could've made an educated guess. I don't know how much of our altercation he saw – after you took the picture. What are you thinking?'

'The killer had to be someone else with a key,' I muttered, low and fast. 'What if Orlagh and Drever were close? Maybe she'd shared the secret of the gallery with him. Cut him a copy of the key in case something happened to her. And . . . his contact card was the last thing she'd looked up on her Rolodex before she died.'

Catalina was listening to all of this with wide, shining eyes. 'So you think Drever might have killed Orlagh.'

I turned to Davina. 'Is there a way she could've found out about you two? Threatened him, maybe?'

'I suppose,' she replied. 'But –'

'Look, why else would he have said you "ruined his life for nothing"? If the only consequence was recasting the lead in a play, I'd hardly call that a ruined existence.' I felt electrified by my string of realisations. 'But if he'd taken an innocent life just to protect the secret . . .'

A vague horror started to play out over Davina's marble-white face. It reminded me of her Lady Macbeth audition – the fear writhing inside her like a feral beast, affecting her every movement. 'But what about Van Der Beek and Barr? Why would he have killed them?'

The second and third murders were the two that didn't fit neatly into any theory, so I zoomed out and looked at it with a broader lens. 'Same as most serial killers, I guess? Did it once and liked the way it felt?'

She adjusted the makeshift eye patch tied around her head. Her movements were timid, careful, hyper aware of her injury. 'So why not kill us too? Why just maim?'

'Maybe he's a sadist. He gets off on our fear,' I mused, again employing that wider scope in the absence of concrete evidence. 'He's toying with us before the killing blow. Men have done far worse things to far more women. It's not totally beyond the realms of possibility that he enjoys inflicting pain. Do you think he's that kind of guy?'

'I don't think so.' Davina's words were like stepping stones over a river; she tested each one for stability before moving onto the next. 'He's the kind of sap who'd risk his career just to save me from sleeping in a cold car. But then again, I've watched enough documentaries to know it's always the ones you least expect.'

Catalina had started nervously folding origami boats from a

stack of book receipts she'd found in her wallet. There was already a fleet of around twenty littered across the coffee table.

'So what are you going to do?' she asked. 'If it really is Drever – but you can't go to the police . . .'

Davina's knee jerked even more erratically. 'Look, I think we should go down to the gallery tonight. Even if we don't catch him, we can take our portraits down and hide them somewhere else. Then at least we'll be safe from mutilation.'

I swallowed hard, my throat ragged as a cliff edge. 'What scares me is that . . . even if we catch Drever, and he's somehow arrested and charged and sentenced, we still don't have a way to remove these anchors. I don't want to be rooted to that painting any more.'

'You want to age?' Davina asked, incredulity puncturing the words. 'Grow imperfect?'

'Not especially,' I admitted. 'But it can't be any worse than this. It's not just the wounds, either. I went to the sitting freezing and half starved. That's how I've felt ever since, no matter how many blankets I wrap myself in, no matter how much food I eat. I feel half mad from it, like a starving wolf.'

Davina stared at me for several beats. 'Me too.'

'You too?'

'Not so much the cold,' she murmured. 'But the hunger. I've been hungry for as long as I can remember.'

There it was.

Even though I'd suspected it of Davina – with her sharp bones and ballerina limbs and feral glare – the confirmation still filled me with despair. I thought of how different the three young women sitting in this kitchen were, and of how absurd it was that we were all, in some way, connected by the same stupid, meaningless demon. Of how even the most strong-willed among us still found herself fixated on something so trivial.

We were bright and young and brilliant, alive with glittering promise, and yet we went to such extreme lengths to keep ourselves small. No matter the cost.

'How fucked up is this?' I said with a bitter laugh. 'The things we'll sacrifice to be beautiful.'

Davina grimaced. 'Girls don't want beauty. Girls want power. And sometimes beauty is the closest substitute.'

I let this idea sit for a moment. My conversations with Orlagh, Catalina and now Davina had followed similar paths. They had all explored the idea that the thing we truly wanted wasn't actually beauty. It was whatever we believed beauty could buy us.

Sex. Identity. Power.

Love.

Suddenly Davina winced, a short sharp sound with anguish appearing abruptly on her face. Her hand raised to her eye again, and her posture sank around her core.

'Are you in pain?' I asked, leaning towards her. I'm not sure what I planned to do, but the instinct was there, to lay a palm on her forearm.

'I'm fine,' she said fiercely, with the distinct air of someone who was not fine at all. 'I still hate you, by the way.' There was an air of performance to the sentence.

'I know,' I said evenly, feeling a little sad for her.

She was an enigma I felt compelled to disentangle; a yarn I yearned to unravel until I found its beginning. I wanted to understand why she was like this, so tightly coiled with hatred, so barbed with defence mechanisms, and yet, in reality, she was a little girl putting on a big show. I wanted to draw a map of our shared ground and chart a path across it. I wanted to understand her, to shine a light on her good parts, because we were so similar that it might illuminate my own.

Catalina began talking once she was sure our contrived exchange was over. 'I want to help you both. Really, I do. It's just that the thought of going down to the gallery scares me, and I don't think physical fighting is my strength, as badass as my DnD character is.' She made the final fold in another receipt. This boat somehow had a mast. 'But maybe I can help you another way. I'm a skilled researcher. I can try and find the Masked Painter, learn as much as I can about this very peculiar magic, so we can free you from the suffering.'

I smiled. 'Thank you.'

'So it's settled, then,' Davina said, climbing to her feet with an aura of adjournment. 'Penny and I will go down to the gallery tonight.'

'Tonight,' I agreed, feeling like someone who'd just agreed to walk a tightrope over a gaping crevasse.

Just one false step from falling to my death.

CHAPTER TWENTY-SEVEN

In the Basil Hallward Theatre, Davina and I had to wait for the second years to finish their rehearsals before we could sneak below the stage. We took a seat in the back row where I'd sat weeks earlier, right after discovering Orlagh's dead body. And despite the fact that I was there with the fiercest adversary I'd ever had, I couldn't deny that it felt good not to be alone.

We sat in terse silence, half listening to Hero and Ursula discussing Benedick's love, until, with a visceral jolt, she let out another involuntary whimper. One hand went to the makeshift patch over her missing eye, while the other dug its fingernails into the velvet arm of the chair between us.

'Are you okay?' I asked softly, resisting the urge to rest my hand over hers. Her moan left an echo in my chest.

'I'm fine,' she snapped.

I knew beyond all doubt that she wasn't fine. I couldn't imagine the pain she was in – not to mention the awful permanence of her injury. The impact on the way she moved through the world. She was a ballerina – that loss of depth perception, of peripheral vision . . .

But from everything I knew about Davina, coddling

and cooing wasn't the way to go. And so I opted instead for distraction.

'What's the plan?' I wrapped my fur coat tighter around me. 'Once we get down there?'

She nodded gratefully. 'Well, as long as our portraits are still there, we can take photos of them, and our matching wounds. And of the dead subjects' ravaged paintings too. It'll at least be proof of *how* it's happening, if not by whom. Then I guess we hide out for a while, behind that screen in the corner. And hope Drever – if he is the killer – comes down tonight. Film him slashing the portraits so we can take the evidence to the police.'

The police. The only place all of this could end. The only people who could really bring Drever to justice. Did that mean I was fated to lose my mother no matter what? Would she really follow through on the threat?

Maybe we'd be able to have Drever charged without digging up the distant past. There was no need to bring the original Masked Painter into it, after all.

Or we could seek our own justice, as Davina had suggested. But I didn't think I had the stomach to take Drever's life.

Whorls of dread snaked around my lungs like adders. 'What if the slashes he makes tonight are fatal? Should we just sit back and let it happen?'

Davina considered this for a second. 'If it's one of *our* paintings, we'll have to confront him. Like I said, I'm good with a knife.' She tapped her front teeth with her fingernail. 'But anyone else . . .'

The callousness stole my breath. But then again, I supposed we'd *have* to let it happen, so the evidence was airtight enough to seal a guilty verdict, despite the absolute lunacy of the method and the weapon.

It was already going to be a stretch, I realised, to get the police on board with this theory – let alone a court of law. At this point I'd come to accept these cabalistic happenings at face value, despite the fact it all defied the laws of physics, of reality. But for a court of law to comprehend it . . .

Through the abstract musings appeared a sudden bone-chilling realisation.

'What about my mum?' I asked, so quickly the words rolled into one.

'What about your mum?'

'Her portrait is in there too.' My stomach cramped uncomfortably. 'If he approaches hers, and it looks like he's going to kill her . . . what do we do?'

Davina's expression betrayed no emotion. 'That's your call.'

Would I throw myself in harm's way to save my mother, no matter how much I hated her? It was a more complicated question than Davina could ever know.

Unless, of course, she did know. We were so horribly similar.

I took a few extra breaths before my next question, feeling the chilled, dusty air of the theatre expand in my chest. 'What about your parents?'

She stilled beside me. 'What about them?'

'Who are they?' The questions already felt like an intrusion, and yet I found myself burning to know. 'What's your relationship with them like?'

'Dunno. I grew up in care.' From the way she said it, it was as though she had to exercise great self-control to say the words at a normal speed, instead of rushing over them as quickly as possible.

'Oh. Were you ever . . .?'

'Fostered? Yeah. Twice. The first time, when I was five or six, actually went pretty well. It was a couple who already had a biological kid, and they wanted to do something *good* to complete their family. They treated me well. I think they loved me, actually.' She swallowed hard. 'But then I started acting up when I was eleven or twelve. I don't even know why, really. But yeah, they ended up sending me back.'

I panged for her. 'That's awful.'

'My own fault, I guess.'

'No, it's not,' I insisted. 'Parental love should be unconditional. They wouldn't ditch their biological child if things started to get hard.'

'Whatever. It's in the past.' She shrugged, but it was so far from casual that I felt almost embarrassed to be witnessing her careful performance.

On the stage, the Watch of Messina gathered to discuss their policing for the night. Dogberry's malapropisms were butchered by a skinny student with shaggy black hair.

'You said twice,' I pushed on. 'Who were your next parents?'

'Parents is a stretch. They took in a boatload of teenagers for the money. I shared a bed with three other kids. Super fun as a fourteen-year-old girl. I left when I was sixteen. Got myself a scholarship at ballet school, and there was a boarding wing so I stayed there. I worked in a bar at weekends, saved up enough to buy myself driving lessons and a car at seventeen. I slept in it during the holidays.'

No wonder she was so wrapped in barbed wire. 'Do you know who your biological parents are?'

'Nope.'

Another similarity we had semi shared, until recently. I hadn't known who my father was, and it had gnawed at me for decades.

The second years finished off their run-through of Act III, and seemed to decide that was quite enough for one night. They hoisted rumpled backpacks on to slim shoulders and lolloped towards the exit, not paying Davina nor me any mind.

'Let's go,' I muttered, once their echoing voices faded from the lobby behind us.

We made the trip through the trapdoor and down the corridor to the gallery in taut silence.

When the narrow passageway opened out into the cavernous room, I could not stifle the gasp.

It was exactly as we had thought.

Camran's picture hang in tatters, the slices matching precisely the wounds on her body. I hadn't seen Van Der Beek or Barr in death, but theirs too were ravaged by a feral blade, the canvases almost entirely shredded as they hung side by side.

The wounds were so wild and imprecise that surely, *surely* the police suspected something sinister. And yet to what could they possibly attribute those strange, seemingly old wounds on the corpses? What knots were they tying themselves into trying to explain this to the victims' families?

And then there was me – and Davina.

We hung side by side, her portrait only hours younger than mine.

At the sight of the laceration over her eye, Davina sank to her knees.

In my own, I barely recognised myself. This was not how the portrait had originally looked, when the paint was still fresh.

Harsh cheekbones jutted through my skin, hollow pockets sinking beneath the razor edges. My skin was pallid, sickly, and there were purple bulges beneath my bloodshot eyes. There were nicks and notches all over my neck and collarbones, and one glaring cut across my face – careful, considered, clean compared to the furious slashes on the others. A calculated wound. For some reason, that chilled me more.

As hideous as she was, the girl in the portrait looked how I truly felt. Starved, exhausted, terrified for her life. I felt a surge of sympathy for her. She looked so young.

I could've stared for hours, but I was keenly aware that Drever could appear at any moment. Davina was still crouched on the ground, as though worshipping at the altar of her own suffering, so I spurred into action. I took photos of my portrait, of Camran's and the other victims, and of Davina's over her shoulder. Then I tucked my phone in my pocket and crossed back to my painting, closing my fingers around the edges of the gilded frame.

But when I tugged – gently, at first – it held firm to the wall. I tried to lift it upwards, imagining it to be fixed by a hook, but it didn't give. Even when I put my whole weight into it, gripping tight and yanking back, it stayed welded to the wall.

Doom gathered in me, dark and churning. A small part of me had hoped we'd at least be able to remove our paintings from the gallery – so that even if we couldn't free ourselves from the shackles, we could keep them safe from further disfigurement.

But the Masked Painter, wherever he was, had not lied.

The anchor was, in all meaningful ways, permanent.

CHAPTER TWENTY-EIGHT

'We should get behind the screen,' I said eventually. 'In case Drever shows up.'

Davina climbed to her feet, pale and dazed, as though seeing the portrait first-hand had made the loss of her eye real. Her movements seemed suddenly clumsier, more laboured, like her body too had finally caught up with the change in depth, in space, in peripheral detail. I offered her a forearm to grab on to, and she looked at it as though she'd never been so patronised in her life.

Once we were behind the fabric screen, she leaned against the back wall of the gallery with her legs stretched out in front of her. Her palm rested over her empty eye socket, fingernails digging into the white skin on her forehead and cheek. As though the eye was still there, hanging by a thread, and she was trying to hold it in place.

The silence between us was jittery, uneasy.

'You know what you said earlier,' she muttered at last. 'Nobody's ever said that to me before.'

I frowned, not following her train of thought. 'Said what?'

'That it's not my fault my foster parents abandoned me.'

Her chest rose and fell with precise breaths. 'And since we hate each other, I don't think you have any reason to lie to make me feel better.'

'I meant it.'

More silence, in which I felt the oppressive weight of the icy lake press down on us from above. There was a distant dripping noise, and the frenzied scuttle of nearby rats, but no footsteps echoing down the corridor towards us.

'Have you ever . . . spoken to anyone about it?' Davina asked. 'Professionally, I mean. The famous parent shit.'

'No. Mum wouldn't allow it. Too paranoid. She didn't trust the client-privilege.' I swallowed. I'd always thought her paranoia was totally irrational, but she had her skeletons to conceal. Her arcane beauty. The murder of my father. 'And I had no way to pay for it discreetly. We might be rich, but she's very controlling of how I spend money. She wouldn't bat an eyelid at a five-grand handbag on the credit card bill, but a single therapy session would make her cut it up in front of me.'

A rattling scoff. 'And it was beneath you to get a job, right?'

Her tone was a scalpel against exposed skin, but it was also hasty, automatic. The barbed wire she'd willingly wrapped herself in.

'I think part of me doesn't *want* to get help,' I continued, as if she hadn't spoken. 'All the trauma is woven into the fabric of my identity at this point. I don't think I'd be who I am without it. Sometimes I worry my whole personality is just "messed-up daughter of an icon".'

The confession sat between us like a dead body propped upright – cold and tragic and absurd.

Davina half smiled, half grimaced. I expected her to mock me, but instead she said, 'It's like the ship of Theseus paradox. If a ship has all of its component parts replaced one at a time, is it still the same ship as before? If I fix all the parts of me that are broken – if I replace them with something shiny and new – am I still the same person as before?'

I pictured myself as a caravel battered by a storm. I imagined a captain gazing up from the harbour, deciding not to try and mend the broken parts, just out of some vague sense of identity. How maddening that would be to the crew.

The paradox might not have directly offered an answer – such was the nature of paradoxes – but at least the metaphor showed me the insanity of my own flawed reasoning.

Of *course* I was worth fixing.

'I'm sorry for what I did,' I said evenly, picturing myself lifting up the closest shattered plank to assess the damage. 'Blackmailing you with that picture. If I could take it back, I would.'

'Well, obviously,' she snarked. 'Look where it's got you.'

An epiphany came to me like a physical blow.

That's where it all started: the word RECAST printed on a damning photo.

If I hadn't made that terrible decision, I would never have entered into Camran's mentorship. And I would never have had my portrait painted. And there was a good chance that

Camran, Van Der Beek and Barr would still be alive. That Davina would still have her eye.

Because if Drever really was the perpetrator . . . he was driven by hatred of me, and latterly of Davina. Without that initial blackmail, he wouldn't hate me at all.

The idea was so profoundly terrifying – that one bad decision from one scared girl could unravel so much of the world around her.

Tears began to spill silently down my cheeks; the guilt, the shame, the self-hatred became too much to contain. Davina didn't notice, at first, but when my shoulders shook and I sniffed fiercely, she turned to look at me.

'Oh, for god's sake.' She gave an elaborate, exaggerated sigh. 'What's wrong?'

'All of this is my fault.' I gestured to the ruined portraits.

She looked at me like I was an unbelievable narcissist. 'How?'

'If I hadn't done what I did to you, none of this would've happened. You'd still have your eye.'

She snorted. 'Unless you took Drever by the hand and forced him to lift the blade, no, it isn't your fault.'

'You don't have to try and make me feel better.' A fat, salty tear trickled over my Cupid's bow and over my chapped lips; a hot sting. Next to Davina's deliberate composure, I felt like a child sobbing over a lost teddy.

'I promise I don't care about you enough to do that.' She kicked one ankle over the other. 'Look, this is a thought experiment, right? How far back does blame really stretch? How strong is the link between cause and effect and culpability? You say it's your fault for pushing Drever towards a certain action, but what pushed *you* towards that action? Your mother's shittiness? Okay, so what pushed *her* into being shitty?'

'The Masked Painter.' I pressed the heels of my hands into my eyes in an attempt to stem the flow. 'Her portrait anchored her to the worst mental and emotional breakdown of her life.'

Davina shook her head. 'You're misunderstanding. Maybe it was the Masked Painter's brush who created that anchor, but what pushed your mother towards that decision in the first place? Her own mother? Society?'

I let this seed of an idea sow itself into my mind, and after a few beats, it began to flower. 'When you put it like that, is *anything* really our fault?'

The thought filled me with a kind of existential relief.

'Not wholly, anyway.' Davina wrapped her arms around herself. 'Of course we have to believe that our actions matter, and we should take responsibility for them. But evil deeds are not created in a vacuum.'

There was a hawkish keenness to her intelligence that I hadn't expected. It made me want to rise to meet it, and yet I found I had nothing of equal intellect to say. It was the same feeling I'd had back in Camran's office – awe mingled with an acute self-hatred.

But maybe it *wasn't* self-hatred. Maybe it was regret. At the things I had wrongly prioritised. I'd put so much value on my exterior that the interior had been sorely neglected. My thoughts had never been given enough space to broaden, to deepen, to develop long tendrils of curiosity.

I was too busy just being hungry.

When I thought about how I felt playing chess – the thrill of it, seeing the perfect move, a glittering rush through my body that felt almost like self-respect – that's what I wanted more of. It felt rewarding in a far deeper, more textured way than thinness did. And when I was fencing . . . it was so different to running, which felt like monotonous punishment. Fencing was all adrenaline: the euphoria of winning and losing. Joy for joy's sake.

Things would be different, I promised myself.

If I got out of this alive, *I* would be different.

'I guess we've both given each other something tonight,' I said, voice rough with emotion.

'What's that?' She sounded almost bored by comparison.

'Permission to forgive ourselves.'

She made a *pfft* noise. 'Definitely not. I'd like you to keep beating yourself up.' Yet there was something lighter than usual in her voice – a kind of jocularity to her normally acerbic wit. A clown with a sad face painted on.

When I didn't respond, she added hastily, 'I'm kidding. You deserve a better mum.' A long, taut beat; a drumstick hovering over a cymbal. 'You deserve to be loved.'

It was as though all the oxygen was sucked from the room; as though my heart had been plucked from my chest by a divine hand. Something dark and morbid inside myself momentarily healed.

Because she had no reason to lie.

She had no *reason* to say something like that to me.

And yet she had.

She had vocalised the one thing I had never truly believed, because the person who was supposed to love me with the fire of a thousand suns simply did not care about my existence either way. I'd always felt like I'd failed some mysterious test as a child, and that the universe would therefore withhold love from me for all eternity. A punishment simply for being who I was. Beyond all hope or redemption – unless I could be perfect.

And yet here was Davina, the girl who hated me more than anyone else had ever hated me before, who had been on the receiving end of my greatest imperfections, saying something like that to me.

You deserve to be loved.

The idea was dizzying, intoxicating, heady with possibility.

Before I could respond – although how could I ever respond to that? – she cradled my chin between her thumb and forefinger, tugged my face gently towards hers, and brushed her lips over mine.

What – ?

Everything in me jolted. I was stunned by it, like a flash-bang had just gone off. Blinding light, ringing ears, a sense of disorientation.

Pure, raw shock.

And then the exhilaration flooded in.

I kissed her back, with more heat to it than I intended, remembering how it felt to first lay eyes on her, the impossibility of her beauty, the magnetic field surrounding her. And now I was *kissing* her.

I laced my fingers through the short crop of her hair and pulled her towards me, marvelling at the softness of her lips, the tingle of her tongue; all the while a sense of euphoria coursed through me like an electric current. A deep, tremulous thrill.

I was kissing *Davina*. The most talented person Dorian had ever seen. The girl so wrapped in barbed wire nobody could ever get close.

Except *me*.

Maybe there was something special about me after all.

I could get into Dorian. I could have Davina.

I was someone.

Her teeth grazed my lower lip, her grip tightened on my jaw until it was almost painful, and something rich and aching began to pool between my legs. My heart bucked in my chest – with nerves or longing, I did not know. Kissing her felt like pressing down on a bruise. I couldn't tell if it was pain, or pleasure, or a potent mix of the two.

Some distant part of me felt guilty. Because in the very depths of my chest, nestled in the place just between my ribs, I knew I really wanted Catalina. I knew my feelings towards her had swelled and deepened. But I also knew that it would destroy me if she didn't feel the same, and I lost her the way I had lost Samara.

Davina was here, now. And despite everything we had done to each other, she wanted me.

I was *wanted*.

Her spare hand traced a fingertip along the ridge of my collarbone, down the curve of my breast, over the peaks and troughs of my ribs, until it came to rest over the top of my waistband. The hook of her thumb through my belt loop, the gentle tug, was enough to unravel me. Goosebumps covered the flat plane of my stomach in seconds, and I shivered involuntarily.

Pressing her palm flat against my hipbone, she pulled the top of my jeans down ever so slightly; ran a finger over the red-laced edge of my underwear.

'Do you want me to?' Her voice was the brush of costumier's satin against bare skin.

Perhaps it was the thrill of having someone like Davina seduce me. Perhaps it was the promise of pleasure after so many months of physical discomfort. Perhaps it was just lust, pure and simple. But I knew, with a singular chime of truth, that I wanted her hand to slip lower more than I'd ever wanted anything.

I nodded, shaking almost uncontrollably, my breathing too loud even to my own ear.

She unbuttoned my jeans with a practised precision. A light flick was all it took.

I gasped at the cold of her fingertips against the softness of me. The touch, so light and yet so sharp, a thousand times more vulnerable and intimate than when I explored myself. She traced the outline of me, dipping into my own wetness before tracing tiny circles over the place where heat was building. The heel of her hand pressed into the expanse of skin and bone above, and I throbbed against it.

Falling into a light rhythm, her other hand slid under my jumper, under the lace band of my bralette, and tweaked me with almost too much force. I gasped, and her eyes glinted with satisfaction.

She was playing me like an instrument, every note crystalline clear, building to an inevitable crescendo. I began to melt into her, to feel myself tightening and pulsing around her hand.

And then –

Rrrripppppp.

'Davina,' I murmured, a gasp, a plea, a warning, and just as I was withdrawing myself – an inelegant backwards scuttle – there was a vicious noise from somewhere in the gallery.

We both stilled, her hand held in the air over my thigh like a claw, fear creeping across her face.

Rrrripppppp.

Canvas shredding beneath a blade.

Horror bloomed inside me; an unfurling blackness.

We hadn't heard footsteps.

It was a miracle I hadn't whispered her name loud enough for the person on the other side of the screen to hear.

Making as little sound as I could, I pulled my phone out of

my fur coat pocket. With it came the tiny origami lion Catalina had given me as we walked across campus. Despite the fear lurching in my chest – or perhaps because of it – the intricately folded paper made me yearn for her.

I cupped it in my palm. A talisman. A reminder of why I was worth saving.

Rrrripppppp.

Another violent shredding of canvas from the other side of the gallery.

Were we about to die?

What would my final thought be?

I couldn't hear anything else – ragged breathing, the squeak of footsteps – over the roar of blood in my temples. I had never in my life been so afraid of something I could not see.

Switching my phone to record mode, I leaned slightly to the side, so that my right eye could just peer around the edge of the screen.

The sensation of a missed step.

There was nobody there.

Unless I just couldn't see the killer from this angle . . .

I tilted my body even further to the side until I had a view of the whole gallery.

It was empty.

Had I imagined the noise?

No. Davina had heard it too. She was still frozen to the spot with the fear of it.

Eyes frantically scanning the room, I did a quick inventory

of the paintings to see if any had been damaged. They were all as they had been before, but –

No.

Angus Arras.

There were three furious stab marks on his chest – one directly over his heart.

His portrait was right by the entrance. Had the killer slipped quietly out after the fatal blow?

Confusion spiralling through me, I lifted my phone and began recording in case they returned.

That's the only reason I caught it. The fourth wound. That's the only reason, in the days and weeks to come, that I knew I wasn't losing my mind.

Rrrrippppppp.

Straight through his mouth, bisecting his lips.

It appeared as though from nowhere – apart from the slightest bulge in the canvas the moment the knife wound appeared.

A burst of silvery light, seemingly emanating from the canvas itself.

And then nothing.

'Impossible,' I breathed.

'What is it?' Davina asked, quieter than I'd ever heard her speak.

It couldn't be. And yet . . .

'I think the killer is behind the portraits,' I whispered, still breathless, still throbbing, my mind spinning off the edge of the world.

CHAPTER TWENTY-NINE

'Thank god,' exclaimed Catalina, as I walked back into the flat without Davina. 'I was so worried.'

And then her arms were around me, and my face was pressed into the soft skin of her neck, and she smelled of fresh-baked cinnamon buns. A lock of her hair tickled my nose, but I found myself not wanting to pull away. I wanted to collapse into her, the safe haven of her, but I felt that if I did I might start crying and never stop. I wanted to apologise to her, but I wasn't really sure why.

'You were?' I asked, ears still ringing, limbs still trembling.

'Davina's alright too, isn't she?' Catalina looked behind me, as though expecting my nemesis-turned-*something* to appear in the doorway.

'She's fine.' My mouth was dry and rough. 'Just wanted to get some rest.

'I was a coward not coming with you.' She pulled away and looked me up and down, checking for injury. Behind her, the kitchen counters were laden with baked goods on cooling racks – cardamom buns and cinnamon swirls and something that looked distinctly like a birthday cake. 'If anything had happened . . . god, I would never have forgiven myself.'

'Why?' I frowned. It wouldn't have been her fault. Not even by the elastic reasoning Davina and I had stretched in the gallery.

She squeezed my upper arms, then turned to flick the kettle on. 'Because I care about you.'

The way she said it was so honest and easy, with not a shard of barbed wire to be seen. What must it be like, to feel so safe and justified in your own emotions? To share them with such candour, without fear?

'What happened?' she asked, grabbing a few mosaic-patterned side plates and piling them with one of each of her bakes. 'You are okay, aren't you?'

'I'm okay. So is Davina.' The memory of our intimacy burned in me, hot and viscous, almost shame-like in texture, but I didn't have the bandwidth to unpack it.

In one breathless rush, I rattled off everything that had happened in the gallery – except, of course, Davina's hands on me – before showing Catalina the footage I'd captured of Angus Arras being carved up from *behind* the portrait.

'So the world will wake up to news of his death,' I finished, studying her stunned face. 'God knows how the police are going to explain it away this time. They must already be scratching their heads after Lyle and Celia.'

'Behind the portrait.' Her Spanish accent was coming through stronger, as though the shock of the video was pulling her back to her roots. 'The killer is . . . behind the portrait?' Killer like *keeler*.

'I don't know how it's possible either.' I took a huge bite of cardamom bun. It was delicious – floral with rose petal, warmed through with complex spices, with a punchy sweetness that melted over my tongue. 'If you don't open a bookstore-bakery someday, by the way, it'll be an immense loss to the human race.'

She was too bewildered to acknowledge the latter part, absently brewing her pot of tea. 'Maybe there's a series of tunnels that wrap around the gallery, and someone has found a way to access them from the back. That way they can kill without ever being caught.'

'I guess that's possible.' I wiped my icing-sticky hands on my jeans. 'But we didn't hear any footsteps at all.'

'The earth is packed tight around there. It likely muffles sound.' She watched my face carefully. 'What are you thinking?'

'I can't put my figure on it,' I replied slowly. I replayed the video on my phone, pausing at the precise part that was playing on my mind. 'It's the way the canvas almost bulges around the knife. Wait – no. It's the way there *is* no knife.' The realisation was the flicker of a forked serpent's tongue. I held up the paused screen. 'See? When the gashes appear – if a killer was slashing through from behind, you'd see the tip of a blade, wouldn't you? But there's nothing.'

I quashed the despair welling inside me with another cardamom bun, still warm from the oven. A kind of giddy euphoria came with it – even though I knew they wouldn't satiate me, I was *eating*. And the fear, the sense of failure, hadn't yet caught up to me.

Because what did it matter if I ate a damn sugar bomb? If the portraits couldn't be removed from the wall, and the anchors were permanent, and the killer was somehow behind the portraits . . . how could I ever save myself? It was only a matter of time before the warning wound on my cheek manifested more fatally. All the starvation in the world couldn't give me power over that.

'It doesn't make any sense.' Catalina chewed the inside of her cheek, causing the now-familiar pucker on either side of her lips. 'I've always believed there's something out there that goes far beyond what the human brain can even imagine. And yet this is proof. It's *proof* that there's something else out there, and I still can't process it.' The words themselves were wispy, ethereal. 'Unless . . . no. It can't be real.'

'Unless what?'

'While you were down there, I checked a few books out of the library about the history of Dorian. I started reading through one to distract myself – by Basil Hallward, who founded the school.'

'I thought you were stress baking?' I gestured to the cakes.

'I can do two things. Anyway, my thinking was that if there was one secret tunnel snaking away from the theatre, what's to say there weren't more? What if there was somewhere Drever could lie in wait, away from the eyes of the rest of the campus? What if there was a secret entrance to the gallery that we didn't know about – a trick wall panel or something? I thought that even if we couldn't catch the killer that way, maybe we could try to block off the entrances to keep the paintings safe. Seal the gallery, so to speak.'

'And?'

She shook her head, a corkscrew curl tumbling loose of its tortoiseshell clasp. 'I couldn't find anything along those lines, really. A lot of the so-called "history" seemed to be myth and legend rather than, like, architectural drawings. And much of the folklore concerned the paintings and mirrors on campus. This piqued my interest, of course, but there was no mention of the Masked Painter or the Gallery of the Exquisite. The author did posit, however, that the paintings and mirrors were not only haunted, but also sentient and interconnected.'

I frowned. 'Sentient and interconnected how?'

'Like a huge, pulsing organism existing alongside – weaving through – the campus. There was a lot of nonsense, honestly, and it was hard to decipher what the author was actually saying. Half of it was pseudo-intellectual ramblings about the philosophy of liminal worlds, and another quarter was a recounting of a personal experience with one of the huge mirrors in Drummond – he'd been physically unable to look away from his own reflection for thirty-six hours, because he was wholly convinced there was something wrong with it. An uncanniness to his own appearance. He wet himself right there on the staircase without noticing. And there was another anecdote about a student throwing an egg at a portrait of her professor, and a bump appearing on the forehead of another portrait across campus.'

I pinched the bridge of my nose. I was so tired, and none of this made any sense. 'Catalina, what in the ever-loving fuck are you talking about?'

'Among all that waffle, there was an analogy that stuck with me.' She strained the tea leaves and placed a steaming turquoise clay mug in front of me. 'Are you familiar with how trees communicate through mushrooms?'

I blinked at her, bemused. 'Is this a hippie van-life thing or a science thing?'

'Both. My parents used to talk about how all the trees in a forest are entangled in complex symbiotic webs of interbeing. They constantly communicate with one another through the enormous fungal networks that live in their roots. It sounds like an acid trip, but it's actually been reputably proven. They have this whole invisible underworld that allows them to move and live as a single organism.'

'I'll never look at mushroom risotto the same way again.'

Despite the situation, Catalina couldn't help the impulsive bark of laughter. 'Did you just make a joke?'

'I did.' I nodded sagely. 'I'm not sure I care for it.'

A broad smile spread over her face. 'Anyway, this book's author proposed that a similar kind of symbiotic system had developed between the paintings and mirrors at Dorian. Allowing them to communicate, to live and breathe as one. To feed on decay.'

I ran my finger over the top of a cinnamon swirl, and licked at the orange-peel frosting. 'I don't understand. What are they communicating? And what do you mean *living*?'

'That's just it. The same way that communication between trees is largely beyond human comprehension, so is the supposed central organism of Dorian. It's like a colony of ants watching the construction of a superhighway – they fundamentally do not possess the intellectual sophistication to process the how, let alone the why.'

Unlike when Davina and Camran said things I didn't quite understand, I didn't feel the same sense of self-loathing with Catalina – more of a twinkling, albeit disquieted, curiosity.

Because . . . perhaps I *did* understand. Not in a way that could be articulated through words and hypotheses, but in a deeper way – one carved from experience, from feelings of ill content.

I thought of the silhouette I'd seen in the foreground of the mirror in Drummond. And in my own bathroom, the way the mirror seemingly glitched, back when I was examining the wound on my face. How it had flipped sides for a split second; that reality-defying lurch, the feeling of the floor yanked from under me. The not-quite-right colour of my eyes.

Speaking of eyes . . . I remembered the arctic-blue glare seemingly peering through my bedroom mirror. I'd been so sure it was Davina somehow.

None of it quite made sense, and yet it made perfect sense. I thought of ambulance lights illuminating the paintings in Drummond, the way their backgrounds shifted and stirred in unnatural ways, as though a torch was being shone into the den of a mythical beast and awaking it from a long slumber.

And I wondered.

'So how does any of this relate to the Gallery of the Exquisite?' I asked. 'And the paintings being destroyed from behind?'

Catalina was quiet for a long while, before eventually murmuring, 'Maybe there isn't a killer. At least not in the way the human brain can understand. Maybe the organism has fed on decay for so long that it's destroying itself from within.'

Dread lurched in my chest, like a falcon trying to take flight without realising it was chained to the ground. 'And in turn, it's destroying us?'

She nodded, face pale in the moonlight. 'That's my fear.'

'So how do we stop it?' I asked, a creeping urgency in the words. Almost a plea – I was subconsciously begging her to know the answer.

'I think we'd have to do that from the inside.'

'How?'

A solemn headshake. 'I'm sorry. I have no idea.'

A vast, empty helplessness sprawled out inside me, underpinned by an aching exhaustion. And as much as I wanted to stay with Catalina, eating cakes and making bad jokes about the situation, I had the burning urge to be alone. To unpack the chaotic events of the evening. To try and wrap my head around everything she had just told me.

'I'm going to try and get some sleep,' I murmured.

Catalina stared out on to the Great Lawn, which rolled

away from Abernathy like a dark magician's cloak. 'I don't think I'm going to be able to sleep. Maybe I'll go back to the library. Do some more research.'

Surveying the mounds of sweet treats dotted around the kitchen, interspersed with textbooks and research papers and her own hastily jotted notes, I was overcome with a wave of emotion – gratitude, and awe, and something richer still.

'Thank you,' I said, swallowing the lump in my throat. The words seemed so insubstantial. 'Your brain astounds me, you know that? The way it makes sense of such enormous ideas.' A strange, wistful smile twisted across my face. 'I wish I was more like you.' And it was true. If I could be like anybody else in the world, it would be her.

'Hey,' she murmured softly, clattering an icing-coated wooden spoon into the sink and crossing over to me. She took my hands in hers, fixing me with a meaningful gaze. 'Don't say that. I mean, I'm pretty great. But you're an amazing person, Pen. You have a heart like a train. And I'm glad to know you.'

Don't cry. Don't cry. Don't cry.

The charge between us grew as our eyes did not shift from each other. She moved her head towards me the tiniest fraction, an almost imperceptible tilt, and something in my chest soared – like a great bird spreading its wings over a vast plain.

But no matter how wonderful the sensation, I couldn't act on it. I squeezed her hands in return, tucking the urge to kiss her into my back pocket. It would've felt cheapened, somehow, after what I'd done with Davina in a moment of frenzied lust.

'Have fun in the library,' I whispered. Disappointment fell behind her eyes like a curtain as our hands parted. I smiled, then winked. 'I won't wait up.'

The last part was a joke – a light-hearted barb at how the library was better than any party, for Catalina.

Little did I know how much I would live to regret it.

Because by the next morning, she was gone.

CHAPTER THIRTY

Clawed hands shook me awake.

'*Penny.*'

Davina's fuzzy black hair was haloed by the blood orange of the sunrise.

'You're in my room,' I said, bleary from sleep. 'Why are you in my room?'

A few hours ago, those hands were very, very elsewhere.

'Something's happened.' She crouched to the ground on her haunches. 'Maybe. I think.'

'Be more specific,' I grunted, reaching over to my bedside table to take a sip of peach iced tea. My throat was dry as baked clay.

Abruptly she stood up again, and began pacing the narrow strip of floor between my bed and my pine desk. 'I couldn't sleep, so I went to make myself a cup of coffee. I saw a figure by the lake, through the window. I don't know why, but I had a bad feeling. How late it was, the way the figure just stood and stared . . . it was like what happened to me the night I lost my eye. I ran out there, but by the time I got to the Great Lawn, the figure was gone.'

My stomach clenched and unclenched, as though my

nerves didn't know how afraid to be. 'Okay . . .'

'I found this on the shore.'

She dug a hand into the pocket of her leather jacket – hastily thrown over silky black pyjamas – and pulled out something that made my heart stop.

An insulin pump.

There was a crashing sensation in my chest, like the rubble of a building hitting the ground after an earthquake.

'Catalina.' The word came out as a choked sob.

Davina laid the insulin pump on my desk, and I stared at it like it was a hand grenade. 'I can't find her. She's not in her room.'

'Have you tried calling her?' The suggestion seemed so simple, so commonplace, that it was almost absurd.

'I don't have her number. Can you?'

Hand trembling, I fumbled for my phone and tapped Catalina's name.

Straight to voicemail. As if the phone was at the bottom of a lake.

No, no, no.

No.

Something bad was happening. Something very, very bad.

'What was she doing by the lake?' Davina peered out of my window, clutching the sheer white fabric of the curtain with taut knuckles. 'Does she swim?'

'Never. She said she was going to the library to research the portraits some more.'

Had she had some kind of breakthrough?

One that had led her down to the lake?

Had the lake . . . summoned her, somehow? The way it had lured Davina on the night she lost her eye?

Did that mean Catalina was injured too?

It couldn't be in the same way Davina and I were wounded. She didn't have a portrait.

Still, the thought of Catalina being hurt . . . it felt like reading a news story about a natural disaster. So tragic it was physically painful. So horrendous my brain bucked against it.

But the fear carried with it an altogether fiercer force. A desire to protect her, to keep her safe, to stand in the line of fire and take the hit for her. To lift up the car she was trapped beneath; to grab her by the hand as she fell from a cliff. It was a bolstering sensation, hot and tempestuous, roiling with desperation.

Think, Penny.

I launched myself out of bed, grabbing discarded clothes at random and tossing them on over my pyjamas.

'We have to go down there.' My mind reeled. 'That day in Lawrie's class, when you were drawn to the swans. How did that feel? Do you have any conscious memory of why you were doing it?'

'I still don't know,' Davina admitted. 'It's a bit of a blur. I was just kind of . . . drawn to them.'

Several large puzzle pieces arranged themselves in my mind. 'The ghost story,' I said slowly, yanking a jumper over my head and stuffing my feet into some boots. 'The girl in the nineteenth century. And the liminal world?'

Davina glared. 'Please try to make more sense when you speak.'

As fast as I could, I summarised Catalina's theory about the pulsing organism behind the portraits and mirrors. A fungal network that fed on decay. A liminal world destroying itself from the inside out.

'So then, the ghost story. The girl was swimming in the lake when a swan attacked her, wasn't she?' I muttered, pressing my palm against my forehead as though it would make me think harder. 'It beat her with its wings and she sank below the surface, unconscious. Someone saw from their dorm window and ran to help, but she'd vanished. Her body was never found. What if it isn't just a ghost story?' My brain was tripping over itself, like a runner in too-big shoes. 'What if the lakebed . . . what if it's some kind of entry point to this supposed liminal world? And the swans are . . . *guardians*?'

It was, I had to confess, an outlandish idea, but everything in me was alight with certainty. If one of these absurd things could be true – if you could anchor your soul to a painting and render yourself immortal – then why couldn't the liminal world? Why *couldn't* the lake be an atrium?

'The girl was getting too close,' murmured Davina. 'Elsbeth Owens. She went swimming, and got too close to the entrance. That's why one attacked her.'

NO SWIMMING – SWANS DANGEROUS.

'Could that possibly be true?' I asked. 'Or is it too mad?'

'No madder than the rest of it.' She was staring at me with a strange expression. Her makeshift eye patch had been replaced by a neater felt one she'd bought online – black, with a tarantula embroidered in tiny silver beads. It seemed almost comical that she'd chosen the beast she knew I was afraid of. Like a kid picking out the scariest Halloween mask they could find, believing it would genuinely frighten their parents. 'So you think if we swim deep down into the lake, it'll just . . . keep going? It can't, can it? It's right over the gallery. It definitely has a bottom.'

I started towards the door. 'There's only one way to find out.'

Davina knew, without words, what I planned to do.

Go in after Catalina.

Please don't let anything bad have happened to her.

Please don't let her have drowned.

Please, please, please. I'll do anything.

I didn't even know who I was begging and bargaining with. I knew only that if I started crying, I might never stop. And so I had to take action instead.

I wrenched my bedroom door open – only to find Maisie standing on the other side.

'What's going on?' A pair of binoculars hung around her neck. Had she been out birdwatching so early in the day?

Almost panting with fear, I looked back at Davina, who shrugged back at me. As if to say: *Tell her. You might as well.*

But I didn't get the chance.

'Catalina's missing, isn't she?' Maisie voice was small and scared. She was scrubbed free of make-up, wearing a pair of wellies and a waxed coat several sizes too big for her. She looked as young and out of her depth as I felt.

Davina frowned. 'How did you know –?'

'The walls aren't as thick as you think. Does this have something to do with the alumni deaths?' Maisie pointed to me, then Davina. 'With your face, and your eye?'

I nodded fiercely. 'Yes, but we don't have time to explain. We have to go and help Catalina. We think she's in the lake.'

Maisie dropped her small backpack to the ground, then her binoculars. 'I'm coming with you.'

'It's too danger–'

'I'm. Coming. With. You.'

Her face was pale but stoic. Determined.

The three of us headed towards the front door, only to hear a key scratching in the other side.

My heart leaped in my chest.

Catalina? Was all of this just a misunderstanding, and she'd gone for an innocent walk with her phone switched off? If she walked in that door right now, I would throw my arms around her, I would hug her so tight, I would nuzzle my face into her neck and tell her I was so glad –

But it wasn't Catalina.

It was Fraser.

Fraser, wearing a full face of drag make-up. False lashes as thick as tarantula legs, elaborate eyeshadow in pink and purple and red glitter, overdrawn lips the colour of a blooming fuchsia.

All at once, everything made sense. The scattered sequins and traces of make-up on his face when there had been no fancy-dress parties. The feather boa slung over the sofa in the kitchen. The general sense that he was hiding something.

At the sight of us standing there, he stopped dead.

'Errrrr. Hi.' A sheepish grin, followed by a shrug of the shoulders. 'Coco Coxx. Nice to meet you.'

Davina sighed. 'Damn it. A poker card I never got to play.'

'Fraser, you look fucking fabulous.' Maisie gave a camp little finger snap. 'But Catalina's in trouble. We're going to help her. That's all the detail I have at the moment.'

'Roger that.' Fraser dropped his sports bag by the door in a puff of glitter. 'I'm coming too.'

Despite the terror of the situation, something warm spread through my chest. I'd never had cavalry before.

For the first time in my entire life, I did not feel alone.

And so, as the sun rose golden over the stark black Crosswoods, together we strode towards the lake where Catalina was last seen, hoping beyond all hope that we were not too late to save her.

CHAPTER THIRTY-ONE

The cold outside was so raw, so absolute, that it almost burned the skin. It was a miracle the lake hadn't frozen over.

Up close the boathouse was in even starker disarray, the royal-blue paint sloughing off like dead skin, the smell of damp rot creeping at its ramshackle feet. The doors hung off their hinges. The whole place smelled of decay; I had no idea how I hadn't noticed sooner.

This had to be the seam between the liminal world and the real one.

It *had* to be.

Standing barefoot on the silty shore, I yanked my clothes over my head, then kicked off my bottoms. For the second time in the last few days, my classmates were seeing me half naked. This time, I didn't care. Because it was on my terms, and because I was doing it for Catalina.

Davina tore off her nightwear next to me. 'Do we have a plan? I feel now's the time to mention that I can't swim.'

I nodded. 'I'll try and get to the bottom of the lake. You try and fend off the swans, if they come for me.'

She pulled a knife from the jacket she'd just ditched on

the shore. Maisie and Fraser looked at us as though we were quite mad.

Clutching the knife blade-out in her palm, we both took the first step into the lake. The coldness of the water was a savage bite; a pain that scrubbed me raw.

I steeled myself, thinking of Catalina. The way the sun illuminated her corkscrew curls. The way her bronze eyes gazed at you as though you were the most fascinating creature ever to exist. Her hands on mine, soft and warm. Her furrowed brow as she folded origami, or measured icing sugar, or read a dense textbook.

The thought of her was like having a candle glowing in my chest, only now I had to watch it flicker and wane, terrified that it would soon blow out.

It was my fault she was caught up in this. I could handle the cold if it meant making this right.

The further we went in, the worse it got – especially around the waist – until the ice water was no longer our biggest problem.

The spectral swans glided over to us, somehow luminescent. Four of them, looming larger by the second. Dawn light threaded through their silver feathers, and their eyes glowed a peculiar obsidian, which shouldn't have been possible. Blackness was not supposed to be backlit.

The hissing from their throats was guttural, monstrous, raking over me like claws or teeth.

I swallowed hard. 'I don't think we're in danger until they raise their –'

The frontmost swan lifted its wings like an angel straight out of hell.

And charged straight at me.

I toppled backwards into the water, gasping at the freezing shock of it. Water stung at my eyes. I could barely see. In the blurred darkness there was an enormous splash, a hissing shriek, a grunt from Davina. And then limpness.

Please don't be her, I thought, but when I rubbed the water from my eyes, I saw one of the huge birds floating on its side, its neck black with blood. The oily crimson seeped into the water around us, staining our pale skin pink.

I fought the urge to retch.

'What the fuck!' Fraser yelled from the shore.

The other three swans charged towards Davina in a semicircle.

'Go!' she yelled at me, both of us past caring who woke up and witnessed this hideous onslaught.

'But –'

'Don't let this be for nothing.' Her lips curled around her teeth as she fell into a boxer's stance.

With one last look at her – bone-white limbs, burgundy lips, black pixie hair, narrow chin raised defiantly – I took a deep breath and dived below the surface of the water.

I wasn't the strongest of swimmers, but adrenaline powered my feral kicks until I was far enough from the swans that I could no longer hear the struggle. I ran my palms over the lakebed; it was surprisingly soft with silt, dotted with pebbles and something slimy.

Not the entrance to the underworld. Just a regular lakebed.

Stupidity pressed in on me like the water itself, but I pushed myself further into the middle of the lake, where the water was deeper. The bottom of the lake curved away from my hands, and despite kicking myself further down, I couldn't find it again. I was absolutely blind, the darkness rendering the water wholly opaque.

I burst back through the surface, choking back the earthy water I'd accidentally swallowed. Treading water, I looked back to the shore where Davina was still embroiled with the swans. Another had fallen, but she was still outnumbered.

Panic crested in my lungs. This plan was hastily conceived, and thus far poorly executed.

What if she lost her life over this?

But no. She couldn't – because the portrait made her immortal.

Unless . . . the supernatural swans had more power than we'd reckoned with?

A threat we had failed to calculate, like a sudden back rank checkmate on a chessboard.

I watched helplessly as another swan beat its ferocious wings in her direction.

This time, they struck true.

Davina sank below the surface of the water in a surge of air bubbles.

'Davina!' screamed Maisie, tearing off her coat before wading in.

Fraser threw himself into the water, cutting his way through it in a confident front crawl.

I had a choice. I could go back and help them save Davina – would two of them be strong enough to fend off the swans bare-handed? – or I could keep searching for Catalina.

Catalina, who might already be dead.

Drowned.

The mental image of her bloated corpse was enough to drive me downwards.

I had to act. Now.

Sucking in air slowly, I let my lungs stretch and expand deep into my belly, until I could no longer hold another breath. Then I sank back below the surface, this time angling myself towards the bottom centre of the lake.

The deepest point.

I kept swimming in dogged breaststroke until my palms hit the floor, but it was more of the same: satin-silt, slick pebbles, something rough and sharp like a crab's grip. Tendrils of seaweed floating ambivalently in the current my body was creating.

Kicking back up to the surface, defeat was already weighing heavy on my lungs. I swam into a more central position – imagining the lake's bullseye from a crow's view – and repeated the process.

Hit bottom. Nothing promising. Back to the surface.

Swim to a better position. Try again. Repeat.

I could no longer see Davina or the swans; my vision was blurry with the effort of treading water, of holding my breath for almost a minute at a time. There was a distant male shout. Fraser?

I had to trust they would be okay. Safety in numbers.

After three more tries, my blood howled through my limbs, and I knew I only had one more attempt before I passed out. If I kept going, there's no way I'd be able to get myself back to the lakeshore.

Deep breath. Dive.

Swim, swim, downwards, downwards, trying to fight the terrifying disorientation of the black water.

This time, my hands took far longer to meet the floor.

My heart surged, thinking perhaps I'd found it, the seam between our world and the liminal space behind the portraits.

But then my finger juddered against rock, and all the hope died.

Catalina. Catalina. CATALINA.

Please.

I manically clawed at the lakebed as though I could dig my way to her, until my vision vignetted dangerously.

I'd been underwater too long. I had to get back to the surface.

But I'd been underwater *too long*.

And for the first time, there felt like a very real chance that I would not make it.

As I pushed frantically upwards like a frog, my lungs were burning, burning, burning, so brightly I felt like I might implode from the pain.

But the pain began to ebb away, dim and soften to a gentle

throb, and that frightened me more. My limbs floated away from me like tendrils of seaweed drifting on a current. My sight bleached furious white, and the fight slid away from me like a waning tide.

It felt like dying.

Oh.

Maybe that was the point, I realised.

Maybe to pass through, I had to let myself enter a transient state.

After all, isn't that what the portraits were? Transient beings, trapped between life and death, existence and non-existence?

Perhaps that was how Elsbeth had passed through this impermeable membrane. She was knocked unconscious by the swans, unable to fight for her life. She let herself drift away, and the ether welcomed her in. And the same might have happened to sweet Catalina.

Could it be . . .?

Was this my way in? Or was I just delirious?

It was a risk.

The greatest risk there was.

The surface was a few more kicks away. If I gathered all my strength and gave it one final surge, I might make it. I could gasp in sweet lungfuls of crisp morning air.

But there was no other way to save Catalina – or myself.

I knew that deep in my bones, in my flesh and sinews.

So I succumbed.

I opened my mouth, let my lungs fill with water, let it weigh me down from within.

Let the beating of my blood fade to a feeble whisper.

After a few long, peaceful moments, the darkness opened its maw and swallowed me whole.

CHAPTER THIRTY-TWO

I choked awake.

There was water in every pore of my body. I was swollen with it, rasping and delirious. I coughed and coughed and coughed, until the coughs became vomit and I soaked my lap with silty lake water.

And then I looked up and around.

I soon wished I hadn't.

It was a labyrinth of portraits and mirrors.

Except the portraits were not human busts and faces; they were the *backgrounds* of portraits. Abstract swirls of colour and shade, peculiar textures and planes of smoothness, shapes and patterns that never seemed to solidify into anything recognisable, all refracted and repeated by vast swathes of silvered mirrors.

I looked down to find that the floor was not the floor at all, but rather a reflection of the sky, which was itself the mirror image of the earth.

I vomited until there was nothing left.

Clambering to my feet as though my bones were made of gelatin, I cast my gaze frantically around, trying to see where there might be a path. A way forward, if not out.

Out.

How was I ever going to get out?

I couldn't think about that now. I just had to find Catalina.

I heard no sobs, no wails. Just silence so absolute it was like death itself.

One step at a time. Don't look up or down, just around.

But it was impossible. The walls of the labyrinth shifted and swirled the second I locked my sight too firmly on them. In one I thought I saw a silhouette of a bust, the outline of a person, but they vanished into nothing as I stepped towards them.

Ears ringing, I reached out my arms and grazed my fingertips over the nearest wall. It seemed to shiver and shudder beneath my touch, then morphed from an abstract fern-like swirl into the rugged peaks of a mountain range from above, then into a mirror clouded with a curious fog.

At the sight of what was inside the mirror, I bit back a scream.

A little girl of no older than four sat cross-legged on a marble floor, a wooden chess set splayed before her. She wore pink denim dungarees, a sunflower T-shirt, and a look of intense concentration, nose scrunched and brows furrowed as she studied the board in front of her.

And she was bald.

Memories flooded my brain like a river burst its banks. Memories I had no conscious knowledge of ever repressing.

Of course.

I'd had alopecia as a child.

How could I have forgotten?

My hair fell out, almost overnight, when I was two. The doctors didn't understand why. By my fifth birthday, it had miraculously grown back, thick and lustrous, the copper of molten coins.

When it first fell out, I don't remember ever particularly caring – I was a kid, and my appearance was the last thing on my mind. Why would I have worried about such a thing, in a world where there was chess, and books, and cartoons?

As I watched Kid Me make a killer knight move in a game against herself, tears stung at my eyes. She beamed, big and bright, then looked around hopefully to see if anybody saw her genius. Her whole body sank when she realised she was alone.

My heart ached and ached at the sight of her, at the thought of all the pain I would later inflict upon her. How could I tell this little girl that I was going to let her starve? How could I tell this little girl that she was worthless without her hair?

This sweet, innocent, lovely little girl. I could not imagine taking a scalpel to her bones – nor could I fathom explaining to her why I wanted it to happen.

I was so perfect before the world told me otherwise.

Trembling, I planted my palms on the mirror, letting my breath fog up the silvered glass.

Could I pinpoint it – the exact date or age at which I learned the importance of beauty? Was there an axis point, a tip of the scales, a hinge between childhood innocence and *this*, me, now? Or was it more of a slow indoctrination, an airbrushed magazine cover, a skeletal catwalk in Paris, a barbed comment from a boy in school? An unflattering photo, a lack of control, a vague sense that I needed to punish myself. An article about acid peels, or toxic injections, or celebrities who'd had ribs removed just to be a little smaller. An exercise in mimicry in order to fit in – copying my friends as they picked at lunches, as they pinched their stomachs in bathroom mirrors, their behaviours ingrained from their own mothers, their own sisters, their aunts and cousins and grandmothers.

Where did it all begin? And what was it all *for*?

The answer floated to the surface of my mind like a dead body in a lake.

My mother had always taught me that beauty was my most valuable currency, and in a sense it was.

It's just that the money – the power – did not flow towards me. It flowed towards the billion-dollar industries. It flowed towards the diet clubs, the shapewear brands, the detox teas. Even my beloved fashion houses, the make-up empires, because really, where were the lines drawn? It was all built at the altar of beauty. Empowerment was just a pretty lie we'd been sold to keep us feeling good about the sacrifices we made day after day. Life after life.

My grandmother, meticulously measuring herself with a pink dressmaker's tape, and my mother, observing, internalising. A generational curse passed down like a set of ancient pearls, impossible to escape from once they were hanging around your neck.

The truth was clearer than ever, and I could never unsee it.

I had sold this little girl's soul to line a rich man's coffers.

Tears sprung to my eyes, hot and ashamed, and my breath caught in my throat. I wanted to reach through the mirror and take her by the hands. I wanted to tell her that she was loved, and she was perfect, and she deserved so much more than what I was going to put her through. I wanted to drop to my knees before her and beg for her forgiveness. I wanted to protect her. I wanted to play chess with her, and bake cookies with her, and go on long walks through the woods and teach her about the different kinds of tree. I wanted to mother her, to sister her, to care for her. I wanted it so much I felt like I could shatter the mirror with my bare hands, if only it would get me to her.

Maybe I could still do all of those things. Because she was still in me.

I just had to save Catalina and get the hell out.

And if I could, I had to find the back of my portrait and sever the anchor. Forever.

I kept going, pushing through the labyrinth.

'Catalina?' I called out, expecting an echo. There was none – the sound dropped dead at my feet.

Another mirror caught my attention: a scene I was all too familiar with.

My past self lying on a chaise longue, the Masked Painter crouched beside me. Carving at my bones.

I had thought I'd hidden my pain reasonably well, but my whole face was contorted with it. And I couldn't help but notice how much I still looked like that little girl playing chess. It was the same girl. Only this time, I was willingly hurting her.

I pressed my forehead against the cool glass.

'I'm sorry,' I whispered.

And the me in the mirror jolted ever so slightly.

All my blood ran several degrees hotter as I realised what was happening.

The voice that came to me unbidden right as it happened.

I'm sorry.

Was it my future self? Echoing from this liminal world.

My mind spiralled and spiralled, a helter-skelter, a tornado.

As I turned away from the mirror, something ten times more horrifying appeared around a corner I hadn't realised existed.

Myself.

Only this version was not in a mirror.

And she was not four years old.

She was corporeal.

She walked as I walked, breathed as I breathed.

Skeletal. Deranged.

The version of me from my portrait.

Our eyes met, and I have never been so profoundly terrified in my life.

We both froze for a moment. My vision swooped and dived, and I clasped on to consciousness with all my might.

She started towards me, a look of pure menace in her eyes.

My eyes.

I turned in the other direction and ran.

Straight into another portrait background, which became a

mirror, and then another silhouette appeared in the middle distance of the brushed maroon pattern, and I screamed at the top of my lungs.

Fingertips grazing either side of the labyrinth's corridor, I kept running, turning corners when they came, not daring to look up or down, nor behind me to see whether I was following.

I ran and ran and ran, as though my life depended on it.

The walls of the labyrinth were unrelenting in the way they eddied like a murmuration of swallows, full of dead ends and trick turns, mirrors that were really portraits and portraits that were really mirrors. One particularly enormous pane of silver was starkly familiar – was this the other side of the one that hung in Drummond? The one in which a silhouette had appeared? – but I couldn't stop for a second.

Around another corner was a corpse.

It was not rotting, not crawling with rats or insects, and yet I knew for a fact the person was dead.

For a single horrific second, I thought it was Catalina. I thought I was too late.

Yet it wasn't her.

Orlagh.

The flowing gown, the bloodied wounds over her face and chest, the vacant eyes staring up at the sky-ground.

Above her was the ravaged portrait she had once belonged to, as though she had fallen straight out of the frame.

I recognised this background – blues and purple, a curl of ocean spray with mottled heather blooms. It was the exact portrait from the Gallery of the Exquisite. Had I found a seam, of sorts?

The material of the thing – for here it was not canvas, but something altogether more ephemeral – had been shredded by a blade.

Footsteps echoed down the nearest corridor.

There was no time to figure out what this meant. I had to keep moving. Keep running from myself, like I'd been doing all these years.

As I stumbled over Orlagh's physical corpse, she twisted around the middle and her hand smacked the back of my leg with an icy thump.

I pliéed out of the way, palms planting heavily on the opposite wall.

Another mirror.

This time, through the ethereal fog I saw my eight-year-old self. Writhing in twisted pink bed sheets, jerking and thrashing my way through a nightmare. The daisy-shaped digital clock on the nightstand read 11.11.

Glancing quickly behind me in the labyrinth, I realised my portrait self had stopped following me through the maze. A mere morsel of relief. Breathing raggedly, I took the spare seconds to watch my younger self thrash and contort in the mirror, remembering vividly those My Little Pony pyjama shorts from my aunt Polly. The soft brush of them against my stomach, the elastic waistband loose from overwashing.

Observing the scene now, I could almost feel the movements

in my own body, could feel the raw terror. I dug my fingernails into the glass. What was she dreaming about? The raves she'd just witnessed? The comatose bodies slumped over stiff chesterfields?

Why did nobody protect me? I wanted to howl.

'It's okay,' I whispered instead. 'You're okay.'

Abruptly, the girl in the mirror startled awake, palm pressed to her chest. She sat bolt upright in bed, her head whipping around the room – as though to find the source of the voice.

And then she turned to stare straight at me.

No no no no no –

Her eyes were wide and somehow blank, somehow *wrong*.

The horror of it all was mounting. It was towering over me like a shadow, ready to swallow me whole.

I ran again, footsteps growing heavy and clumsy. Tears were streaming down my face now, overflowing with the certainty that this could not possibly be real, it was just another one of my nightmares, and yet I *knew*, I knew I was really here, in this terrible liminal space, and there seemed the very real chance I would not get out again.

Were Catalina and I trapped here forever?

Would I ever find her?

Eventually I fell to my knees, lungs still choked full of water, and I pressed my forehead against the sky-ground, letting my hot sobs wrack my whole body, and I started begging. I don't know what I was begging for – or who I was begging to – but I felt it right to the bottom of my very being, a visceral litany of *please please please please stop* . . .

And then a voice. At once achingly familiar and something entirely new.

'Penny?' A sharp inhale of breath.

I looked up slowly, fearfully, mortally petrified of who I might see.

At the sight of the figure in front of me, my heart folded in on itself like a dying star.

My mother.

CHAPTER THIRTY-THREE

This was not the mother I had left in a drunken stupor in her lonely mansion.

That mother was cold, distant, ambivalent towards my very existence. Porcelain skin, flowing bronze hair, those cheekbones, that *body*, yet so devoid of emotion, of maternal instinct, that it had made me feel fundamentally unworthy for nearly two decades.

No, this was the mother from the painting.

Green eyes dulled to a mossy grey. The skin around her mouth sagging into low jowls. Lacklustre grey hair shot through with tepid ginger. Her hips wide and swaying, her breasts full and drooping like roses at the end of a long summer.

It was her, but it wasn't, but maybe it was.

Which one was real?

'*Penny*,' she whispered hoarsely once more, and then she ran to me.

I couldn't explain why I was not afraid of her, the same way I was afraid of my own doppelgänger. I couldn't understand why, as she barrelled towards me, at once familiar and strange, I opened my arms wide and let her embrace me. I couldn't fathom the flood of emotion that ruptured in me, a breaking dam, a tidal wave, the furious gush of a river hurtling towards the ocean, as we fell into each other.

She was a few inches taller than me, and my hair was soon warm and wet with her tears. I pressed my face against her chest and sobbed too, without really understanding why.

Pulling back only a fraction, she cupped my face in her warm, rough hands. 'It's you,' she murmured, the words bleeding into each other. 'It's really you.'

'And you're really you,' I croaked, so certain that it filled me with a deep, penetrative ache.

'Oh, my girl.' The tears fell in unashamed sheets, and I could barely see through my own. 'I love you. I love you so much.'

I wanted to say it back, but I couldn't. I just shook and shook and shook, wrapping my arms around her ever tighter. I felt like that four-year-old in the mirror, small and afraid but, for the first time in living memory, *comforted* by my own mother.

'I'm sorry,' Mum said in a rush. 'I'm so, so sorry.'

'What for?' I asked, but I knew. I just wanted to hear her say it.

She sniffed fiercely, pressing the heels of her hands into her eyes to stem the tears. I keened with recognition – I did the exact same thing. 'For everything that imposter version of me has put you through for . . . god, for your whole life.' A whimpering noise. 'You deserved so much more.'

'How do you know?' I asked, suddenly hot with

embarrassment. 'Can you see it? All of it? What's happening out there?'

Now that we were a little apart, I noticed that the dress she'd worn in her portrait was in rags around her heavy-set frame; it had literally burst at the seams. The violet swathes barely covered her.

'Certain scenes play out in the mirrors,' she explained. 'The big moments. Watching helplessly as that . . . as that . . . *horrible* version of me slowly destroyed you. My baby girl. My beautiful, brilliant girl.'

The back of my throat tasting of silt, I choked out, 'I never felt like I was enough for you.'

'My love, you are all I ever wanted in my life. You are all I ever needed.'

'But I still couldn't keep you sober. I couldn't make you happy.'

'It should *never* have been your job to make me happy.' The words were both fierce and tender. 'I was supposed to make *you* happy, make you warm and safe and loved. I have watched four-year-old you play chess against yourself too many times to count. If I could have just got down on the floor next to you, asked you questions about your ideas and your strategies . . . god, I would have done anything. I would *do* anything. And it is the greatest agony I have ever known to realise I will never get those years with you back.' Her whole body wracked with sobs.

Tumbling emotions gathered speed in me, a snowball turned avalanche, until they were so ferocious I was terrified of being buried beneath the aching weight of them.

It was everything I'd ever wanted to hear in my life, and yet the circumstances were so far from how I imagined. Why couldn't I have just had this mother all along? I hated Orlagh, hated the Masked Painter for stealing this woman from me.

But like Davina said, where did the blame ever really start? Did I really hate Orlagh and the Masked Painter? Or did I just hate the world that had pushed my young, naive mother into this ruinous decision?

The pain of what could have been was almost too much to bear.

'My dad . . .' I started, but I didn't know how to finish. Didn't know what I was even trying to say.

She sank to the ground. 'I robbed you of that too. Although I suppose without this grotesque choice of mine . . . I wouldn't have met him. And you wouldn't exist.'

It was true. I was quite literally born from my mother's insecurities. Was it any wonder I was the way I was?

Mum took a deep, steadying breath. 'You know, by now, who he is. The Masked Painter. But your father's real name was Basil. Basil Hallward.'

Basil Hallward.

The name was so familiar. When I finally placed it, I gasped. 'The founder of Dorian?'

They'd named a whole theatre after him.

'The one and the same. He named the place after his first-ever subject – Dorian Gray. What better place to find a constant supply of new image-obsessed subjects than a drama school?'

The cold simplicity of it took my breath away. A whole elite institution built on this rotting heart – built on the narcissistic fears of people just like me. The pulsing organism of the underworld growing stronger and stronger beneath it. Could it ever be destroyed, without destroying the whole of Dorian and everyone tethered to it?

'Do you know who the new Masked Painter is?' I asked. 'I was never able to figure it out.'

Mum shook her head regretfully. 'I'm afraid I don't.'

'Have you tried to get out of here?' I whispered.

'Every single moment of every single day.'

'Does that mean I'm stuck here now too?' My voice was tiny and afraid even to my own ears.

'Oh god.' She ran wrinkled hands over her face. 'You're here. You're *here*. Are you alright? Are you hurt?'

I was hurt in too many ways to name, so I answered a different question – one she had not asked.

'The paintings – people are being killed through them. From the inside. From in here. We think . . . we think the organism is destroying itself. And I think it took my friend Catalina.' *Catalina*. The thought of her was an axe to my heart. 'Did you see Orlagh? Her corpse is just back there.'

Mum's face twisted, half sadness and half disgust. 'I saw her.'

'I just – I don't understand.' My mind was beginning to pinwheel once more. 'Which version of her is real? The one out there? Or the one in here? Are *you* the real you?'

An immediate, insistent nod. 'I'm almost certain of it.'

I shuddered. Because that meant the skeletal, haunted version of me that had started to chase me through the labyrinth was the real me too.

So what did that make *this* me? The imposter?

Or were we both real, in a sense?

And most importantly – how could I destroy one without destroying us both?

I had to believe there was a way to bring us back together into one body. One single body, free from horrifying anchors, from portraits connected to a liminal underworld where nightmares lived and breathed. To bring this soft, lovely mother out into the real world too.

My heart grew a hundred sizes at the thought. It was everything I'd ever wanted.

'I love you,' I said, and I felt it so sharply it was like the tip of a sword against my heart.

But it did not have the impact I expected. Mum started shaking violently, leaning back against the grey-silver painting behind her and sinking to the ground. Like a marionette doll cut loose of its strings. 'Oh, baby.'

'What is it?' I asked, crouching down beside her. I wanted to hold her hand in mine, but it still felt too strange to initiate physical contact with her after so long being treated like a leper.

'Everything I have ever done has been out of love for you.' The expression of her face was not one of love, though – it was one of horror.

'What do you mean?' I asked, feeling frantic now, wrong-footed. My pulse skittered like a stone skipping over water.

My mum's body stilled, and she stared at a fixed point on the sky-ground, her eyes pinned wide. 'When I watched Orlagh lure you into the Masked Painter's lair, the way she had me, I –'

'It was you,' I finished, as my brain finally caught up.

My stomach turned over, feeling like a slab of raw meat inside me.

'You killed Orlagh.'

CHAPTER THIRTY-FOUR

'She hurt my baby,' my mum whispered. She dug her fingernails into her palms, mouth twisted into a knot. 'The hatred I felt for her . . . I just wished I'd done it long ago, before she had a chance to snare you too.'

I shook my head. This couldn't be happening.

In both worlds, my mum was a killer.

'Orlagh was trying to help me,' I said, my voice high and thin.

'She *believed* she was trying to help you, Penny. But I knew it would destroy you, the way it had me.'

I knew I should be disgusted with her. I should revile her actions, because they were *wrong*, so deeply wrong – she had taken a life. And yet something primal and tender inside of me glowed with it.

My mother did love me. She loved me so unbelievably much that she would kill anyone who hurt a hair on my head. She would do anything to protect me.

How could I hate her? This was what I wanted from her all along, wasn't it?

'How did you do it?' I fixated on the logistics to avoid the painful, unsettling emotions roiling in my ribcage. 'Do you have a knife or something?'

'Mirrors can be shattered,' she muttered, as though it was irrelevant. 'And shards can be blades.'

I rubbed my stinging eyes. The tears had stopped, and some of the adrenaline was ebbing away, and I felt overwhelmingly exhausted. It was a side effect of feeling safe, I realised. Because even though this situation was anything *but* safe, I felt protected nonetheless. A lioness and her cub. I longed to rest my head in her lap and fall asleep, curled up like a cat as she stroked my hair.

I thought again of Aunt Polly when my cousin Pippa was a baby.

You're a good girl, such a good girl. Feathery eyelashes drifting carelessly shut, the smell of milk and baby sick on the air.

I had wanted it so much I felt like I might die from the pain of it.

Again I forced my brain to focus on facts, not emotions. If we were going to get out of this – so that I might have those moments for real – I needed all the facts possible to formulate a plan. I couldn't be distracted by yearning right now.

'Were they all you?' I asked of the murders. 'Celia and Lyle and Angus?'

She slipped back into that trance-like state, as though trying to shield herself from guilt or shame. 'When I first destroyed Camran's painting, it felt like I had created a kind of opening back into the real world. Those tears in the canvas sent new air rushing in, and it struck me that I might be able to climb out of them.' Something in me leaped up, like a flame to flint. 'But by the time I realised what was happening, they'd started to seal over again. I couldn't even get a fingertip through.'

I remembered how entirely ravaged Celia and Lyle's paintings had been, side by side on the gallery wall, most of the canvas in ruins. Understanding swelled into a full circle. 'So you wrecked two more, this time making far larger holes to try and climb through.'

'It sounds cruel, but they had lived long lives. And in truth, I would have done *anything* to get to you.' I saw her battle the lump in her throat. 'Anything in the world, Penny.'

'But it didn't work.' Obviously – we were still here. 'Why did you wait so long between Camran and those next attacks?'

'It took me that long to find more portraits. I think the labyrinth understood what I was trying to do, that I was trying to compromise it in order to free myself, and it kind of twisted and rerouted everything to disorient me. For nearly a week I was trapped in the same mirrored corridor.'

I couldn't think too deeply about the hellscape we were trapped in without feeling nauseous; unsettled on a fundamental level. 'And Davina's eye . . .?'

'That was on purpose.' A defiant smirk. 'I saw her strip you half-naked in the master and subject class.'

It was a hideous thing to have done, but my mind was focused on something else.

What *other* moments between Davina and I might she have seen?

My cheeks burned hot and furious. 'Did you see anything . . . after that? With Davina?'

'Not in any of the mirrors, no.' The relief that our moment in the gallery remained a secret was a cool ice pack on my face. 'Why? What happened?'

'We kind of reached a truce,' I said quickly. 'She battled the swans to help me get in here.'

Mum pursed her lips at this. 'Two decades in here, watching you suffer from afar, has kind of intensified those overprotective maternal instincts. I can't say I regret it. She hurt you.'

The words were a blanket wrapped around me in the cold depths of winter.

This is all I wanted, I thought, cupping the feeling to my chest like a single lit candle.

But there was one more question – one I had been avoiding, because I was afraid the answer might shatter this reunion.

'So why did you wound my face? Why all the little cuts and scars?' I mumbled, fingers going to the purple wound bisecting my cheek.

Silence spread out over several moments like frost over the Great Lawn. Then, finally, she sighed and said, 'Desperation. I needed to lure you here, somehow. I needed to make you afraid enough that you would somehow find your way behind the portraits.'

Surprise jumped in my chest. I didn't understand this reasoning at all.

'Why would you want me to come here?' I asked, baffled. 'You said yourself that we're stuck. That you've tried for years to break free.'

She took a deep, steadying breath. 'Because I think I've figured it out. I think destroying your own portrait is such a powerful act that it could create a hole in the seam large enough to climb through. When I was carving up Angus Arras, this version of him that exists back here found me. We struggled and fought, and he managed to grab hold of my mirror shard. I was standing in front of his portrait, and when he lunged at my face with the blade, I moved out of the way at the last second.

'When the mirror slashed into the canvas by Angus's own hand, there was this huge flash of white light, and this hideous *screaming* noise that didn't come from either of us. Angus died instantly, and his canvas glowed silver-white for several seconds longer than usual, the light flooding through the huge hole he'd unwittingly created. But I'd been blinded by the flash, and I didn't move quick enough to get through.'

I tried to process all of this, but there was a missing piece.

'Why did you lure *me* back here, though? Couldn't you have just tried it again with somebody else's canvas? Now that you know how to do it?'

She shook her head, tucking a loose lock of white-grey hair behind her ear. 'The chances of somehow finding one of the other subjects behind here, let alone tricking them into stabbing their own portrait, were incredibly slim. I was trying, of course. But then you arrived.'

Was I just being slow? Or did none of this make any sense?

'Okay . . . so how does this help us?' I replied, and for once I didn't seem to care about looking or feeling stupid. 'If I destroy my own painting, it'll destroy me too. I'm still stuck.'

After a fleeting burst of agonising resignation, Mum's eyes fluttered shut.

And then I understood.

'No. You don't mean . . .'

She was going to sacrifice herself.

'I can destroy my own painting and give you enough time to climb out.' Her voice was so heavy it pressed down on my chest like a physical presence. 'We just need to find the other version of you so you can step through together. So you can both be free.'

'But you'll *die*.' My heart felt like it was caving in on itself.

She opened her eyes at last. 'But you'll live.'

Shaking my head fiercely, I whimpered like a wounded rabbit. I couldn't make it this far, to finally meet the mother I had always craved, only for her to be snatched away from me so soon. 'I can't let you do that.'

'I've had a while to ponder the alternatives, but I don't think we have any choice.'

My mind scrambled for flaws, loopholes, anything to highlight how terrible this idea really was. 'What about Davina? I'll be free, but she won't. She has nobody back here to offer themselves as a sacrificial lamb. I don't want her to be in danger.'

'She won't be. The only danger is me. I'm the one wielding the blade. With me gone, nobody will have any reason to hurt her through the portrait. The others back here . . . they won't go slashing up the portraits just to try and poke a finger through. By all accounts, their other selves are doing rather well in the real world.' Again that awful twist of the lips, so pained and desperate. 'Their children aren't suffering, like you were.'

Wrapping my arms around my knees like a lost child, I pressed my forehead into my thighs and felt the warm rush of tears once more. 'Mum, I . . . I can't say goodbye to you. I want you. *This* you. I want us together, out there, living. This can't be the only way.'

'Oh, my love.' She crawled over to me, wrapping her arms around my hunched form. 'By all means, if you can find another one . . . I'm all ears.'

I thought and thought and thought. I thought for so long that days might have gone by in the real world, weeks, but no other alternatives appeared.

Where had I arrived in the underworld? Could I find that exact spot again, and hope it took me to the lake?

But I had been unconscious when I finally slipped through the ether. I had no idea how it happened, in actuality, and I didn't think it would work the same in reverse – falling unconscious into the bottom of the lake did not seem like a fantastic plan.

So it was one of three options: certain drowning, living in the underworld in perpetuity, or losing the mother I had wanted since I was a child.

Silently, desperately, I wished for a fourth option to materialise. A devil of some kind, who might be willing to bargain. Because there was very little I would not give up in exchange for both of our survival. I would make us the ugliest hags in all the world, I would make us poor beyond measure and talentless as earthworms, if we could simply be together.

But this was no Faustian tale, and no devil appeared.

It felt profoundly lonely that even hell itself had deserted us.

'Even if I agreed to all of this,' I said, 'none of it matters until I find Catalina.' Another horrible suspicion smacked me around the face. 'Mum . . . did *you* lure her here? To try and force me to follow?'

Mum's eyes widened. 'Of course not. Of *course* not, Penny. I have no idea what happened to her. But from what I've seen of her, she seems like a smart girl. Maybe she figured it all out, and decided to come down here and free you herself.'

Could that be true? Did she really care about me enough to be so reckless with her own life?

'Or the swans just attacked her,' I reasoned. 'The way they did the girl from the ghost story. In any case, we need to find her. Can you help me?'

Mum wrapped her arms around me once more, thick and warm. 'Of course. Anything for you, Penny. Anything. And while we're at it, we have to find the other you too. We need her for this to work.'

I clambered to my feet like a foal who'd been born mere seconds ago. I was dizzy and faint, hungry and cold, and so deathly afraid that the simple act of breathing and moving like a human being seemed insurmountable.

It wasn't just the imminent loss of my only living parent, or the realisation that I might be too late to save Catalina, or the idea of trying to claw through a temporary gap in the ether before it sealed me in here forever. It was the willing pursuit of the other me – the one I had sentenced to this terrible existence. The uncanniness of seeing another you live and breathe and walk and think and *feel* . . . it was profoundly wrong.

'It's terrifying, looking at her,' I said as we started walking unevenly, side by side. 'The other me.'

'Doppelgängers are freaky enough, let alone ones who actually *are* you.'

'Do you know where your own portrait is? Will we be able to find that when the time comes?'

'As long as the labyrinth doesn't shift again, I think I should be able to trace the path to it. I make sure to memorise it every time it moves.'

Sure enough, she seemed to know where we were going.

'But how do you memorise it?' Everything around me seemed to warp and eddy before my eyes. 'Even when they don't entirely shift, the backgrounds never stay still.'

Mum nodded. 'They do, but there are fundamentally two

types of panes – mirrors and paintings. They're arranged in different orders in each corridor. I've trained my brain to think of mirrors as white and paintings as black –'

'Like a chessboard.' I couldn't hold back the laugh.

'Exactly.' She gave a funny smile. 'They're just ranks and files. All I have to do is remember the sequences of each corridor and I have a good idea of where I am.'

There was a hooking sensation in my chest. 'I was absolutely robbed of you.'

'To think that I gave it up to stay beautiful . . .' Her voice sounded like a physical wound. 'It destroys me. It absolutely, existentially ruins me. I love you. I just love you, okay?' She slid her hand into mine and squeezed. The palm was warm, fleshy, wrinkled. Perfect.

Every time we rounded a corner, I held my breath, unsure what was more terrifying: finding Catalina, or not finding her.

What state might she be in if we found her?

How long might we spend looking?

But the next corner turned into another empty corridor. I recognised a hideous brushed maroon velvet background with a silhouette in the distance. The hue and texture reminded me of the seats in the Basil Hallward Theatre. My *father's* theatre.

'Have you talked to her much?' I asked. 'The other me.'

She shook her head. 'She's only been here a few weeks, and she's absolutely terrified. Whenever she sees me, she sprints in the opposite direction.'

My stomach lurched as there was a crack of thunder and a flash of lightning in both the ceiling and the floor. The mirrors seemed to rattle in response. I shivered in my swimming costume, still wet from the lake. 'How have you not gone insane? Two decades here . . . it's purgatory.'

'All this time, I focused on you.' Mum let her fingertips run along the walls, almost with fondness. 'I savoured the snapshots the mirrors gave me, no matter how painful they were to watch. The raves I took you to . . . my god.' Her teeth gritted. 'But at least I was seeing you, hearing you, despite being unable to touch you. It was sweet, perfect torture. And so whenever I felt myself losing it, contemplating taking a mirror shard to my own wrists – I just thought of the next time I'd get to see you.'

Everything in me wept.

I had been enough all along.

I let the thought of this marinate. 'So, in a way, when you were watching those awful moments through these looking glasses . . . you were there, in a sense.'

'I was.'

If there was such a thing as retrospective comfort, this thought gave it to me.

Around what felt like the hundredth corner, I heard the unmistakable sound of hyperventilation. Raspy, uneven breaths, high-pitched and deeply afraid.

Hands grazing the cold silver of a mirror pane, I steeled myself and walked into the next corridor.

There I was.

The real me – with enough murderous fear in her eyes to burn down the underworld.

Kneeling over Catalina's lifeless body.

CHAPTER THIRTY-FIVE

'CATALINA!' I screamed, lunging towards the limp figure on the mirrored sky-ground.

Fury and grief propelling me forward, I tackled my doppelgänger out of the way with a skeletal *ooft*.

'What are you doing to her?' I yelled, the voice echoing around the labyrinth a thousand times in distant loops.

My doppelgänger raised a bony hand and slapped me clean around the face.

'Trying to save her, you stupid bitch!' she snarled, wresting me off her with surprising strength.

I fell back on to my heels with a jarring shudder. 'She can still be saved?'

But my doppelgänger was once again hunched over Catalina, pumping rhythmically on her chest. Then she brought her lips to Catalina's, holding her ski-slope nose and breathing air into her lungs.

For several moments, I was powerless to do anything but watch.

My thoughts and emotions were a frantic carnival. Hope and fear and loss. A peculiar kind of relief – watching even my tortured, starved doppelgänger work so hard to save Catalina, a girl she'd barely had the time to get to know before I imprisoned her here . . . maybe I was a good person, deep down.

And Catalina had seen it all along. *You have a heart like a train, Penny.*

After what felt like an eternity teetering over a dark precipice, Catalina's limbs thrashed suddenly and severely, then she vomited lake water all over the floor.

'She's alive,' I whispered, tears falling down my cheeks. I crawled over to her. 'Catalina. *Catalina.* I'm here.'

But she was not awake. Not conscious. Her body was alive, but barely.

'Her pulse is thin and weak,' my doppelgänger said. The voice wasn't how I thought I sounded. 'Erratic. But it's there. If we don't get her out of here soon, though . . . We need a doctor. We need a doctor very, very soon.'

'She's diabetic,' I muttered, dropping to the ground beside her. I pressed my forehead to Catalina's and fought the urge to sob – it was blueish, marble-cold. 'She's probably hypoglycaemic right now. She's been down here far too long.'

'Then we need to go,' the other me said. Then she looked up at me, her expression so utterly heartbroken that it reminded me of the little girl playing chess against herself. 'How could you do this to me?'

'I think you did this to yourself,' I whispered. My mind was on a sickening fairground ride, and I wanted to get off. 'If you're the real me . . . you made this decision.'

Seeing myself moving and talking independently of me . . . it was like staring into a mirror that had a brain of its own.

Wrong wrong wrong wrong this is so wrong –

I had never been more afraid in my life.

Streams of water slicked down the mirrors and paintings, but it never pooled at the bottom, just vanished into the trick floor, which was also the sky.

'We have a plan to fix this,' Mum said, so sensible and capable, so motherly. I could imagine this version of her dusting floury hands on an apron so she could help me with my homework. 'Please, listen.'

'You're you,' the doppelgänger said, suddenly rooted to the spot. 'Mum?'

'It's me. And I love you.' Illogical jealousy coursed through me. 'Alright? I love you, and I'm here to help you.'

My doppelgänger's eyes shone, and she nodded, dumbfounded with emotion. I knew the feeling.

I listened as my mum explained the plan, and every inch of me railed against it.

She can't die, she can't die, she can't die.

But other Penny took it better than I did. Then again, she's the one who'd been stuck in this purgatory for weeks, cold and starved and terrified. The need to escape must have burned far brighter in her.

I wanted so badly to refute my mother's plan, to suggest we stay down here longer and figure out another way, but we couldn't.

Because Catalina would die without imminent medical attention.

We had to move. We had to move now.

'How are we going to –' I started asking, but my mother had already hoisted Catalina over her shoulder in a fireman's lift, the raw strength so incongruous with the mother I'd always known.

Then again, didn't they always say a mother could lift a car off a baby if they had to?

The four of us set off once more. As our broken crew rounded the corner, we were met with another figure, and my stomach twisted again.

Blonde curls tumbled to rounded shoulders. A curvaceous body in a pink gingham swimsuit. Watery pale blue eyes and plump, rose-tinted cheeks. I didn't recognise her from the gallery.

'I heard everything,' she said, her voice posh and wobbling. 'Your plan to escape. Please. You must take me with you. I beg of you.'

'Elsbeth,' my mum said softly, and it clicked into place.

Of course. The girl who went swimming in the lake was attacked by swans, and fell through the ether.

Every inch of her trembled.

She didn't have a portrait. She hadn't made this awful decision. And yet she'd been stuck here anyway – for an unfathomably long time.

'Do you know how long you've been here?' I asked her

gently, as though trying not to spook a squirrel into darting up a tree.

But our new companion was steadfast. 'Years.' She frowned, as though she could work it out by rote counting. 'Decades, even. I fell through the lake in eighteen ninety-nine.'

I fixed a sympathetic expression on my face. 'It's been over a century.'

The rosiness blanched from her face. She shook her head vehemently. 'Impossible.'

'I'm sorry.' And I meant it. What a horrible, horrible thing, to slip through a crack in the universe and never find your way back.

'Everyone I knew – everyone I loved . . . they'll all be gone.' Her bottom lip wobbled, and she bit down on her knuckles. 'They're all dead?'

'I'm so sorry, Elsbeth,' my mother said coaxingly. 'But we can still take you with us.'

Elsbeth began to scream.

It was bloodcurdling, ear-shredding, almost inhuman. A wounded animal, a grieving widow, a mother who'd lost their daughter. So much pain and fear that hearing it made your lungs crumple inward.

And then she started to lash out, pounding her fists against the mirrors and walls, hairline cracks appearing in the silvered glass.

'Elsbeth,' Mum shouted. Louder still, 'ELSBETH!'

No response. Elsbeth began slamming her whole body

at the mirrors, as though trying to smash through with sheer brute force.

Catalina still hung lifelessly over my mother's shoulder.

'Mum, we have to go,' I muttered urgently. 'We don't have time for this. Catalina . . .'

'She comes first,' my doppelgänger finished fiercely.

Mum nodded.

Leaving Elsbeth behind, we hurried down the next corridor, Mum's breathing becoming more and more laboured as she carried Catalina. I watched in amazement as, despite her exhaustion, she studied the panes of the labyrinth – mirrors and paintings, black and white – to figure out the route. She must have built an incredible map in her mind, like learning the longest, most complicated chess game ever played.

After a few minutes, Elsbeth's distant howls faded away. Either she had given up, or we'd moved far enough away that we could no longer hear her.

When my mother stopped dead and stared at a charcoal-grey background with gold constellations, I knew we had reached our final destination. We had marched to her execution like guards escorting a death-row prisoner to the gurney.

'When the gap appears, the light will be blinding.' Mum's tone was low and urgent as she lowered Catalina to the ground. 'Memorise the size and shape beforehand, close your eyes, and be ready. Waste no time. Can the two of you lift Catalina?'

My doppelgänger looked at me and nodded.

I stared at the background of the portrait as the constellations rearranged themselves into Orion. Water slicked down it in dark, oily rivulets.

'What if it doesn't work?' asked other Penny, and still the sound of her – my – voice made all the hairs on my spine stand on end. 'What if it doesn't work, and you die for nothing?'

Mum took my hand, then my doppelgänger's, and again I had the childish feeling of not wanting to share her. 'I won't have died for nothing. I will have died for *you*. And you are everything.'

As she turned to hug me, a thousand thoughts pinballed through my mind.

I love you.

I need you.

I will miss you – this you – forever.

But I couldn't say any of it, and nor could my mother. Instead we just held each other and wept softly, and it felt as though these thoughts were beaming directly into each other's chests – a warm, painful current, both healing and devastating.

It was the cruellest trick the world could have played. To give me everything I'd ever wanted for the briefest of moments, only to make me watch as it was wrenched violently away.

Other Penny watched, an impenetrable expression on her face, and I swore inwardly that I would heal her. As soon as we got through this, I would never stop healing. I owed it to my mother – I couldn't squander my life after she had given her own for it. Right now I could not imagine caring about calories, about pounds and inches, about control or punishment.

I just wanted to live.

And I wanted Catalina to live too.

Mum pulled away from me, and with a final loving look, turned to face the painting.

My heart writhed and jumped, and I felt its pulse in my ribs, in my temples, in my throat.

Don't do this, the little girl inside me wailed, but I knew it had to be done. There was no other way to save Catalina – or myself.

Mum withdrew the mirror shard from a hidden fold of her dress, then studied the portrait for a long time. It must have been a strange, torturous prospect, to end your own life without actually wanting to end it. To force your hand to lift the blade, anticipating the pain, then the nothingness. I wasn't sure I would have the strength to do it.

I could barely watch.

Doppelgänger Penny and I hoisted Catalina up between the two of us, flanking her on either side. As Catalina's head lolled on to her chest, a corkscrew curl tickled my nose, and it was everything I could do not to break down and sob.

Our bodies were mere inches from the back of the canvas.

Mum sucked in a final, courageous breath beside me.

The mirror shard lifted.

I closed my eyes, anticipating the bright white flash but praying it didn't come.

It came.

Bright, brighter than anything, so bright it burned the back of my eyelids.

A piercing, spectral scream that came from neither me nor my mother but from the pulsing organism itself.

Don't open your eyes. Don't look back. Just climb.

I pressed my body forward, hauling Catalina through with us, but someone grabbed me from behind. Another feral scream, not from the portrait but from the person yanking me back.

Mum?

No.

Elsbeth.

What –?

Then I understood. She was trying to get through first.

And I was barely strong enough to resist her shoves.

Our seconds ran down in the struggle.

Please! I tried to scream at her, but my throat was too tight with terror.

Other Penny's cold, bony hands closed around mine and pulled, harder than I thought her capable of, and she tugged both me and Catalina through the hole in the portrait.

Falling through the ether felt like nothing I had ever experienced.

It was cold and searing hot, neither solid nor liquid nor mist, at once deafeningly loud and horribly, absolutely silent.

And then we hit solid ground.

The polished hardwood of the gallery floor.

Peeling my eyes open, the first thing I noticed was that there was only one of me.

Looking frantically around, there was no sign of my

doppelgänger, just Catalina slumped horribly on the ground.

Had it worked? Had both Pennys become one? Or had Elsbeth somehow hauled her back to the other side? Had this all been for nothing?

In the split second it took to study my mother's eviscerated portrait, another head appeared through the hole in the ether.

Blonde curls.

Elsbeth.

Her shoulders, then her torso, and she was nearly through, and I hated her for what she had almost cost me, and –

The hole in the ether shrunk sharply shut, cutting her off at the waist.

For a single horrific moment she was suspended in mid-air, eyes open in a silent wail, her body welded to the wall like a taxidermied stag head.

And then she fell to the ground, her corpse sawn off at the hips.

She did not bleed, and no entrails spilled out; it was as though the ether had cauterised her shut.

I opened my mouth and screamed like I'd never screamed before.

I screamed for my mother – dead now, in every form – and for the unspeakable horror of the half body in front of me.

I screamed for Catalina, who I might not be able to save if the gallery was still locked from the outside.

I screamed for myself, all the versions of myself – baby and girl and young woman and doppelgänger – and everything we had just lost, and for the life we had just regained.

When the screams finally ran out, and my throat was raw and hoarse and shredded, I crouched over Catalina's body, pressing my face into her soft stomach. She was breathing, but not very convincingly.

Please please please please please don't die please don't die I need you I need you I need you so much, please –

Then I heard footsteps running towards us.

Hope surged in my chest.

Davina, Maisie and Fraser burst through the entrance to the gallery, all of them wet and panting but *alive*, and they ran towards me and Catalina and they were talking in soft, urgent voices, and Maisie was sprinting back up to the theatre to call for help, and I couldn't understand any of it, the frantic murmurs, Fraser's broad hand rubbing my back, Davina cupping Catalina's jaw and begging her to stay with us, and I so badly needed to stay awake, stay present, to save our perfect, perfect friend, but my vision swooped and dived, and then

everything

went

black.

CHAPTER THIRTY-SIX

One week later

My mother's funeral was a strange affair.

Most people don't have to share the grieving of a parent with the rest of the world, but the turnout was so substantial that the small church had to hire security. Peggy Paxton was to be buried in the tiny village she'd grown up in, and the single street was suddenly swarmed with fans and journalists and photographers. It was a national event, but that didn't make it feel any less personal or devastating to me.

Aunt Polly and I rode in the same taxi to the church.

The sky was a blank winter blue, the sun hanging low and sombre over the rolling fields of the Scottish Borders. Neither of us spoke, or cried. We had said everything that could possibly be said over the last seven days. My mother's death had always felt like a looming inevitability, but it was still far more painful than either of us could have ever anticipated. But we talked, and we hugged, and we shared memories. We sorted out the death admin. We laughed and cried some more. We started down the long, winding road of grief.

Now we just had to grit our teeth through the public bit.

Aunt Polly had been with her when she died in the real world. I tried not to think about how horrific it must have been to witness the sudden and shocking evisceration of your sister's body. I hadn't asked what state the corpse was in – I didn't want to know. I wanted to remember my mother as the person I had met in the liminal world pulsing beneath Dorian. Warm and clever and loving and kind and selfless and *brave*.

All the things I wanted to be myself. The things I wanted to stay with me.

But of course, I was grieving this real-world mother too – she was the one I had lived with for eighteen years. And though she had made my life a misery, for the most part, I had a new-found sympathy for her. I understood why she had been that way – a mental illness made permanent by a single shallow decision she'd made when she was young. How narrowly I had escaped the same fate.

I chose to believe that, for all her faults, what she had said after my Lady Macbeth audition had been true.

I'm so proud of you, darling.

I knew for certain, now, that those emotions did exist in some version of her. That made them real, in some way.

The saving grace of the whole experience was that Catalina had made a full recovery from her near drowning.

The moment I had wrenched through the portrait with my doppelgänger, Davina had felt a visceral yank towards the gallery – an almost physical pain, as though the organism she was tethered to had sustained a critical wound. She, Maisie and Fraser had sprinted down there as fast as humanly possible. Their quick actions saved Catalina's life – the paramedics got there just in time to administer insulin. She'd spent a few days recovering from pneumonia in hospital, where she Dungeon Mastered an extremely elaborate heist campaign with two elderly women on her ward.

She met me at the village church, alongside Davina, Maisie and Fraser.

My cavalry.

I had asked them not to wear black. They were my bright spots in the dark, and I wanted them to show up like that on the worst day of my life.

Davina refused, of course. She wore her patented black leather jacket and skinny jeans. But Catalina dressed in clashing burnt orange and sage green and mustard yellow, Maisie wore a bright pink houndstooth coat with a matching headband, and Fraser came in full drag make-up – purple and red and lashings of gold.

Aunt Polly went to talk to the minister, and I walked over to my friends. Davina was leaning against the wall of the church, one foot pressed flat against it, chain-smoking cigarettes. But the other three enveloped me in a group hug, arms interlocking around my shaking body.

'Hi,' I whispered to them, dimly aware of the paparazzi shutter clicks all around us. I tried to block it out. 'You all came.'

'We had to drag Davina,' joked Maisie. I could smell her sweet, floral perfume. 'We promised there might be some small children here to terrorise.'

I hugged Catalina tighter than any of them. I'd barely seen her since the gallery. 'Are you okay? I'm so sorry. I'm so, so sorry.'

I didn't have the guts to ask whether she'd purposefully gone in after me, or whether a swan had dragged her under.

'I'm fine.' She kissed my cheek in a casual continental way, and it left a warm imprint on my skin. 'But you need to stop apologising. It's getting a bit annoying.'

'Is nobody going to tell me how amazing I look?' grumbled Fraser. 'Honestly. You make such an effort for no –'

'Fraser, you look fucking fabulous,' said Maisie, Catalina and I all at once. We all started laughing, and I knew it wouldn't look good on camera, breaking into hysterics on the day your mother was lowered into the ground, but for once in my life I didn't care how it looked on the outside. I cared how it felt on the inside.

Davina dropped her cigarette butt to the path and squashed it beneath her black boots.

'I think that's against the Ten Commandments,' I said pointedly.

She shrugged, digging her hands into her pockets. Things had been a little awkward since I'd told her it was my mother who carved out her eye. 'You alright?'

I nodded. 'Yeah. I'm alright.'

It was strange, but ever since the experiences in the liminal world, Davina didn't scare me any more. And in the absence of fear, there was also an absence of lust. It was as though the spell she had over me had been broken, and I couldn't fathom *why* I'd ever wanted to share those first intimate moments with her.

Davina was like the demon that had controlled my mind for so long – dark, alluring, persuasive, but ultimately destructive. And now that I'd seen what darkness could truly cost, now that I'd barely escaped with my life, I no longer wanted anything to do with it. I wanted to choose the light.

Still, it was almost *nice* to have chalked up a normal teenage experience: kind of regretting my first sexual encounter, but knowing it would make a good story one day. All of this would, in time.

I gestured towards the entrance to the church. 'We should go.'

Catalina held me by the hand as we walked, and its warmth felt like a miracle. I would never forget how it felt to see her limp, lifeless, cold and blue as the lake itself. I didn't want to let her go, and so I didn't. As we slid into one of the foremost pews, Aunt Polly eyed our interlaced fingers with a knowing smile.

The funeral itself was a blur of droned hymns, sobs from near strangers, and overwrought declarations of how inspiring a person Peggy Paxton had been.

I doubted they'd be saying that if they knew of my mother's sins. The dead bodies in her wake: Orlagh, Celia, Lyle, Angus.

Over the last week, I had waited for the truth about the murders to come to light, somehow, but it never did. Perhaps it never would. And perhaps that was for the best. Keeping the Gallery of the Exquisite a secret might be the only way to keep Davina safe – because her own portrait hung there still. She was still vulnerable. She was still cold and hungry, and likely always would be.

Besides, what good would the truth *do*? My mother, the killer all along, was dead. She had died to save her daughter. There was no more justice to be served. Nothing that would bring the victims back.

One loose end did torture me – the fact we'd never been able to track down the second Masked Painter. My mother had manslaughtered the first, but who had painted me? And why?

I might never know.

After the final hymn – 'All Things Bright and Beautiful', ironically enough – we all filed out of the church. Only friends and family were invited to attend the burial, but I could still feel the presence of the paparazzi lurked in the trees surrounding the cemetery. Watching, capturing, selling. The cycle that would always repeat. The sentient organism that spread not just beneath the grounds of Dorian, but through our whole society, feeding on fear and decay.

The maple coffin was lowered into the ground. My cousin Pippa sobbed into Aunt Polly's dress, while Catalina kept holding my hand tightly. Her rings were digging into my skin, but I didn't care. I glanced over at the others to see Davina staring intently at a worm wriggling in the bare earth. Fraser wrapped his arm around Maisie's shoulder, squeezing affectionately, and she glowed. Maybe there was hope for the two of them yet.

The burning sensation of being observed continued to intensify, until I finally looked up.

There.

On the other side of the grave, standing behind my mother's old model friends, was a tall, spindly man in a black trench coat.

Staring straight at me.

Our eyes met with a surge of recognition.

And then he was gone.

CHAPTER THIRTY-SEVEN

A few weeks after my mother's funeral, it was opening night for *Macbeth*.

Without the portrait, it wasn't long before my hair started shedding again in clumps. After everything that had happened, it shouldn't have felt like a big deal, and yet the sight of those seaweed strands circling the shower drain still felt like uncanny buttons of mould, like liminal underworlds beneath haunted mirrors, like something deadly and *wrong*.

By the time it came to the opening night, most of the bottom third of my hair had fallen away, leaving me more exposed and vulnerable than ever.

The green room in the Basil Hallward Theatre – my *father's* theatre – buzzed with activity. We were around twenty minutes from opening, and I was fully costumed in a flowing green velvet dress with Renaissance ribbons. My copper hair was pinned carefully around the bald patches, and as I studied my reflection in the mirror, I thought I looked rather like Princess Fiona from *Shrek*. The realisation made a sincere smile crack over my face, if only for a moment.

But as I heard the audience excitedly chatter their way into the rows of maroon velvet seats, any meagre joy in me vanished. I was horribly, debilitatingly nervous. My stomach clamped around itself, roiling and gathering speed like a tyre hurtling down a hill. In just a few minutes, a thousand eyes would bore into me beneath the heat of the spotlight.

Behind me, Fraser was having a final run-through of his soliloquy with Banquo.

'Are you okay?' Catalina asked, pulling over a stool so she could sit beside me. At the sight of her, something in me eased, and there was a flutter of wings in my chest – a stark contrast to the oily dread in my gut.

And I realised, for perhaps the first time, that there were good nerves and bad nerves. The gentle quiver, the fizzing in my veins when I saw Catalina was wholly different to the disquieted angst I'd felt around Davina. The way I felt before a game of chess – excitement, anticipation, hope – was a different breed entirely to what I felt right now, about to go on stage in the biggest role of my life. Perhaps those sensations were a kind of gut instinct. My heart, my inner child, telling me what I really wanted.

How many times since arriving at Dorian had the voice in my head told me I shouldn't be here?

Maybe I'd misinterpreted that message. Maybe it was right, and I shouldn't be here, but not because I wasn't talented enough. Because I didn't *want* to be. Not really.

For so long I had chased the things everyone else lusted after without stopping to consider whether it's what I truly wanted. It's why I starved and plucked and preened in the name of beauty. It's why I spent my teenage years doggedly attending audition after audition, even though they made me sick, in the name of success – because success might make my mother love me. Hell, it's why I was carried away on Davina's current on the cold floor of the gallery – because everyone else wanted her, and yet in that moment, I could make her mine.

But the truth was that I didn't want fame. I wanted joy.

I didn't want beauty. I wanted identity.

I didn't want sharp love. I wanted soft love.

And so, in that hairspray-filled green room, I turned my head towards Catalina, so that I was looking at her not in the mirror but face to face. 'Is Davina here?'

For a split second, she looked utterly crestfallen. I grabbed her hand and squeezed it beneath mine, the gemstones of her silver rings pressing into my palm. 'Not like that.'

Catalina swallowed hard and nodded, gesturing over my shoulder to where Davina sat in the corner of the green room, sulking at her phone. Drever had roped her into helping with the costumes.

I got to my feet and crossed over to my nemesis turned reluctant ally, turned broken lover, turned almost friend.

She looked up as my shadow fell over her.

'Come for one final gloat?' she snarked, and for once all I could do in the face of it was smile.

'No. I've come to give you what's rightfully yours.'

Slowly I slipped one shoulder off my dress, then another.

My fingers unzipped the stiff side, and the whole dress dropped to my ankles, revealing my white body in seamless beige stage underwear. My figure was already softer from the weeks spent properly nourishing myself, and I thought of how starkly different this moment was compared to the one in the master and subject class. How much more in control of my own life I felt.

Davina stared at me like I'd lost my mind. I hooked the dress up with my foot, catching the velvet folds in my palm. The fabric was warm.

'Do you still remember the lines?' I asked her, feeling the room's eyes on us.

She nodded, dumbfounded for maybe the first time in her life.

I handed her the dress, and she took it. 'Then go knock 'em dead.'

Swivelling on my heel, I walked back to where Catalina sat. She was staring at me with something shaped like awe.

I was overcome with the urge to cup her beautiful jaw in my hand, to graze my lips over hers, to sink into her loveliness, her kindness, the sunny way she saw everything. But the moment wasn't right. I didn't know if she felt that way about me, and I didn't want to put her on the spot in front of a now rapturously attentive audience.

Instead I gathered my clothes in a careless ball, squeezed her shoulder as she had so often squeezed mine.

'Break a leg,' I whispered, with a secret smile just for her. 'Come find me when you're done?'

She nodded, gaze full of wonder and maybe, just maybe, something richer still.

And then without looking back, naked but for the pale slips of fabric covering my most private parts, I forever left the theatre my father had built in the name of rotting beauty.

*

A few hours later, Catalina found me cross-legged on the kitchen floor, surrounded by towels. Bath towels, tea towels, any towels I could find. I wore my rattiest old pyjamas – a Pokémon T-shirt faded from white to grey, and some joggers with a hole at the knee. A big bowl of salty-sweet popcorn sat beside me, studded with M&Ms and Maltesers. Apparently the inner child I was on a mission to feed loved chocolate.

Her face had been scrubbed free of claggy stage make-up, and her eyes were a little pink, as though she'd rubbed too hard with a make-up wipe. She was panting like she'd run straight here, instead of hanging around with the rest of the cast. There was no sign of Maisie or Fraser behind her.

'How did it go?' I asked, grinning madly.

I was absolutely giddy with relief. I would never have to set foot on a stage again.

'It was okay,' she said hurriedly, as though keen to get to the real question. 'Davina fumbled a few lines, and the stage direction was woeful since she hadn't been to any rehearsals.

But the crowd still loved her.' A deep breath as she sat down opposite me. 'Penny, what happened?'

'I'm leaving Dorian.' Her eyes flew wide. 'It's hard to explain, but . . . even though I've only been healing for a few weeks now, it's given me a whole new clarity. When you're that hungry for that long, you feel so horrible in your own skin, and so everything in your life feels *wrong*. But when you finally start to feel right in it again, it shines a spotlight on what actually *is* wrong. And Dorian was wrong.' I shrugged, as though it didn't matter, but in truth it mattered more than anything. 'I have never wanted this. Not really. I just lost sight of that, for a while. And it's like . . . with my mum gone . . . I don't know. I feel sad. I feel so, so sad for what might have been. But I also feel free. Like I can start living my life for me.'

'I think that's the bravest thing I've ever heard.' Her cardigan sleeve had slipped off her shoulder, revealing that tattoo along her collarbone. 'What will you do instead?'

'I don't know. Maybe I'll be a chess bum. Maybe I'll take up fencing again. Maybe I'll just swan around living on my mother's inheritance. Or maybe I'll find another thing I truly love, now that I finally know how to listen to my gut instincts.' I clutched my hands together in my lap. I felt so young, but in a nice way. Like I had so many luxurious decades sprawling in front of me, and I could do with them whatever I wished. 'I don't think I have to have it all figured out right now.'

'Of course you don't.' Her smile was sunny olive groves and

old books and the smell of rich earth. She gestured around. 'What are the towels for?'

Her eyes finally landed on the clippers plugged into the charger by the sofa, and she frowned in confusion.

'I want you to shave my head,' I said, with another deep grin.

'What?' She looked equal parts terrified and horrified. 'Penny –'

'I promise this is not a Britney meltdown.' Sitting forward on to my knees, I turned around so my back was facing her, then carefully lifted up my remaining sheets of hair. I was glad I couldn't see her reaction. 'I have alopecia. I had it as a kid, and it came back at the start of term. I've been losing more hair than ever since my portrait was destroyed, and I want to take charge of this. I want it to be on my terms.'

I let my hair drop over my back and turned towards her. The expression on her face was unreadable.

'Are you sure?' she asked softly. 'I mean, I'll do it. Of course I will, Penny. But I just want you to be sure.'

I nodded. 'When I was in the liminal world, I saw my child self in a mirror. I was around four years old and totally bald. Alopecia. I'd totally forgotten – I think all the trauma thereafter erased vast swathes of my childhood memories. But as soon as I saw her, I just thought . . . god, you were so perfect before the world taught you otherwise. I felt like I was looking at my true self. I was wearing these adorable pink dungarees, and playing chess, and I just absolutely did not care about my hair. I want that girl back, Catalina.'

And so we shaved my head.

The buzz of the razor over my scalp filled me with those fluttering good nerves, and as my hair dropped away from me in heavy clumps, it felt totally and utterly right.

When it was done, I studied my reflection in a little Swarovski-studded pocket mirror my mum had given me for my eleventh birthday. I was perfectly and absolutely bald, the ridges of my skull highlighted in pools of golden light around us. The scar on my cheek was stark, but I looked at it with nothing but fondness. My real mother had carved it to save my life. I would always remember her love, her sacrifice. Now it was a part of me forever.

That elusive, slippery thing: identity.

'How do you feel?' Catalina asked, nervous at my silence.

Laying down the mirror, I looked straight at her. She beamed at me, a glistening, radiant smile, and the fluttery wings in my chest intensified. Her curls were still pinned back from her face, as they had been beneath the wig she wore on stage, and her skin shone with a dewiness that made me think of ripe fruit and gushing waterfalls.

'Thank you, Catalina.' My voice was a whisper, hoarse with emotion.

'What for?' she asked sincerely, as though she genuinely didn't realise what she had done for me.

'Well, first there's the obvious. You saved me. You solved the mystery of the portraits with your intellect instead of a knife. I would still be tethered to that hideous gallery without you. But it's more than that.' I swallowed hard, my throat suddenly full of emotion, and I couldn't find the words. 'I'm just . . . I'm so glad you're in my life.'

At this her eyes filled with tears. She nodded, but said nothing.

In that moment, I knew what I felt towards her was how love should have felt all along. Good nerves. A blend of admiration and attraction, the deep desire to care for her, to protect her, to keep her safe. To give her pleasure; to be with her, truly *with* her. To be around her all the time, because she made me feel good about the world – and about my place in it.

'I would really like to kiss you,' I said, almost too quickly, as though I was trying to capture the dregs of adrenaline still in my body. 'But if you don't want that, please know that your friendship is more than enough for me. Because you're the most –'

Before I could finish, her lips were on mine. They were soft and sweet from mango lip balm, with a warm saltiness from her tears. She cupped her hand around the back of my naked head; ran her fingers over the ridges like it was the most beautiful thing in the world.

Everything in me sang.

It was soaring, it was yearning.

It was release.

It was hope.

Maybe love did not have to be carved with a scalpel.

EPILOGUE

The portrait arrived on my doorstep on my nineteenth birthday; a cold, crisp day in March.

It was wrapped in brown parcel paper, secured with precise squares of rose-printed washi tape. On the back, '*for Penny*' was scrawled in cursive marker. There was no address.

The sender had delivered it personally.

A cold dread slicked over me as I pulled it inside.

After leaving Dorian, I had sold the townhouse my mother had left to me – auctioning off most of the expensive and meaningless objects inside – and bought myself a small, airy flat in the Old Town. It was a neater, more manageable place in which to grieve. Catalina, Davina, Maisie and Fraser had helped me decorate it at Christmas. Coloured fairy lights and garish blue tinsel, homemade sugar cookies strung on the boughs of a wonky tree, cheesy Bublé playing as we sipped at eggnog and watched Fraser perform his new Coco Coxx act for us.

Family, or something resembling it.

The demons in my mind had not vanished entirely, but they seemed a lot smaller, somehow, like trivial gnats I just had to swat away whenever they appeared. Because the feeling that stuck with me long after I left the liminal world was the pain of what could have been. It was a profound yearning that ached in every chamber of my heart – I would have done anything to have the mother from behind the portrait with me now. And yet it was done. She was as gone as the mother I'd grown up with. What could have been would never be.

All I could do was not make the same mistakes with my own life. If I lay on my deathbed with the knowledge that I'd thrown away the richness of my humanity, my joys and passions and hopes and dreams and fear, all in the name of temporary beauty . . . it would feel a thousand times worse.

And so I lived my life in a way I hoped my child self would be proud of. I started fencing again, once my body was strong enough. I joined a chess club, and was suddenly surrounded by people from all walks of life who thought the exact same way I did. Weekly sessions were held above a dingy pub – the furthest thing from the glittering grandeur of Dorian I could imagine – and we'd stay there for hours every Monday night, analysing positions and debating theory and going far too deep into pawn structure. I hired a coach. I read every chess book I could get my hands on. I entered every Scottish tournament that was going to be held that year.

Good nerves.

The nerves as I unpeeled the mysterious brown package, however, were not.

As the parcel paper fell away, I could not stifle the gasp.

It was a painting of my mother.

My *real* mother.

The woman I had met in the underworld. The mother I had yearned for all along. Mossy-green eyes shot through with pink blood vessels. A puffy, bloated face; low jowls hanging from the jaw. Straggly grey hair. An eminent humanity shining behind her like a backlight. The whole thing charged with a metaphysical tension.

And I knew exactly who had painted it.

Him.

How did he know where I lived? My gaze snapped around the living room, as though he was about to jump out from behind a curtain. Like I was being watched.

I thought of the strange, intense-stared man at my mother's funeral, and the disquiet swelled in my chest.

It had been him. I was sure of it.

He was still out there, lurking in the shadows.

Was this portrait a gift? Or a threat?

I tried to steady my breathing, to steel myself against the realisation that no matter how deeply I healed, there would always be a dark underworld waiting to prey on my moments of weakness. On my insecurities and imprecations. I just had to stay vigilant. Remind myself every single day that I was worth saving. That my beauty was the least interesting thing about me. That chasing it would only ever leave me hollow.

My heart panged as I ran a finger over the gilded frame, wondering what my mum would think if she saw me now. Would she applaud the shaved head? Support my decision to drop out of Dorian, as she had too? From the brief but beautiful moments I'd shared with the real her, I felt that she would, on both counts.

As my finger moved from the frame to her aged face, a peculiar jolt shot up my wrist. I yanked my hand back from the painting, a sickly sense of disorientation coming over me.

A strange nausea with no clear origin.

The feeling of oily water trickling down a mirrored surface, disappearing into a floor that didn't truly exist.

Somewhere deep in the background of the painting, a shadow flickered.